AVID

READER

PRESS

Born and raised in Echo Park, California, Brando Skyhorse is a graduate of Stanford University and the Master of Fine Arts Writers Workshop program at the University of California at Irvine.

His debut novel, *The Madonnas of Echo Park*, received the 2011 PEN/Hemingway Award and the Sue Kaufman Prize for First Fiction from the American Academy of Arts and Letters. He is also the author of *Take This Man: A Memoir*, and coedited an anthology, *We Wear the Mask: 15 True Stories of Passing in America*.

Skyhorse has been awarded residencies at Art Omi, the Key West Literary Seminar Residency Program, and was a recipient of a Rockefeller Foundation Bellagio Center fellowship. He is an Associate Professor of English and the Director of Creative Writing at Indiana University in Bloomington.

For speaking engagements and First Year Experience inquiries, please contact the author at brandoskyhorse.com.

ALSO BY BRANDO SKYHORSE

The Madonnas of Echo Park: A Novel

Take This Man: A Memoir

We Wear the Mask: 15 True Stories of Passing in America

My Name Is Iris

BRANDO SKYHORSE

A NOVEL

AVID READER PRESS

New York   London   Toronto   Sydney   New Delhi

Avid Reader Press

An Imprint of Simon & Schuster, LLC
1230 Avenue of the Americas
New York, NY 10020

First Avid Reader Press trade paperback edition July 2024

AVID READER PRESS and colophon are trademarks of Simon & Schuster, LLC

Simon & Schuster: Celebrating 100 Years of Publishing in 2024

For information about special discounts for bulk purchases, please contact Simon & Schuster Special Sales at 1-866-506-1949 or business@simonandschuster.com.

The Simon & Schuster Speakers Bureau can bring authors to your live event. For more information or to book an event, contact the Simon & Schuster Speakers Bureau at 1-866-248-3049 or visit our website at www.simonspeakers.com.

Manufactured in the United States of America

1   3   5   7   9   10   8   6   4   2

The Library of Congress has cataloged the hardcover edition as follows:

Names: Skyhorse, Brando, author.
Title: My name is Iris / Brando Skyhorse.
Description: First Avid Reader Press hardcover edition. |
New York: Avid Reader Press, 2023.
Identifiers: LCCN 2023001692 (print) | LCCN 2023001693 (ebook) |
ISBN 9781982177850 (hardcover) | ISBN 9781982177867
(trade paperback) | ISBN 9781982177874 (ebook)
Subjects: LCSH: Immigrants—Fiction | Identity (Psychology)—
Fiction. | LCGFT: Dystopian fiction. | Novels.
Classification: LCC PS3619.K947 M9 2023 (print) | LCC PS3619.K947
(ebook) | DDC 813/.6—dc23/eng/20230130
LC record available at https://lccn.loc.gov/2023001692
LC ebook record available at https://lccn.loc.gov/2023001693

ISBN 978-1-9821-7785-0
ISBN 978-1-9821-7786-7 (pbk)
ISBN 978-1-9821-7787-4 (ebook)

This book is for K.R. and R.K.

If we forget ourselves, who will be left to remember us?

—CHERRÍE MORAGA, *Native Country of the Heart*

One

Whenever I ask my mamá what her first memory of America was, she says, "Who cares about me? You were born here."

You were born here. That's my first strip of memories, my parents taking turns to berate me whenever I misbehaved or, later, asked about their pasts to deflect an imminent punishment. Never "Stop doing that!" or "Be quiet!" or "Finish your dinner!" It was "You were born here! It is something you can never lose. Don't forget that."

"How can I?" I shouted. "You tell me every day!" I was five when I said this.

"Ay, ¡qué malagradecida!"

I had no life before America the way my parents did. I am a second-generation Mexican-American daughter of Mexican immigrants, meaning that of course I was ungrateful. I heard about my parents' sacrifices and how they forded an endless river of prejudices so often it sounded like a polished comic routine. When I was born, a white nurse asked my father, Gonzalo, "English is okay, Dad?" Through a haze of drugs and pain, my mamá, Dolores, sprang upright in her hospital bed and shouted, "Lady, we speak English!"

My mamá, who is proud of her English but rarely uses it aside from talking to me, enrolled me in English-only classes at our elementary school. Mr. Chela decided the Spanish-language program was a better fit. The idea was parents could better help their children with their homework in a language they understood. Dolores refused. School was for *me* to learn English, not her.

"I don't want you to be a slave in America," my mamá said.

"Teacher told me Lincoln freed the slaves!" I said proudly.

Mamá rapped me on my butt with her chanclas, twice. Once, for being disrespectful, and twice, for wasting my knowledge.

"Use your smarts for good," she said. "Not backtalking tu mamá."

Mr. Chela threatened to transfer me to a school in the Valley an hour away on an old, wheezing school bus, thinking Mamá would back down.

"If they talk to you in Spanish," she said, "answer in English. If you don't, the school will take you away from me and we will never see you again."

My mamá and I ended up in the principal's office, two scolded women sitting in moldy, oversize chairs. Dolores shouted at Mr. Chela while I trembled that someone would come and snatch me away.

"Cálmese, señora," he said. "Somos mexicanos, ¿verdad?"

Dolores slapped away his proffered high five and said, "Show respect for a woman."

"My own kids are in Spanish-language classes," he said. "Your daughter is not ready."

Dolores rolled up her sleeves and said, "Look at our skin. I am lighter than you. Who is more American? Who deserves to learn English more?"

"You're crazy," Mr. Chela said. "But you win. Now please get out of my office."

Mamá tells these stories often, at family dinners and to strangers at tiendas pushing plump babies in shopping carts. My father, Gonzalo, whose English is tentative, shy, like a child hiding behind a parent's leg, has long ago mastered his passive head-nod-in-agreement. He is my mamá's physical responsibility and repays her care with a benign acquiescence. Before his erratic hand trembling got him fired and then made him unemployable, he was a hard worker, which is how every Mexican describes their dad. On Gonzalo's job sites, white men with clean nails called my father "a solid guy," which he repeated with pride. (We do not say "retired" in our house; trabajadores *never* retire.) Watching endless TV fútbol matches, Gonzalo's body molded into his recliner and never left, my father's confident, masculine hands disfigured into catatonic pincers for his remote controls.

Dolores and Gonzalo were born in Mexico. They didn't share, or explain, what life there was like for them. When I asked, they said, "Everything is here. Who cares what came before? Did you forget already that *you were born here*? Act it!"

Growing up, Dolores asked me, over and over, "What are the rules to live in America?"

I didn't understand why, but I knew the answers well:

Speak English in front of strangers. No Spanish anywhere outside the house.

Walk far—but not *too far*—from gringos on a sidewalk until they have acknowledged you. Call any gringo you meet "sir," even if they are young. Call any gringa you meet "ma'am," especially if they are old.

And never, *ever*, cry in front of anyone, even if you think they are your friend.

"Do that," my mamá said, "and they'll let you become anything you want here."

Two

My name is Iris Prince. I was born Inés, and would have stayed that way had my seventh grade teacher not kept stumbling over my name and gave me a new one. Now even my parents call me Iris, proud of the fact that someone in America was thoughtful enough to give me an American name.

I'm in my early forties with a healthy child, living in a secure, slightly upper-middle-class income bracket. I lock my doors at night, never cut in a line or disobey a posted sign or a command from a uniformed person, have excellent cholesterol, and good, mechanically stimulated orgasms. (I'm not ashamed of my agency.) I am happy with the person I have become and am content with the life I carved out from a modest poverty. If not for minor slights and grievances, I have no bad memories at all.

I am a success. America believes in me.

A few months ago, I left my husband of sixteen years. Leaving Alex surprised him, which was itself a surprise. Why was I unhappy, he said, when he showed up for his daily chore list without excessive complaint, his reliability adjusting like a thermostat whenever I was irritable or dissatisfied. This made suggestions of counseling or divorce feel hyperbolic, absurd, even dangerous. "Think of Mel," he said, our nine-year-old daughter. Why do you demand reason, he asked, when you are so incapable of it? Why couldn't I accept, he insisted, that we were a content, functional couple who made responsible parents and it was far too late to expect any more from life, or from each other, now?

What, *exactly*, did I want?

It's not that I disagreed with him. When I read magazine stories about women starting over after a divorce, I thought, *Why did you bring this on yourself? Why didn't you pick the right person? Why should I care? Couldn't you have worked harder to stay together?* Where are the stories of women who sacrificed their happiness to stay in a loveless marriage so their child doesn't grow up in a broken home and become a delinquent? Put *those* women on the cover of *People* magazine! Those are *my* heroes.

I knew from when I was eleven years old what kind of married life I wanted. My fantasies were projected onto a yard-sale Barbie with a detached arm that kept popping off. I wrote "Mr." on that arm because Mamá didn't want to waste money on a headless Ken. "Mr." had a reliable job—he was an air traffic controller—and our cardboard box dream house was in a perfect little neighborhood called Lilac Village. It was far from the noisy airport (where Hot Wheels stood in for planes), in order to ensure my plastic toys got a good night's sleep, but close enough so that my one limb of a husband didn't spend precious hours stuck on the busy McDonald's place mat freeways when he should be at home helping take care of our daughter, a stuffed donkey named Gwen.

Eres una niña extraña, my mamá said. Very strange kid.

When I was older, I knew I wanted someone who could handle being with a responsible, college-educated Mexican American, ascending the staircase of our American Dream in tandem with me, through tireless work and deferring immediate pleasures to benefit our future family. That's a very specific kind of man, one I had never expected to meet before I was twenty-five. College was for men like Richard Cameron, a white upperclassman who decried "flat-assed güeras," spoke better Spanish than I did, and interlaced his arms and legs with mine in bed when we were naked, using Starbucks adjectives like "demitasse" or "mocha frappe" to describe my skin color. We met in a dorm room for what I thought was a poli-sci midterm cram session. There, a dozen people drank cheap beer while Richard rambled in frantic bursts and jumped on his bed, shouting, "I'm not afraid of any of you!" When he asked me for the eighth time, "How tough was your neighborhood?" I lied and said I saw a guy shot in the head during a carjacking. "Nine one one is a joke!" he said, pumping his fist in the air until his knuckles scraped the popcorn ceiling, then asked for my number, wincing in pain.

I hated him touching me. Sex with Richard felt akin to leaving a copy of myself behind with him. I didn't want to have that experience of loss too many more times. Who knew how many copies of yourself you had before you ran out? Who knew what that person would do with the copy of you that stayed with them after you broke up?

My best friend, Gertie, said, "Terrible sex does unforgivable things to a woman. Dump him."

Richard dumped me instead. He learned how dissatisfied I was by accessing my email account without permission, then blamed me for having such an easy-to-guess password, turning his violation into a teachable "I'm trying to make you safer" moment. Last I heard, he'd hooked up with a married white graduate student. What did their interlocked, white-on-white fingers reveal to him? Did he hold her ass's lack of buoyancy against her?

Alex wasn't like that, ever. Alex was easy. On our first date I shared a list of world destinations I wanted to see but never would because of a crippling fear of flying. He didn't pathologize me or insist I needed therapy, but sent videos of people walking atop the Great Wall of China, or a safari jeep driving alongside wild elephants in South Africa, or time lapses of the northern lights in Alaska. Every experience I said I wanted. Seeing the world from my desk chair on a turkey sandwich and diet soda lunch break, I knew I could fall in love with this man.

Alex was the same kind of responsible, college-educated Mexican American I was. We are everywhere in my generation except in movies and television. We are everywhere here in the state where we live, in local government, and in positions of authority at stores and banks, where we can make decisions without having to check with a white person first. Like every Mexican American we knew, we worked for everything we had and we hated those who expected handouts. Ours was a punitory worldview meant to exclude and wish suffering on those who didn't work as hard as we did, even if that included members of our family (like my sister, Serena).

When Alex and I married, my goal was to save for a modest one-level house with no stairs in case we had children right away, with a tiny space for a garden. I spent hours browsing the dining room displays of home furnishing stores, picturing my perfect tiny family around the dozens of various tables—stone, wood, glass— and envisioned how we would engage with one another. The stories we would tell around that table to make each other laugh, and the ways we would pass the time together. These moments were the true happiness I was working for.

Alex knew this about me. I never changed what I wanted. But we didn't have children right away.

His parents, Kevin and Cynthia, who had no interest in being grandparents, had bought us—him—a let's-kill-the-kids town-house with three flights of steep staircases and sharp corners on everything (even the banisters) that was too far from my work. On the ground floor was a sliding glass door that opened into an un-fenced backyard bordered by an empty lot, where cars parked late at night in the corner closest to our property. Their interiors were lit up by cell phones, wispy smoke slithering out of their windows. In the morning I found used condoms, burnt tinfoil squares, and plastic pen casings.

"This area isn't safe for a child," I told Alex.

"We don't have kids," he said. "We can always put up a fence or something."

Our property's grounds were harsh and desertlike, so I tried tending a sand garden out front with a patchwork of all-season plants—white sages, succulents, cacti—along with cosmetically similar solar rock lights that fizzed an anemic firefly brightness at night. I selected rocks from a catalog of rock palettes, learning the difference between axinite, apatite, and serpentine. All the rocks were uniform in size, granular color, and stone consistency with my neighbors' properties. I arranged the stones in a constant rotation by color and size around the centerpiece of my "collection," a translucent dufrenite mineral from southern Maine.

I made the best of it. But, really, how much could you do with fucking rocks?

Once, when Cynthia visited to try and sell me Herbalife products for my parents and sister because she heard they were "big in the Hispanic community," she said, "This space is so hostile. Are you and Alex in couples counseling?"

As in-laws, they sent us unsigned birthday and holiday cards that were advertisements for multilevel marketing companies. We had closets full of artificial, orange-flavored weight-loss powders, and trapezoid storage containers that didn't seal. On Christmas they'd miss the six-course dinner I spent hours cooking, then show up after dark, with Kevin dressed in a Santa tank top and shorts, butchering Frank Sinatra carols and drinking scotch until three a.m.

After one particularly raucous night when Santa Kevin slept on the couch, I told Alex, "Next year, we're either in a different house, or we're having a baby."

Alex's lingering resistance to children had melted into indifference, which by my thirties was good enough for me. Melanie (spelled with an *a*, the way my white yoga teacher spells it, not an *o*, like that Mexican pop star) was what my doctor called an "easy" pregnancy and what I called an assault on every orifice of my body. I was warned by books with panic-inducing titles about swollen extremities, the accumulation of fluids, the combinations of fist-clenching stiffness and jolts of migratory pain, every part of my anatomy rebelling against me. I hadn't prepared for my thoughts to do likewise. My anxiety levels fluctuated between maddening and ravenous. During my last trimester, I instructed Alex (who offered to handle my chores, then bombarded me with endless questions and texts about whether he was doing them right) to treat any form of conversation between us like 911 calls—emergencies only.

To quell a creeping dread of postpartum depression, I took daily walks before and after work. I slathered Melanie in sunscreen and set up a baby hammock next to my front yard rock bed. I strapped Mel on my back in an eco-friendly hemp sling and participated in a gentrifying downtown calendar of activities: fun runs, farmers' markets, Wine on Main Street Wednesdays, and glass pumpkin patch charity auctions. These activities attracted the same people who organized "Not in my backyard" protests, and as a new parent genuinely concerned about our neighborhood, I migrated to these events, too, drawn by promises on the colorful flyers of finding like-minded community. I picketed with a random cluster of middle-aged housewives and their bored children chanting, "Keep Us Safe!" while holding pink signs decorated with glitter outside a planned homeless shelter three miles from our home. I reasoned that its twelve-minute driving distance was too close to a park where I would likely take my child to play. I lectured able-bodied men outside the local food pantry on the virtues of plant-based diets, reminding those who said they weren't "commie vegans" that "you can't be a beggar and a chooser, too."

One day, a friendly schoolteacher named Allie, who I befriended on a methadone clinic picket line, met up with me for a "girls' date" at a smoothie shop. We laughed about our favorite dumb Christmas movies and our shared last-trimester affinity for dark chocolate bars and crunchy peanut butter. I thought I'd made a new friend.

She leaned in and said, "Do you know who the enemy is?"

"Oh," I said. "I don't think so."

"I can't say too much in public because everyone's phones are listening to us," she said. "I'll send you some links!"

Clicking through Allie's sites—the lurid colors, their inflammatory pictures and hateful language—made me physically retch. Served me right for trying to make a friend as an adult.

Quickly, I realized a simple fact: these people were *nuts*. When had everyone gotten so crazy? Being this nuts—and this angry—was scary enough, but it was also time-consuming. What kind of good parent could be this angry all the time? How could you maintain this level of constant agitation and paranoia and know anything about who your child really is?

Once I gave birth, everything and everyone who wasn't my immediate family exhausted me. Show me a mother with time for close friends, anyway. I didn't have the inclination to expose my feelings to a world that might reject them. A high school friend I no longer speak to said becoming a mom would give me a clarity I desperately needed. "Becoming a parent softens people," she said, adding, "but I doubt that will happen with you." She was right. Parenthood hardened my resolve to protect and secure, to be skeptical of insincerity, and to, above all else, physically adore and love my child.

So when Alex asked me, over and over, *What did I want?* I wanted my husband to do the same. He never did.

Fatherhood, too, like my leaving him, caught Alex by surprise. He was present, but he wasn't *there*—just like my own father, Gonzalo. Alex thought his parents could protect him from its responsibilities, the way they'd inoculated him from the work and chores I had to do growing up. When I was old enough to hold a broom and not drop it, Mamá had me cleaning house. Even after I moved out for college, when I came home every weekend my mamá enlisted me and Serena to help clean the house. I did the counters, while Serena was told to sweep. She'd sneeze up a storm, do a fake cough routine, and say, "Mamá, I can't breathe!" Dolores then gave her trash duty. "Mamá, it stinks!" Dolores scolded her to be quiet and stay out of the way. So Serena ended up on the couch watching TV, and I ended up dusting, sweeping, and taking out the trash. My mamá had a clean house and I had a sore back.

In the same way my parents spoiled Serena, Alex was too permissive with Mel, and didn't set enough boundaries. He handed our daughter off to me like she was groceries he wanted me to carry up a flight of stairs. I stayed quiet longer than I should have, hoping he'd somehow change, evolve, or by accident let himself fill up with wonder at each new way Mel explored the world. Instead, he retracted, burrowing into his phone, his laptop, his television, his widening half of the bed.

We fought about the age a child should start making her own bed, and he got me blacklisted from a local online parents listserv when they found out I assigned Mel a daily chores list that included physical labor. ("You make your child sweep floors *and* wash dishes?" Damn *right* I do.) I told him to stop giving Mel unlimited screen time, and to stop running to the freezer for chocolate ice cream when she screamed for attention.

"Relax, it's vegan," Alex said. "Why do you treat Mel like a wicked stepmom?"

I am a vigilant mother and know two styles of parenting: push, or surrender. My mamá pushed me. Then she got old and surrendered to my sister, Serena. Melanie grew up learning a clear, specific routine that I established, and Alex ceded input into, before Mel was a year old. She understood from an early age that she had responsibilities and rules she must follow. Our family ate together at all mealtimes. No screens or phones at the table and only one hour of screen time per day. The rules were easy to enforce, at first. Then her tantrums hit.

"I can't teach a crying child," I'd say to her. "No brats in my house. Stop crying so you can learn."

Every lesson, no matter how emotionally grueling, ended with me giving Mel hugs, kisses, or some form of physical affection. I wanted her to know she was loved, and a child can't learn that if you only tell them. I don't live for my daughter. I live to never let her doubt for a moment that she is loved and she can be fearless.

I fell out of love with my husband at one of his parents' pool parties in Hyde Heights, a two-hour journey through inhospitable desert colonized by flotillas of strip malls, then to roads in the cold gloom of crumbling smoke-colored hills, with Mt. Burnett (whose name has been under "historical review" for the past seven years) poking through rings of smoggy haze. These were weekly events with swollen, furious retirees drinking local, desert-grown rosé wine, endless cans of light beer, eating rounds of frozen cocktail wieners and tortilla chips with un-spiced "American" tomato salsa. Kevin and Cynthia, who were Mexican Americans themselves, proselytized to their selected coterie of friends how terrible and foreign the world outside their artificial-turf backyard had become.

I'd met them at what was meant as a celebratory meal for Alex's first real job—a position he had wanted, applied for, and gotten. "Your birth name's Iris?" Kevin asked. "*Really?* Never met a Mexican named Iris before."

"Oh," I said.

"I mean that in a good way!" Kevin said, and double-pumped my hand.

He introduced his wife, Cynthia, as "a fan of God, Ronald Reagan, and real work."

"You enjoyed college?" she asked me. "You can thank me, as a taxpayer who helped pay for your education. No offense."

"Oh," I said again. What I thought was *I went to a private school on a scholarship and I owe you nothing.* How elegantly she had shifted the burden of being offended onto me. I whispered to Alex, "Aren't both your parents Mexican?" I knew Kevin was—he couldn't pass for anything but—yet wasn't sure about Cynthia.

Alex said, "They are. But they don't mean *us.*"

"Which 'us'? I don't understand," I said.

Alex never explained. I had never met this kind of *us,* this kind of Mexican American—*malinchistas,* my mamá called them—before. I never thought I was the target of Kevin and Cynthia's speeches—*I was born here*—yet their diatribes flowed freely on visits that grew louder in volume and more tediously bitter and, at my insistence, less frequent over the years. His parents were a conspiracy theory jazz combo, improv-ing off each other's prejudices and resentments, rewarding each other for their mutual disinterest in the world beyond their cul-de-sac.

These hatreds invariably led to Alex and Kevin having a hostile relationship for years. Any conversation, no matter how banal, could lead into bitter arguments between the two. I sat mute by Alex's side during what Kevin playfully called "colorful discussions" because I thought I could learn who Alex really was, what he really cared for and believed. Perhaps, then, I could understand why he acted as aloof and distant as he did, or attribute those needling things about his personality to his father. That never happened. I thought these men had strong opinions, when in fact they were simply opinionated—they couldn't be moved. What I accepted was that my husband and Kevin had a genuine passion for articulating the other's weaknesses and watching each other explode in a rage. They enjoyed hurting each other. It was almost a sport for the both of them, one that Cynthia didn't condone but didn't really dissuade, either, as long as they didn't interfere with her numerous social get-togethers.

I didn't mind their parties, as copious amounts of booze was freely available. I liked speaking my mind and, after two or three glasses of white wine, enjoyed being Alex's "challenging" wife who gave shit to people who, ideologically, I probably had more in common with than I did with my "everything everyone says is a problem" sister, Serena. I understood where shit talkers were coming from. They want someone to listen. But, my God, if you stop listening to their tonterías? I wore a LEGALIZE SCIENCE T-shirt Serena gave me to one of their parties. Gone was their facade of collegiality and friendship. "Now you're just betraying your ignorance, Iris."

That day, Mel was playing with Alex and Kevin in the pool, when she called him "Abuelo." Kevin handed Mel to Alex and stormed out of the water.

"Grandpa," Cynthia corrected from the deck. "He's Grandpa in this house."

We raised Mel to be bilingual, but accepted that Spanish was prohibited in their home, meaning Mel had to abide by their rules. (My Spanish had long fallen out of favor, like a once beloved toy.) I saw Alex motion to follow Kevin, I guess to apologize, but Alex knew I did not want Mel unsupervised in the pool, so he stayed with her in the shallow end. I watched them from behind a frayed magazine, then went to the kitchen for a tumbler of ice water. In the three minutes it took me to return, a concerned group of murmuring adults and quiet, still children were huddled around Mel's motionless body, laid out on the deck.

"She was under the water for less than a second," Alex said. "I swear."

I pushed everyone aside and pumped my child's stomach as she choked for an excruciating thirty-seven seconds before I helped her puke out globs of gastric juice onto an Elsa beach towel. I breathed in Melanie's precious, vomit-scented exhales while Alex's parents led a round of applause.

"Thank God Alex was here," Kevin said. I glared at Alex, who said nothing.

"She's so well-behaved, who knew anything was wrong?" Cynthia said.

"My child is polite and kind because that is ten thousand hours of teaching and patience and pain and tears that I put in!" I shouted. "She's not mean and boring like you."

Kevin said, "Damn, now we're talking! Get her, Iris!"

I said to Alex, "Go and start the car."

An urgent care doctor confirmed Melanie had swallowed too much chlorinated swimming pool water, but would be fine. When the doctor left, Alex said, "Please don't speak to my mother that way again."

I said, "You're sleeping on the couch tonight."

That night, Mel came to me in a nightmare. She was floating underwater, her chestnut hair undulating like ivy, her face frozen in an astonished gasp.

In the cold gray morning after you've slept apart from your spouse, you can attain a specific clarity about what's important to you. How quickly do you want them back in your bed?

I told Alex I wanted to separate unless we went to couples therapy.

"Therapy means questions," he said. "Questions mean fights."

"Then let's fight and figure this out," I said.

For several months, our therapist asked questions—good ones. But they didn't lead to fights at all, rather an overlapping series of calcified stalemates where no question was ever fully answered but merely tabbed, like on a browser, leading to another "for next time" conversation, and an evolving set of grievances. Alex stammered, shut down, folded into his own silences, but he never fought. Driving back from our sessions in a brittle stillness, I realized that what once had felt like security had become a hard, uncompromising drift apart. Alex and I were fiercely disengaging from each other, a steady, irreversible uncoupling. Our therapy sessions and dinners were our only shared hours together, united only by routine and hunger. How much of the last months of our marriage had been me with Mel in one room, my husband on his computer in another, castled in our silences?

Dolores said my separation was inevitable because "you took your marriage *so seriously*—you're like a white woman." When Gonzalo drank a dozen Tecates at El Camino's pool hall every weekend and came home late, Dolores would sit and read on the couch until she heard him fumble with the locks. Then she'd scare him with a sartén she wielded like a six-shooter and force him to sleep on a cracked wicker chair on the front porch. She'd leave the front door security gate unlatched when she drove to work at four in the morning, which meant their fight was over. Eventually, as Gonzalo aged, he got tired of pool, and sleeping outside every Friday and Saturday night, so he stopped.

My fights with Alex were static and indifferent. We were too tired to argue for more than five minutes at a time, the length of my typical at-work lunch. While Melanie yelled, screamed, laughed, and made herself present, we walked around the house in stockinged feet, creeping into and out of shared rooms, bickering with each other's shadows.

The end—*my* end—happened over a simple text from Alex: *Sorry, running late, forgot the dry cleaning.*

I had reminded him three times. Now I had to wear the skirt with the soiled white stains on the hem again. I would have to dig through my closet for a pair of clean tights I knew weren't there. My hands slipped washing a coffee mug in the sink, where it shattered.

My husband would be home in fifteen minutes. I cried for ten, cleaned up my own mess, then wrote to myself on my phone, *Start looking for houses.*

I browsed homes online the way my husband looked at porn, surreptitiously at night, in the farthest corner of our house, so I wouldn't risk being discovered. He never caught on, though he asked odd questions suggesting he thought I was on a dating site. I met a broker I liked, Susanna, a young Latina who dressed the way I did for work: neutral-colored pantsuit, tiny earrings, and conservative flats. I used to drive straight to Mamá's house after work without changing, but got tired of Serena sniping at me.

"Gawd, you dress like a gringa," Serena would say.

"This is business appropriate," I said. "It's Kate Spade."

My sister said, "Looks like Kate Spade hates boobs."

Susanna and I met after work every other day for two weeks, until one Saturday I found a neighborhood that seemed ideal. With its forever green lawns and generous hardscaped distances between properties, the houses were isolated, private, but part of a community, too.

A beautiful, perfect community. Just like Lilac Village from my childhood.

The house was in a semi cul-de-sac, nestled in the short end of an L-shaped corner with no home across the street from it, nor any homes directly on either side. The closest properties were clustered at odd, semi-adjacent angles, meaning that you could see everyone that came by but almost nobody could see your home unless they went looking for you.

"This home's part of an HOA," Susanna said as our footsteps echoed across its polished, hardwood floors, "but they're really hands-off around here. And they won't bother you at all. I can tell. Just follow the rules."

"The rules?" I asked.

"Yeah, super-basic stuff like no crazy outdoor projects, no loud music, don't trash your property, no front yard barbecues, et cetera. Anything that makes the area more beautiful is okay, but it has to look like what everyone else is doing. We had this Korean family that grew gochu red peppers and summer squash in their front yard. They were pretty to look at, but they didn't check with anybody. The family said they'd get rid of the offending produce but instead packed them into tiny concrete planters in their backyard. So the HOA got them out. I was sympathetic, but people complained about how smelly the garden was even from behind the house, and the family had signed a contract, so . . ."

"You have to follow the rules," I said. "I completely agree."

"I'm glad you get it," Susanna said.

We paused at a multipaned bay window that looked out at the crisp, precisely trimmed Irish-green front yard and the symmetrically balanced and distributed houses throughout the neighborhood. In the distance were violet thistles, red and sandbar willow bushes, crepe myrtle trees, and a clear untrammeled view of my cul-de-sac. I saw waves of asymmetrical white picket fences, showers of windblown jacaranda blossoms, and palm tree fronds hissing in the breeze. I paused at this spot a half dozen times during the walk-through and thought, *Mel and I could be happy here.*

"Look out there, Iris. Your daughter deserves a home like this. So do you."

Yes, I thought, *yes yes yes.* This is where I wanted Mel and I to belong.

I put in my bid that night. I kept my hopes grounded, but a spotless credit record and years of diligent savings in my own separate banking account (at Alex's insistence) made borrowing hundreds of thousands of dollars easier than the process of leaving my husband. My offer was accepted Monday morning. I would own my own house, and as long as I followed the rules, nobody could take it from me.

That night, when Alex asked me if I'd gotten takeout for dinner, I told him we were done. I was moving out, and Mel was coming with me.

"You're not as fearless as you think you are," Alex said, looking to hurt me. "But do what you want to do."

I wanted Alex and I to tell Mel together that we were separating, one of the last things we could do—no, *owed* her—as a couple. He refused.

"I can comfort her when you're done," he said. "Don't say anything that will embarrass me."

I stammered through a simpering explanation laden with bad metaphors I thought would be easier for a nine-year-old child to understand. Mel grabbed a teddy bear from her stuffed animal shelf.

"I'm okay, Mamá," she said, and pressed Fudgie into my quivering hands. "I want you to be, too."

I was proud of her in that moment. I had raised a sturdy girl who needed no consolation when a man left. What more could a mother want for her daughter?

Moving day was a joyless carousel of trips between the two houses, transporting overstuffed plastic tubs and flimsy, dumpster-salvaged cardboard boxes filled with things that seemed less necessary with each pass—obnoxiously scented candles, a ball pit of flaky bath bombs, unsent Christmas cards from a no-longer-intact Prince family. Mel tired of carrying things and squatted in our new front yard atop a nubby box elder tree stump.

"Mommy, are we done yet? I'm starving!"

"Use your 'Only for Mommy' voice, please," I said. I didn't want to cause a front yard scene on our first day. This had to be a street where neighbors leered behind curtains or blinds. Otherwise it wasn't the neighborhood I wanted it to be.

Our new single-family home was near the center of North Vecino, a reasonable five freeway exits away from Alex's townhome. In that eleven-and-a-half-mile distance apart was a new zip code, a much better school district for Mel, and high-end grocery stores that my relatives would cast me into hell for shopping in such a profligate way. *Did we raise you to spend ten dollars on juice from a fruit?*

North Vecino was a perfect distance from the freeway. Close enough to encourage sensible growth, but far from the urban area the highway had sliced through. Leaving the highway off-ramp, you could see the neighborhoods change, a metamorphosis from gritty streets to suburban oasis. The street signs were brighter, and gone were the potholes, strip malls, gaudy colored murals of unknown Mexican heroes who were uniformly men, Spanglish signs painted in mismatched primary colors (PARKING ATRÁS!), gas stations with attached check-cashing liquor stores, lone outpost branches of formerly chain restaurants, Spanish signage, loiterers, the homeless, even pedestrians themselves. Sidewalks narrowed, then vanished. Streets and driveways widened. Lush traffic circles of green space were everywhere. Homes receded from their front lawns, their entryways retreating behind the daylight buoy lights that hugged box gardens and walkway coastlines. Spray paint markings, not on walls, but from surveyors' cans, discreet lines and X's on the ground and front lawns, a never-ending season of renovations and home improvements. In the distance around North Vecino's freeway sound barriers were a painted Möbius strip of nonexistent desert and mountainous horizons to obscure the views and dampen the hostile roar of traffic and collisions.

Our new neighborhood traffic circle was isolated from the main boulevard and its neutral off-beige-colored houses were within eyesight of each other, yet also a healthy walking distance apart. Two- and three-bedroom Horizon houses (like mine) on the south side, four- and five-bedroom Laramie houses at the circle's equator, and six-bedroom Le Roman homes with pillars anchoring the corners.

Cute blue trash bins on Tuesdays, big bright yellow ones on Thursdays. It was a neighborhood where everything made sense.

Every night, Mel and I walked around our neighborhood traffic circle in the quiet, dusky hours around dinnertime. It was a vibrant area: families playing in the park, dogs being walked, and children running without worry about speeding cars before being ushered into their homes at sunset, like a line of buoys being hauled in from the ocean. You could see inside the heart of these houses through floor-to-ceiling glass. Empty, immaculate, showplace living rooms, the faint glow of alarm lights and expensive machines pulsing in the dark like luxury stores after close. And—paradise!—stacks of unattended packages left on the porches. On alternating lawns were mounted cardboard signs: lawn care advertisements, security system warnings, poop 'n' scoop reminders, and outside almost every house, small pink placards with floating golden halos for an election ballot measure that passed several months ago: YES ON PROP 3 = GET ON THE BAND! On the signs were a detached clenched white fist with a gold ring floating around the wrist.

"See how safe it is here?" I asked Mel.

"It's so quiet!" she said. No music, no backyard parties or barbecues, just the ghostly pallor of internal screen lights flickering like dying fires. "Of course it's quiet here," my real estate agent had told me. "People work for a living during the day."

I wanted to live where the land had no memory. I had earned the right to forget who I was, too.

A month or so later, in a quiet afternoon of pen scratching and murmured paper rustling, my marriage was over. Ours was a civil separation. I had Mel during the week, while Alex took her during the weekends, a perfect arrangement as it would turn out. No one raised their voices or hired contentious lawyers neither of us had money for. I was grateful Alex and I didn't have friends, something neither of us realized until Alex said we should list who gets to keep which friendships and both of us held up blank sheets.

That first night I found a tub of Alex's things I must have taken by mistake. I had packed up fast because I didn't want my doubt and insecurity to convince me they had my best interests at heart, the way they often did. Inside the moving tub was a small electric keyboard and a shrink-wrapped copy of *Songwriting for Dummies*, photo frames with no pictures in them, a red leather passport holder for that trip to Portugal we never took. I'm not trying to sound bitter about what he or we didn't do. Our mutual priorities slid out of view. This happens when loving people lose their passion in a crowded room of obligations and absurd arguments over forgetting their bills' auto-pay passwords.

My younger sister, Serena, texted that I should leave his things on the curb in garbage bags "con los perros" to teach him a lesson. She's big on teaching lessons, but not on receiving them, so I stacked Alex's items in organized piles that he could collect on his first weekend visit with Mel. I felt uncomfortable for a while with some of his things being here. Hypnotized by my and Mel's clothes in the dryer, I thought I should drive everything of his back to the house—*his* house—right away, as if getting every single one of Alex's things out of this space would somehow purify our new home, a kind of emotional exorcism to guarantee Mel and me total independence. I held my resolve. I was trying to teach my body—my *self*—that I didn't have to race to do anything for a man anymore.

At the end of moving day, I was un-showered and sleep deprived, my tingling shoulder and back muscles aflame in knots. I imagined a long soak in a lavender bath, but the thought of cleaning and scouring our only tub coated with dust and patches of sticky pubic hair almost broke me.

I remember my first morning as a single mother. The arid expanse of loneliness in an unshared bed. The quiet that rolled in, like a cloak, settling as a deep chill on the bare floors. The blistering anxiety that clung to me for months that stemmed from *not* having to track anymore whether Alex took his pills to help him outrun his middle-aged lethargy.

And the fear. I don't need to say what kind. A woman will understand what I mean.

Can I do this alone? Does my daughter still love me? Is there anyone out there who will like me again?

It's hard to feel likable when your whole life has changed in a night.

Soon, the fear ebbed away. I don't know where it went, but little by little, Alex and I fell into a cordial schedule of "hangs" (as Mel called them) and weekend visitations, which suited us both. He was a much better weekend father than he had been day-to-day. The fact that he knew his fatherhood had a time limit, that he could give Mel back to me on Sunday night, made him freer, relaxed him in ways that helped me see the man he used to be, but couldn't be as a full-time dad.

In three months' time, I had established a new routine, guided by a series of specific birdlike chirps throughout my day. The coffee maker emitted three fast beeps in the morning. Four sharp blips when I finished brushing my teeth. One long confirming beep, then a series of sparrow trills to turn off the alarm system. A cluster of pleasant marimba GPS noises that guided me to Mel's new elementary school, to my office, then the five o'clock after-school-care dash back across town, until a shrill batch of sharp tones in our darkened basement told me my laundry was done.

I hampered Mel's warm clothes and took them into her bedroom. Unlike her old space, this wasn't down two flights of stairs from our master bedroom, and it had a window facing the front yard. She'd had trouble sleeping the last few weeks in the old house while her things were packed up and wanted night-lights and a screen playing cartoons with the sound low to dilute the darkness. We hadn't broken the habit yet.

"Here's your blanket," I said, collecting crayons and paper with two sets of handprints from the floor. "I folded the rest of your things, but please put them away tomorrow, okay?"

"Rub the blanket on my face, Mommy!"

"Can you say, 'please'?" I asked.

"Daddy says I don't have to say 'please' if I'm not raising my voice."

"I said 'please' when I asked you to put away your clothes, didn't I?"

"Yes, Mommy," she said.

"We say 'please' in our home."

"Please," she said. "Blanket!"

I rubbed a dryer-warm blue fleece blanket on her fair-skinned cheeks, which glowed like tiny amber halos. She laughed, a giddy hiccup that delighted strangers. When I take her to the pastelería near my parents' house, her cheeks are squeezed and plumped by handsy señoras, and she's laden with free sweets. *¡Tu niña está* *muy flaca!* At upscale supermarkets, where I do most of my shopping, white women ask me, *"Who* is that child's mom?" and stare in disbelief when I tell them I am. Thanks to Alex, Melanie's skin color would never be the light-to-burnt umber mine is. My lighter-skinned Mexican cousins would never call Mel "la prietita" behind her back like they did me, and Mel's future white friends won't hedge on inviting her over to their pool parties. She would never need to learn, on her own like I did (because Dolores refused to tell me), about when it was advantageous to be more Mexican, or American. Stud earrings at work, hoop earrings on weekends with my Mexican girlfriends. English only in the office, Spanish solo en casa después de las cinco y solamente con la familia. Console my white friends that racism doesn't exist (which of course it does), and console my Mexican friends racism was the reason they didn't get that job they wanted (which of course it wasn't). Living in the middle made me insane sometimes. I was too dark to pass for white, too white and educated to be a "real" Mexican, as if being educated and going to college had turned me pocha. I had to tight-rope walk across two worlds without falling into either: ni de aquí ni de allá.

That was my world. But it already wasn't my daughter's. A lack of pigment, thanks to Alex's melanin, gave her a different path. It's not my place to say, "How tragic." It's my job to help her learn how to take advantage so she can stay safe.

"I want to tell you what happened today," Melanie said.

"You have two minutes," I said. Since our move, Mel had learned that if she confessed to an endless string of "bad things" she did or thought during the day, I would stay in bed with her and listen.

"The last time I was at Daddy's house, I said I hate boys," Mel said. "But I didn't mean it."

"I hate boys sometimes, too," I said. "We don't hate Daddy. Please don't do it again."

"I can't find my Snoopy chanclas or my Tigger."

"Where did you leave them?" I asked. "At Dad's?" I had mentally started a list of things I had to go back to his house and search for. I asked Alex countless times to assemble a box of things Mel or I left behind, but that is not how he's built.

"I was climbing the wall outside and had to leave Tigger behind because I couldn't carry him with me. My chanclas fell off. When I climbed back, they were gone."

"Were you playing down the street?" I asked.

"No, Mom, the wall. Out there." Mel pointed at the window. "When are we seeing Daddy again?"

"Honey, we don't have a wall." I snapped off each appliance and light, then peered out Mel's window into abject darkness, one question behind my child, which happened whenever I stayed up past eight o'clock. Our streetlight, for some reason, wasn't on. "Dad's picking you up this weekend, just like every weekend."

"I wish you didn't turn off the lights in here."

"Big girls don't need night-lights. Mommy's real tired, but your Tigger is probably at the old house. We'll get him this weekend."

"But, Mom!" Mel said. "You can't leave me to the elephants!"

"Do you mean elements?"

"Yeah. The elements. And the elephants!" Mel said, and laughed.

"Time to go mimis," I said. "I'll open the door a little."

I padded on bare feet down our hallway and fell backward into a new king-size mattress. In the last days of our marriage, I fantasized about sleeping in a bed I wouldn't have to share. Yet in all this new unclaimed space I was being swaddled between sleep and waking, as if insomnia had long arms and hands that held me down. That's how it felt not to share a bed with my husband.

Ex. *Ex*-husband.

Later, I don't know when, I heard a young woman speak in a clear voice: ¿Qué eres?

I usually dream in English. Serena, who dreamed in Spanish, ridiculed me about this.

"Ay, ¡qué blanquita!" Serena would say. "What kind of Mexican are you?"

"I can't control how I dream!" I'd say, more hurt than annoyed.

"Nobody's fooled. Love and anger live in your first language.

Even en tus sueños you wanna be a white girl, Eye-reez." She drew my name, Iris, out into a mangled hiss that sounded like a curse.

Deeper into the gray area I went. Asleep, then almost awake.

In that last, crisp second of sleep, I dreamed that I saw myself from above. I gasped for air, my hands clutching my throat to breathe. Then I heard two voices. One voice was my own, the other a scarred, off-accent duplicate, foreign, transformed.

I reached inside my mouth, felt no tongue, yet the words came anyway.

¿Qué eres?

I had to remember my Spanish to translate.

What are you?

I woke up, maybe a minute or two before my alarm, to the sound of a door squealing ajar. Melanie was purr-snoring alongside me. "You hear that?" I asked. "Did you hear her?" Mel didn't rouse.

I shambled to the galley kitchen with its panoramic tri-paned bay window. Each day since we moved in, I sat by this window and imagined what I could do here. This view was the reason I wanted to live in this house. I could see and envision any future—my future, Mel's future—from here. A small garden where Mel and I could plant neighborhood-approved plants and flowers. A mildly gossipy coffee club of casual neighborhood acquaintances drinking from oversize and charmingly chipped porcelain mugs with our names on them (and I already had the mug! *Iris Prince*, it says in a loopy cursive). Time spent with, not adjacent to, my daughter. I relished the joy and satisfaction I felt from following the rules and reaping my success.

I was ready, at last, for days of mostly inconsequential first-world problems. I was ready for a new life.

I fumbled for a coffee mug on the second shelf of the top left cabinet. At last, every item in my house had a home. A final confirming *beep*. I poured the coffee, swiped my eyes left and right to savor this inspirational view.

Outside, in front of my home, was a wall.

Three

When you see something outside your house that shouldn't be there, there's no vacillating between holy and profane exclamations: *What is that? Oh my God! What the hell?* Usually, you don't even realize there's a menace at your front door at all. There's a silence first, a holding in of one's breath. In that long, labored quiet, you are acknowledging something that shouldn't be, but is. You are also grasping for some kind of reason, an explanation that pulls the breath out of you and lets you exhale. When the rational thought does not arrive, a new kind of breathlessness occurs, a giddy, fatalistic thought that says, *I knew something like this would happen.*

Out there was a Wall. Capital *W* Wall.

I was stunned at its size—the actual enormity of it, which ran the entire front length of my property—but after that moment of shock I still didn't know exactly how to process what I was seeing. Mel told me about it last night. I thought she had been confused. It wasn't there the day before. It shouldn't have been there today.

Yet there it was.

The front door was unlocked, a few inches ajar. *Did Alex try to come inside my house last night? No, he doesn't have keys. He wouldn't.*

Did I wander outside last night?

I slipped on sandals, stupefied, a full coffee mug in hand, and walked to the wall.

It was about four feet high, rising to just around my chest, maybe three to four feet wide, and was around a hundred feet long from one end to the other, dividing my perfect green front lawn in half. The wall blocked the neat circular skipping-stone pathway that ran from the street curb to my front door, meaning I'd have to walk a good fifty feet around it just to get to the street every morning. It stopped where my adjacent neighbors' expansive lawns began, meaning they likely couldn't see the wall, since their homes were so far from the street. From a distance, they would likely see a seam in the horizon, spilling out a mirage haze like the kind you see when you stare into the distance long enough. Just a trace outline of the wall itself.

I walked the length of the wall until I stood on its opposite side, looking at my house from behind it. The wall was cool to the touch, made from natural stone—maybe blue limestone brick, if my old HOA rock knowledge was right?—with several layers of weathered face, and smooth stone slabs for a ledge. Depending on where I stood, the wall either radiated or absorbed light. It felt solid, immovable, and was, if I am being honest, aesthetically pleasing. Maybe the kind of "raise your property value" retaining wall I would have hired a contractor to build in a year or two, but without it blocking my path, of course.

I skimmed the street. Trash cans were undisturbed in their driveway cutouts. Silver and chrome luxury SUVs winked in the morning sun. Not a person in sight.

A heady morning balm lingered in the air over a horizon of isosceles-shaped roofs. Beyond that, smoke rings from a gang of stubborn brush fires ringed distant mountaintops. One large gun-metal cloud hovered overhead, flaunting its pillowy belly that I imagined, if sliced down the middle, would gush a flood of sunshine. The weather here was so immutable that the sky could be mistaken for a painting.

There was nothing here I didn't see yesterday.

I stared at my house from behind the wall and propped my coffee and phone atop it. I searched for "walls," lost my grip, and dumped coffee on the wall.

This time, I gasped, "Oh no!"—a silly cartoonish response.

Tepid liquid trickled down its side. Where the wall met the ground, I thought I felt a dim pulsing under my sandals, a faint but insistent thrum that was oddly comforting—nostalgic, even—that drew me to sit down in its shade.

There, I heard that detached, unrecognizable but familiar voice again: ¿Qué eres?

I shot up and saw Mel standing in the doorway. "Mommy? Did you find my Tigger and chanclas?"

I caught my right sandal on a beveled, quarter-size thorn of blue-pink glass that poked out from the wall like a polished baby's tooth. The strap was torn in half. A step more and my ankle would have been sliced open. Ándate con pies de plomo, my mamá, Dolores, said each day before grade school. ¡La tierra se mueve sin avisar!

"They're not here, sweetie."

Mel crossed the threshold and padded onto the porch in bare feet.

"No, Mel! Stay there. Mommy cut her sandal on something." I thought about hurdling over the wall if I had a running start, then remembered I wasn't twenty years old. I walked the long length of the wall back to the front porch. It felt like a needless, punitive journey I would now have to take every day.

"I told you," Mel said.

"Mommy's sorry," I said, and hugged her. "I was tired and confused. I'm going to listen to you from now on," I said. I meant it, too. "That wall's taller than you," I added. "I don't want you climbing it anymore. How did you get over it yesterday?"

"It's bigger," she said.

"What do you mean?"

"It wasn't that tall last night," Mel said.

A dissonant alarm chime from my phone drowned out my follow-up questions. We had fifteen minutes before we were running late. To start accommodating our route to a new school, I set my alarm early to make sure we had enough time for both of our morning chores. Melanie had to start every day opening her bedroom shades. If her bedroom was dark, I marched Melanie back around. At our old house, Mel had to make her bed, wash her face, brush her teeth, pick out her shoes and clothes, and be dressed and ready for breakfast before Alex and I sat down to join her.

I found nothing remarkable about my child being able to do this without complaint. By the time Melanie was nine, she had mostly grown past, and through, her incalculable shock waves of tears, screams, tantrums, shin kicks, forearm and shoulder bites, slammed doors, and a hundred thousand *I hate yous!* Alex never hesitated to compliment me on my mothering skills, but my exhaustion and fatigue were unexceptional. I never complained about child-raising and had no patience for those who did, in conversation or online. *You chose to get pregnant, didn't you? Then choose to spend time with your child every day and tell them what you expect from them.* My pain was my business, not the internet's. I didn't have a child for the likes.

No excuses, Mel, I'd tell her. *An excuse is like saying, "Eff you."*
What's an eff? Melanie asked.
You'll never know, I said, *because you won't make excuses.*

Now Mel and I rushed to wash up and dress. In no time came the three-minute countdown before leaving the house.

Three minutes left: grab Melanie's lunch that I premade and prepacked the night before, along with Mel's screen in a childproof container from its cracked wall-mounted charger.

Two minutes left: lock Melanie in her rear seat, check the harness and straps, then double-check it, then double-check the double check.

One minute left: walk around my car to the driver's side, swallow my second cup of coffee from a reusable stainless-steel tumbler, a gift to myself after broiling in a black gown for ninety minutes at my outdoor master's degree commencement ceremony. Cost, with degree: $58,024. (My alumni key fob was free.)

Was it a sunglass or an eyeglass driving day? Like every day here, today's sun was the same as yesterday's, hidden in a partly cloudy sky. I had until I walked to the driver's side to decide what to wear. Otherwise, I would lose my train of thought answering Melanie's daily round of questions.

"Mom! I gotta get the go!" Melanie shouted from the car.

"Okay, we're going." Melanie's old kindergarten teacher had told her she was a "go-getting" child. Since then, whenever Melanie was impatient or bored, she'd say, "I gotta get the go!" I couldn't channel Mel to do anything specific with this initiative except race her to the next activity.

Like Momma, like Mel, Alex would say.

At the driver's-side door, I was out of private time. I chose eyeglasses. I hated how they made the skin around my squinting eyes pucker, but in them I could see things clear, plain, verified by others.

There was a fucking wall in front of my house.

I didn't have time to ponder what this meant. I had to take my daughter to school and get to work. In hindsight, I wasn't seeing things as clearly at the start of that dry, endless mirage of a day as I should have. Or, I guess, every day that came after.

I drove too fast out of our traffic circle over a row of speed bumps separated by a pair of permanent "safety" bollards, then through three sneaky maze bends onto Grand Vecino Street, one of two main boulevards in North Vecino. I'd memorized the trees along the route because I wanted my daughter to learn something aside from gorging herself on screen time, which she couldn't have until our drive home. Seeing her head droop over her screen like a wilted flower moving to sunlight whenever she turned it on was enough for me to set a daily time limit.

"Look, Mel!"

I followed her head in the rearview mirror. *There*, I said, at the corner, *that's an oak.* At the intersection with the church, *a box elder, like the stump in our yard.* Overhanging the impossibly clean (and loitering-free!) gas station parking lot, *a cottonwood.* On the drive approaching Leland Elementary, *ash and sandbar willows.*

"How many of those do you remember?" I asked.

"Why are we always late for school?" Melanie said.

"Mommy tries to do ten things in a space where six will fit."

"You drive slower than Daddy. He drives faster and we're never late when we go places."

"Daddy doesn't drive you to school anymore," I said. He rarely did when we lived together, but I was learning that divorce makes a child nostalgic for an absent father.

"Don't you love me as much as Daddy?"

"Dad does exactly what you see him do. I need more time for the things you don't see."

"That's not what Daddy says!" Mel said.

"I know, cariño. Daddy says a lot of things. But mommies have no reason to lie. Sometimes my plans take longer than I think."

"But, Mom," Melanie said, "that's not how *my* plan goes."

When, and how, had she learned to talk this way? Freely, with such confidence, as if we were equals? She was a fourth grader. I was grateful Mel was a girl, though. This was as much pushback as she gave me. Flexing her authority at this age was a delight because she had limited autonomy. I knew this wouldn't last.

"I get scared when I'm late," Melanie said. "Do you want me to be scared at school?"

What the hell are they doing to fourth graders in school? I thought. *When I was nine, the only reason I was scared was—* But, no. I didn't need to think about her today.

"Parents are supposed to get nervous," I said, "not kids. You don't have to worry about anything except listening to Mommy. And Daddy. Get your stuff ready."

I fished from the glove compartment the Leland ID placard and flicked it in the lower right-hand corner of my windshield. While researching the school, I discovered, aside from its superb academic reputation, some commotion about an archivist revealing that the school was named after a long-dead KKK member. A petition was circulated to change the school's name. Overnight, several North Vecino "community groups" argued the archivist's historical research work was sloppy and actively promoting an "outsiders' social justice agenda." The petition was unanimously rejected by the school board. Since the name wasn't changed, I had to believe it wasn't true, but my memory—a busy parent's memory—was slippery about community history. What did it matter, anyway? Leland had resources a hundred times beyond Mel's old elementary school. Who, or what, could help Mel now? That's what I cared about.

I turned left—a new morning drop-off pattern circulated last week to decrease idling and "help save the planet!"—into a driveway loop. Without my sunglasses, I was blinded by a caravan of SUVs and expensive sedans that shot forth sunlight, taxiing to a disembarking curb where spray-painted palm trees with bulgy cartoon eyes pointed to the school. The country and state flags were at half-staff again because of a new mass shooting, but I didn't remember which one. I couldn't keep track of when the mourning period of one calamity ended and a new tragedy's grief began. It was easier to lower a flag than imagine a screaming child's last breath. I had much less trouble imagining it.

"I want you to be happy," I said. "Not nervous. Happy means following the rules. You're special to me, but if a teacher or a police officer says you did something bad, I'm taking their side. Do you understand?"

I heard Melanie's fingers fidget with her harness. No follow-up questions, a dangerous sign from a child. Had I confused her?

I turned on the hazards. In our daily drop-off routine, I'd ask, *You want me to unlatch your seat belt, or do you want to do it yourself?*

You do it, Melanie would reply. When I opened the back car door, Melanie would wait with her arms raised. I'd lift Mel up and kiss both cheeks before she'd run to school.

I heard the clicks of Melanie's harness in time with the metronome turn signals. What was she doing back there? The child locks on her harness would not make it possible for her to release herself—unless I had forgotten to snap the straps in place, which I never, *ever* forget to do.

"Melanie, you have to wait for Mommy," I said.

"It's okay," Melanie said. "I know where I'm going." Then she leapt out of the car, dashing through the school gates before I could snap off the hazards. In the back seat I discovered—sure enough—that I hadn't locked her straps together properly.

There was enough time to fix my sandals before work if I could find the materials at the supermarket. I wouldn't discard them after spending seventeen cumulative hours across six days hunched like a question mark over the kitchen table scrolling through dozens of gardening sandal options on different shopping sites, weighing excerpts from hundreds of collective anonymous "Plus" (*Nothing can break these straps!*) and "Minus" (*Save your money!*) reviews. This broken strap was my punishment for buying a sandal with a middling batch of concurring *You get what you pay for!* comments. I couldn't remember when strangers' opinions became essential to my decision-making process, but I wanted the security of sifting through and learning from a collective's errors and failures. I didn't have money to waste being wrong about what I bought.

Lo que hoy parece barato, mañana puede ser caro, my mamá, Dolores, would say. My toes curled into a tense fist. I knew this was my fault for "saving" eighteen dollars.

While I drove, I resisted calling Alex about the wall and instead tried the realty company, where I learned they had no record of my agent, Susanna, having worked there. "But I started here last week," a woman said with an icy, lunging twang in her voice, "so I could be mistaken."

I explained what happened.

"You built a wall on one of our rental properties?" she asked.

"I have a mortgage. I'm not a renter," I said.

"You sure?" she asked. "We deal almost exclusively with rentals."

"I'm sure," I said, sounding unsure. It was hard for me to challenge a stranger's confidence.

"I'm just the office manager," she said, and typed loudly on her keyboard. "Let me talk to a senior agent and get back to you."

Halfway between Mel's school and my office was FARM, a "hypermarket" in its own shopping island that, as of the move, was my new local grocery store. I found it by accident when I asked five different coworkers in three separate departments if there was a grocery store near work to save a few minutes on my commute home. Each recommended the generic brands–only grocer by the freeway overpass that was several miles out of my way—the "ghetto" outpost. I discovered FARM by accident when I swiped my map function right instead of left. Later, I saw three of my coworkers at FARM on separate occasions. Each time they glided past, our eyes locked in split-second recognition until they flinched, their head back down to their phone, its glow a dehumanizing mask.

In the "hyper" part of the grocery store, alongside dangling placards that read GET ON THE BAND!, were eighty-nine-dollar sandals. I considered buying them, but the sandals were a specific in-store brand I couldn't read reviews of. I wouldn't change my buying habits now. I *misread*—and was not *misled* by—the online reviews. My system *worked*.

I could resist the sandals. I couldn't resist the sixty-three-dollar hiking skirt with the soft cat paw–like fabric. *I'll take Mel hiking*, I thought, rationalizing the purchase.

It took me three minutes to find materials to mend my sandals that would hopefully extend their life another month or two. I then spent another ten minutes I couldn't spare roaming FARM's aisles, *just because*. My grocery store was a hypnotizing experience—who knew? My old neighborhood's grocery store was unruly: floors doused in a hazardous mix of ammonia and bleach; spoilt, out-of-season fruits; cracked glass panels in the fish and meat counters where graying chicken lingered until it reappeared, repurposed, in the deli's prepared foods and sandwich cooler. My stomach churned in each overlit, medicinally scented aisle, exasperated at how to make a wholesome dinner for my family every night.

Alex would reply, every night via text: *Let's do takeout.*

In FARM, I browsed as if at an expensive department store. How many tiny, delicate cooking tools I never knew I needed! So many kinds of cooking oil I could try! Were five kinds of dark chocolate pretzels too many—or not enough? Could I distinguish between nine varieties of vegan mayonnaise? I could hear Dolores, and in my mamá's echo, my younger sister, Serena, say, *¿Qué mexicana necesitaría "vegan mayonnaise"?*

It was the principle of access, knowing such choices existed, and a freedom to imagine options I never thought possible. Would a fourteen-dollar salad dressing reward my family with that much *more* salad satisfaction? Could Melanie taste the difference in a vinaigrette made from hand-pressed apple cider? I found my rationalizations in an open clearing of food-safety articles discussing how a certain kind of basic ranch dressing was synthesized from a strain of dairy product that had been suggested to cause elevated cholesterol in children. *Better ingredients meant keeping Mel safe.*

Roaming the aisles, I could understand, in a way, why my co-workers misled me. Perhaps they thought I'd be unnerved by the ratio of white to other-skinned shoppers, or how the support staff—the aisle packers, box lifters, floor waxers, but not the cashiers, *never* the cashiers—were, predictably, brown. In different spaces with this ratio, there was a fifty-fifty chance of my being mistaken for an employee. "Are you *sure* you don't work here?" someone would ask, and I'd laugh. Then I'd tell the kind-ish, older, and invariably white woman who asked me, "No, but I'm sure I can find someone for you who does." How could I tell my colleagues, *I understand. I'm not bothered by these moments, and I don't make a big deal out of things that aren't one. I'm not like my sister. I'm not like them.*

I'm me. Iris Prince.

Or maybe they were trying to keep me from fomenting dissatisfaction with the way I had structured my life. I naively imagined these people cared not only about me, but the various, brilliant, and exciting potential lives I saw for myself based on what I bought at a grocery store. A new life that began under the LOCALLY SOURCED, NEVER FROZEN banner. Shrimp cocktail with fresh dill sprigs, made for the handpicked group of friends I was bound to find in my new kind of cul-de-sac. In the three months I'd lived there I saw my neighbors every day—taking their trash cans to the curb, walking dogs, parents chaperoning their children on Sunday afternoon strolls. (I wasn't ready to explain Alex's absence yet.) I was going to change that, as soon as I had the time.

I'd invite people over to a Sunday luncheon with paper invitations. We'd start with an artichoke française platter and discuss a book that we read together, something literate that wasn't a bestseller but also wasn't an abstract wonky bore-fest for out-of-touch snobs. Glasses of Andover Estate sauvignon blanc paired with lemon macaroons from the bakery case on an outdoor deck, and conversation that would tiptoe and flirt with provocativeness to demonstrate how similar I was in mind and belief with my neighbors. There would be no need for discomfort when we saw each other on the street or at the grocery store later; I was with friends and they were with me. With each sip I could reveal that what some mistook for distance in me was in fact the same desire for safety we all shared and, like a car's rearview mirror, I was much closer to them than I actually appeared. I had no actual race- or gender-based biases, *just like them, of course*, but fairly structured ideas about safety, order, and truth. Rules mean structure, structure means order, and order means safety, which means a life without fear. That was how my mamá raised me. My success—*which any Mexican American could duplicate*—had come from following rules. A second glass of wine, defenses down, we could laugh together at our shared "solutions" for a safer way of life, like giving homeless people one-way bus tickets out of town, but in the spirit of keeping children, *our* children, safe. I idolized planned communities like North Azulia, devoid of pedestrian-friendly areas, or social places that encouraged congregation, with streets that dead-ended into a never-ending series of loops. In a place stripped of the dirty, unsafe elements that make a city a city, I saw true safety and, therefore, happiness.

Locally sourced, never frozen.

In my car, while I affixed a color-disguised hardware tape to my slashed sandal strap, I spotted stacks of clean, pink disposable razors by the store's dumpsters. I assumed someone had dropped them from a delivery, so I carried them to the guest relations counter. There, a perky teen told me that it was FARM's policy to leave them out for "persons experiencing houselessness." During my new home reconnaissance drives in my waning marriage's late afternoons, I saw on North Azulia's fringes packs of loitering men in snow hats and oversize leather overcoats roasting in ninety-degree heat. It was rumored on social media that they were rounded up nightly by North Azulia PD and dropped off at the city limits.

"So you want me to put these back where I found them?" I asked.

"We'd really appreciate that," the teen said. "Have a mindful day!"

Outside, I weighed the razors in my hands. *Why don't you get a job? Or be a Mexican and get three?*

With a stern heel stomp, I cracked their pink handles like eggshells. I was proud of how the taped patch job on my sandals held up under that much pressure.

From FARM it was a shortish drive to work, a journey through endless "traffic reduction" roundabouts, with each jagged turn adding an extra minute or two, including the road that my GPS mistook as a lane instead of a path. A five-minute straight-line drive became a twenty-three-minute excursion, making me late. With anxiety flooding my thoughts like rushing water, I parked in a far corner of the parking lot, changed into office shoes and, in a last second impulse, my new hiking skirt.

My office building occupied a bizarre, zigzag buffer zone between West Vecino, where my parents and sister lived, and North

Azulia. When I started here, I was given a luxuriant narrative of the area's history. I vaguely remembered from college something about orange groves and the Mexican braceros that had farmed and lived here, but that knowledge, like the groves themselves, had been swept away. I didn't know this land's history, but had instead collected a new knowledge to live in its present, a code to understanding success here, now, pieces from a secret American dialect I felt privileged to have. For example, a cardinal direction before a place, or a noun preceding a landform, meant "affluent." Before my last work promotion, I took my family to Walker Beach, which had free parking but too many cholos grilling cheap cuts of Tupperware meat on portable hibachis. I discovered via my phone West Gaia Beach, which charged ten dollars to park, had Korean BBQ food trucks with jackfruit bowls, and a beach layout that discouraged interaction. ¡Adiós, Walker! *Better sight lines to keep an eye on Melanie at Gaia*, I told Alex.

Inside the office building lobby, one of our safety coordinators, Eric, manned the security oval. He was a short, dark-skinned Mexican American from southern México who listened to banda and narcocorridos—*loud*—in his Chrysler PT Cruiser on his lunch breaks. In México, his skin color would relegate him to the bottom of the social ladder. Here, he fiercely revels in pro-Americanness, and how good it is that everybody has to follow the rules, no matter their wealth or skin color. I have to present my ID whenever Eric is working. "You wouldn't last a day in México," he tells me, tapping my ID card. My white coworkers don't have to show ID, unless they choose to. I attributed this to bringing Serena on "family open house" day. Eric demanded she show a form of picture ID.

"¡No eres la ICE, cabrón!" she shouted, walking past him. "¡Mejor te enseño el culo!" Since then, Eric has "teased" me by asking when Serena was going to bring back unas buchonas from México for him to marry, like he was El Chapo.

There's not an aspect of my life that hasn't been made more frustrating by introducing Serena to it. Her peanut allergy meant that on Halloween, instead of chocolates, our house gave out pencils. The kids would shriek, "¡Aquí no! ¡Dan puro pinche lápiz!" *The fucking pencil house.* She revoked my ability to blend in, and I hated her for that. Sometimes my daughter made me feel the same way, which made me hate myself for not being able to give Mel the gift of an anonymous mom.

I work a corporate office job because my high school friends said I would be a great schoolteacher. Knowing of what my mamá called my taste for "lo bueno de la vida," this knowledge of being ideally suited for a low-paying, high-stress, and heavy-workload job terrified me. When I learned what teachers made in a year, then in a lifetime, I taught myself, in the following order: Excel, PowerPoint, InDesign, and how to gingerly accept "constructive feedback" on my already conservative makeup and earrings, and on the neck-to-ankle work clothes that I could afford on a starting salary.

I landed in Marketing Compliance, with a title and responsibilities that were the Goldilocks level of order taking and giving—just right. I have been here eleven years and change. It's a job impossible to leave, as it's at a pivotal location on a hierarchical ladder with career skill sets that people in my industry assured me cannot be applied elsewhere.

A year into my employment, I learned I made thirty-five percent less than my white male counterparts. Five years and a promotion later, I made fifty percent less.

"I'm sure they respect you," Alex said. "Remember our agreement about our work: don't complain, put your head down, do your job, go home. Just hang in there." Where else was there to *hang*, anyway?

On my circuitous walk to my gray and off-white officle, I regularly overhear tiny peppercorns of discontent from my white male senior colleagues about Irena, a nonexistent coworker that is a blend of my own name and that of Karina, a Mexican-American colleague who has been here two years longer than I have and who I am frequently mistaken for. I'm half a foot taller than Karina, have shoulder-length hair to Karina's pixie cut, with her skin color two shades darker than mine, a difference visible even under racks of fluorescent lighting. I used to worry I would be fired for something management thought Karina did (or vice versa), but I realized Irena—who has been blamed for losing reports, deleting files, crashing the servers, even taking extra donuts from the break room—is a much-needed boogeyman for white coworkers. *Irena can't be fired because . . . you know . . .*

I'd been at the company a week, when Karina initiated a conversation. She'd been mistaken for me nine times in five days.

"I counted," she said. "If people are going to keep thinking I'm you, tenemos que conocernos, ¿no?"

We got drinks at what my mamá would call a "cha-cha" North Azulia restaurant serving expensive margaritas and "Tacos on a Stick" as a featured entrée. I was curious about what our meeting would be like, since I had no friends left over from school. Friends, I learned, meant anxiety, with the innumerable ways we could disappoint each other. It was a stilted conversation until the second round of frozen margaritas arrived. "Relax about work," she said. "I'll keep counting how often we're mistaken for one another. White people need metrics before they can be embarrassed or convinced. When they get to ten times, I'll say something. 'Ten times? Oh my, I'm so sorry that happened to you!'" she said, and cackled.

We hated and were aggrieved by the same things our "gente" did. We both felt the same pit in our stomachs when a major crime in the news had a perpetrator with a Hispanic surname. She asked determined, pointed questions—was I *first* or *second* generation Mexican American; were my parents working-class, middle-class, or paisas?—and seemed satisfied with the answers.

Karina said, "I didn't move away from chuntis to live next door to them again. They're not really *us*."

I nodded in agreement. "When do we finally get to be safe? Because if Mel and I are safe, then, and only then, can we be *us*. Right?"

"Uh, you're drunk, chica!" Karina said, and laughed.

Karina dubbed that night our first "tequila talk" bonding session. *Let's do this next Friday!* I thought we crossed an invisible friendship threshold. When I saw Karina the following Monday, she acted aloof, indifferent. I invited her out several times, but we never went out again.

One Christmas, inspired by a video I saw on social media, I organized at work a used clothing drive for a church. On the next to last day of donation, fourteen bags of clothes disappeared. Later, I saw a donations receipt on Karina's desk with an amount she intended to write off on her taxes. Before I could mention it, Karina brought her college diploma and her mortarboard to work and displayed them on her single officle shelf. Written on the mortarboard: *Orgulloso nopal en la frente.* (My diploma was hanging in my mamá's home, like any good Mexican child's.) *I paid for this with my time and my womb,* Dolores said, *so it belongs to me.* Here, these items served no purpose other than to prompt awkward office conversations.

"Do you know what it says on the mortarboard?" she asked me. "Can you translate? I know you don't really speak Spanish, but you can't forget where you're *from*." Karina could, depending on who was listening, use her Mexican identity as a brace or a cudgel. "This is who we are. I mean, who *I am*. I don't want to speak for *you*."

When I saw Karina in her officle, she said, "¡Qué bonita falda! The grocery store ones, right?"

"Oh, I didn't know you could buy them there," I said. "But thank you for the compliment!"

My work evaporated the hours into a daily cluster of braided kinks in my neck and shoulders. Around late afternoon, the management company called.

"I did some checking, ma'am," the caller said, proud of the advantage her youth gave her in this interaction. "There are two addresses that are very similar in our system. One of them had an exterior facing wall listed in its description, the other didn't. But it's not clear if the address you gave us was inputted correctly in the system and the agent that inputted this information is no longer with our organization."

"What are you saying?"

"We're pretty sure that property had a wall when you bought it," she said. "So there's nothing really we can help you with."

"Pretty sure?" I asked. "There was no wall on this property yesterday. I'm not imagining this. I know what I can see. I mean, what I *didn't* see."

"Ma'am, you are free to re-list the property, however you will likely incur a significant financial penalty by prepaying your mortgage in its entirety."

"No, I can't . . . do that," I said, embarrassed for some reason to use the word "afford," and to acknowledge something as universal as not having hundreds of thousands of dollars available to pay off my mortgage. "I mean, I don't want to leave the house. I love it there. It just has a wall that wasn't there yesterday."

"A wall that wasn't there," she said.

I felt a sense of breathtaking helplessness you get when talking to someone devoid of empathy. "Can you at least send somebody out to take a look at it?" I asked.

"We can put you on the work schedule, but I can't guarantee a date or a time. What would you like me to put down as the reason for the visit?"

I didn't want to mention what Mel told me about the wall's growing height, but I didn't know how to communicate the sense of discomfort, anxiety, and unease I felt about . . . well, a wall popping out of my front yard.

"Put down 'wall,' " I said.

"Wall?" she repeated.

"Wall," I said.

"Fine," she said, and I heard her type four keys loudly. "Just as a courtesy, our records show you have been at your property for three months. Due to the recent passage of Proposition 3, you need to present a state-issued band account number to continue paying any state utility bills such as gas, electric, et cetera. Please adjust your auto-pay accounts accordingly."

I had forgotten about this, adjusting between two different lives. "I didn't think I needed the bands for that."

"You need a band as proof of residency to receive any state, re-
gional, or local service. Is there anything else I can help you with?"

"No. Thank you very much, *ma'am*," I said, and hung up.

Before we separated, I gave Alex the paperwork to enroll both of
us in the band program because he was patient with "techie" stuff.
The materials came from the state in an oversize white envelope,
the kind I got my college acceptance letter in. (I've lost the letter,
but my mamá kept the envelope, as she said she'd never seen me
so happy as when I pulled it out of the mailbox, before or since.)
Along with the applications was a form letter and color insert
I kept at work, showing the bands "in action." They had a glass
"watch" face, a barcode on their reverse side, and an adjustable
strap.

I handled the glossy form letter, which had written, in matte
gold, blue, and green colors: "It's easy. It's fast. It's secure. It's good
for the environment—and for You. All state and public services
tracked in one location, right on your wrist. WELCOME TO THE BAND!"

I knew, in a vaguely informed voter way, that Proposition 3 was
a "green" initiative conceived by a mercurial, bland nineteen-year-
old college dropout. The heiress to a supermarket fortune, she got
the band idea doing a secret shopper visit at one of her father's
stores. In a few months, she had secured several billion dollars in
start-up funding to create a new "one-stop" scannable state ID
wristband that would store all state data and benefits in one location. Test-marketed successfully at her father's grocery store chain,
the band would facilitate paying for and receiving state and public
services, act as a driver's license (physical cards would eventually
be phased out), help users regulate a household's water usage and
garbage output, serve as proof of residency for your child's enroll-
ment in school, and potentially save the state millions of dollars
by curtailing fraud and abuse. Any private business that accepted
state benefits would require band scanners to ensure monies were
being received by their proper recipients. It would offer "extras,"

too, such as merging its "patented" skin temperature monitoring and "wellness technology" with your health records to schedule doctors' visits and medicine refills. I thought how something like that would be a nice thing for my parents to have so I wouldn't have to ask my father how his health was and be constantly lied to when he said, "Bien, bien."

It sounded convenient and fair. My sister said I was gullible and blind.

The band was decried by its detractors as the largest state government assault on individual freedoms in American history, which I didn't like the sound of. Its proponents countered that it was guaranteed to make our state and our streets "safer," something that was important to me, too. Months of advertising and social media posts made me feel less and less informed the closer we got to Election Day. There were televised and streamed debates I didn't watch, town halls I had no time to attend, and as the initiative was endorsed by environmental groups and personal liberty think tanks, it was hard to determine which side was "right," or even what kind of outcome the band would have on my day-to-day life, if any. Karina said on a Friday afternoon elevator ride that she was "totally voting for it" and promised to forward me crucial information, but never did. Serena texted me article links marked "VOTE NO, URGENT!," but my sister's urgency and activism never extended beyond what she could do on her phone. I didn't know what to believe, meaning I trusted nothing beyond my personal experience. Anecdotes are, for me, the best rejoinders to what I've been told is the truth.

I called Alex at my workday's end.

"Sorry to bother you at work," I said.

"No, it's fine," he said. "How are you? How's Mel?"

"We're okay," I said.

"Everything at your house still okay? Faucets work, stuff like that?"

Asking about working faucets? When did Alex become handy? Ignore it. And don't mention the wall.

"It's been three months. We're fine," I said. "Since you brought up water, I need one of those bands to pay my utility bills. Did you enroll us?"

"I did mine," he said.

"Just yours," I said, exasperated. "I'm sorry, I should have asked for the papers back."

"No, I couldn't set you up. You need to upload a parent's US birth certificate on their site, or take it to a center. That's where you get them. It's a lit ring around your wrist. The entire band glows gold—that's how you know it's working. They're kinda cool."

"And you can't get one without a parent's US birth certificate?" I asked.

"Doesn't matter which parent but, yeah, one of them needs it," he said. "That's why, you know, I couldn't activate yours." He knew, as I did, that both my parents were born in Mexico.

"Was that always part of how this thing worked? I mean, how are normal people supposed to get everyday things done?" I asked, and thought about my own vote.

"It's a verification system. To prove you qualify for things. I mean, I guess there's exceptions, but I don't know much about how that would work. I can't imagine it would be too inconvenient to figure this out."

No, of course you wouldn't imagine, I said to myself.

"I already sent in Mel's paperwork," he said. "She's all set. One of us just needs to take her to a center with the code they sent me. I haven't done it yet because . . . I wasn't sure what school I should say she was going to."

"She's going where she goes now," I said. "That's not changing. It's a better school."

"Right," he said. "Better."

"I'm still at work," I said. "Can you drop my paperwork off at her next pickup? You can give me Mel's code, too."

"Sure," he said. Then he blurted out, "I miss you guys."

"I gotta pick up Mel," I said. It was the after-school Cinderella stroke of five. There was a silence while each of us waited for the other to speak. In that silence, I held the band color insert photo. The band looked light and insignificant.

———————

I arrived at after-school in time to catch Melanie skipping through the gates. *She's still a kid*, I thought. *I still have time with her.*

Mel shouted, "Hi, Mom!" and buckled herself into her seat, but instead of plugging into her screen, took out pencils and paper and sketched her hands.

"Mamá," Melanie asked, "am I pretty?"

"Who said you were pretty!" I shouted.

Damn, I thought, *too fast. I said that too loud, too fast, too angry.*

I learned "pretty" was a good conversational opener for sidewalk genealogists: complimentary, while being nonspecific enough to set up increasingly pointed follow-up questions. "Pretty" led to "Where is *she* from?" which led to "Where are *you* from?" which led to "No, *before* here?" "Pretty" meant different, and different meant trouble.

"Mrs. Hunter called me 'pretty,' " Melanie said.

"I know Mrs. Hunter," I said. "She cares about you and what you learn. That 'pretty' is a compliment."

"You never say I'm pretty," Melanie said. "Do you think I'm pretty, too?"

"I think you're pretty . . . smart," I said. "Muy lista."

"¡Muy lista, Mamá!" Mel said. *God, how I love her.*

Mel was immersed in drawing until we parked at home. The wall was coated, end to end, top to bottom, with glittering specks that twinkled on its surface.

"Mommy, ¡mira! It's bright and sparkly!" Melanie said.

"Go and change for dinner."

"Mamá, you see? It's different. Shiny!"

"I do, Mel," I said. "Please go inside."

"But why?" she asked.

"Let Mommy check it out first, okay?"

"Okay," Melanie said, and ran around the wall, inside the house.

Embedded in the wall were glints of shaving razor metal.

Hundreds, no, *thousands* of tiny, sparkling slivers, winking in
the sun. The wall was smooth to the touch. *What does this mean?*

"It means you used to be nicer," a young girl's voice said.

"Who's there?" I asked.

Sitting atop the wall—all of a sudden, *there*—was a young Mexican girl, maybe six or seven, wearing a bright orange T-shirt with
an iron-on Cookie Monster decal, and lime-green pants.

"Remember me," she said, a command, not a question. When
she spoke, I knew who she was.

"Brenda?" I asked. "You're dead. You died."

"I know, how sad, *boo hoo*. But here we are."

"This isn't real," I said. "I thought about you this morning. You
were on my mind and now I'm making this up. You're not real.
Are you real?"

"It's what you're seeing," Brenda said.

"Are you the reason this thing's here?" I asked. "I can't accept
ghost girls *and* magic walls."

"Ghost girls! Fun! You mean those girls in movies that have
long hair that cover their face so you don't know who they are
until they pull their hair back and ew, creepy! Yeah, they're cute.
But they aren't real. Neither are magic walls. You *know* who I am.
And what this is," she said, and kicked her heels against the wall,
swinging her feet that didn't touch the ground.

"I knew who you were," I said. "Do you want me to avenge your
murder or something?"

"You?" Brenda said, and laughed. "Don't be silly. If I did, I'd be
thinking up another plan fast! You don't help people."

"I'm a mother," I said. "I help my family with their bills. I help
my child every day. I give her food, clothing, and a safe place to
live. What have you ever done?"

"You mean before I was murdered, Inés?"

"Why are you being such a smart-ass!" I shouted. "It's not my
fault you died! You're a ghost and you are supposed to be at peace
and respectful and full of kindness and goddamned gratitude that
you're in a better fucking place!"

"Cálmate, Inés."

"That's not my name anymore."

"I'm not here to make you change. I'm a reminder."

"Of what?" I asked. "I'm fine the way I am. I'm a good mother and a good person. And I'm safe. You taught me how. Because of you, my daughter and I are safe."

"You are? Fun!" Then Brenda swung her legs over the wall and jumped. I leapt atop its ledge after her. She was gone.

Mel had been watching me from the kitchen bay window.

"Get ready for dinner!" I shouted, then swung myself over the wall. Something crunched underneath my sandal—a finger's-length pink shard of disposable razor handle.

After an awkward evening tuck-in when Mel asked, "Are you okay? Should we call Dad?" I found in a moving tub, almost as if it had been placed there for me to discover, a manila envelope with newspaper clippings that Dolores saved years ago for me. I'm not sure why she collected them. I emptied the pages onto the bed and sorted them by date. They felt like old skin, translucent and delicate between my fingers.

When I was a little girl, Dolores, Gonzalo, and I moved into a tiny converted garage behind my uncle Agustin's house. "You can hang your clothes here," Agustin said, and pointed to a row of nails under the lone window. "One nail per person. That's what the last family did." There were fourteen nails attached to the wall. Fourteen people living in one garage.

Rats gnawing at the plasterboard and my father's snoring kept me up at night. In my paper-thin sleeping bag, I told myself, *When I grow up, make sure Mamá and I never have to live this way again.*

When a rat attacked me at night for the third time, we moved to what my mamá called the "cholo" courts, a housing development built alongside the dead riverbed, and lived in a small second-floor apartment with a broken dead bolt and a police-split doorframe. Gunshots crackled in the distance like popcorn. Bass from roaming cars shuddered our plastic windowpanes. Police helicopters flooded our backyard with "Nightsun," bright searchlights on the hunt for runners. On Friday and Saturday nights, I heard Dolores curse out, over her sewing, "Malditos paisas," whose heavy cowboy boots tripped up the stairs at three a.m. They laughed, chain-smoked, and knocked over empty Tecate cans on the outdoor landing. Dolores made me sweep up the butts and collect the cans for recycling cash.

Most days, I finished my homework early and then sat by a window and read. Sometimes, I offered to help the holdout German or Italian grandmothers banging their two-wheel shopping carts up the stairs, but they shooed me away in languages I didn't understand. On the weekends, they played loud music on their record players and cut down my mamá's clotheslines.

I had spent two summer days blissfully reading books indoors alone, when I heard a scratching at our punctured screen door.

"¿Estás en casa?" the voice said. A six-year-old girl leaned her forehead against the shredded mesh, peering into our home. "You want to come out and play?"

"Mamá, ¡es para ti!" I shouted. "¡En Inglés!" Dolores shouted from the kitchen.

The girl lifted the screen door up off its hinges and walked inside.

"You can't come in here!" I said.

"Why not?" she asked.

"Because this is our house! No sabemos quién eres."

"Oh," the girl said. "Me llamo Brenda. I live downstairs. Come outside and play?"

Dolores found us standing there, blinking at each other. "¿Por qué me llamaste?" she asked me.

"I want to play with her," Brenda said to Dolores. "¿Ta bien?"

"Sí, bien," she said. "¡Ándale!"

"Mamá, are you crazy?" I asked. "We don't know who she is!"

"Está chavita," Dolores said. "¡Fuera de aquí!"

I sulked on the outdoor apartment staircase, peeling black paint chips off the railing and flicking them into the air.

"I have a hopscotch downstairs," Brenda said.

"It's not yours if it's on a sidewalk," I said. "One game."

"Okay, fun!" she said. After five games, I ran to my apartment and came back with books. "How do we play with these?" Brenda asked.

"We don't," I said. "We read them. They're in English. You should be speaking English as much as you can."

"You can read," Brenda said. "Can I draw?"

"Yes," I said, "*Tranquila*. Those are the rules."

"Fun!" Brenda whispered.

While I read, Brenda rolled out butcher paper atop the thriving grass and weeds we sat on.

"Put your hand here," Brenda said. She traced my hand with a pink pencil. Then she traced her own hand next to mine, and colored them both in.

"We're friends," Brenda said. "Fun!"

Every morning that summer, Dolores opened the front door to let our noisy, rattling plastic fans oscillate the hot air out. Then Brenda appeared, scratching at the screen door. "Can Inés come out and *plaaaaay?*"

"Where do you come from?" I asked. "I don't ever see you coming."

"Were you looking for me? Fun!"

"¡Váyanse de aquí, chicas!" Dolores said. "Go be outside."

I shooed Brenda to a patch of brown scrub grass by the dumpsters to play what I called "The Married Game." We ate gritty "cakes" made in Brenda's only toy, an Easy-Bake Oven. I pretended I was an impatient father waiting for my meal and Brenda had to make me the perfect dinner. I enjoyed saying grouchy things to Brenda I copied from television—*The boss man made me skip lunch, I'm starving!*—but Brenda was an annoyingly joyful play partner. Her kindness was sincere and unbreakable. I felt, even then, behaving as if I was happy for the benefit of others was hard. Mamá wanted me to smile in every photo we shared together. Meanwhile, my distant father, Gonzalo, was smiling in every picture his family wasn't in. When I saw framed photos of him from this period years later, standing in bars holding a beer and a pool cue, grinning, relaxed, I wondered, "Who *is* that man?" Then there were my titas, primas, and white women in the large, over-air-conditioned, neighborhood-adjacent, English-language supermarket who kneaded my cheeks and said, "My, what a *gorgeous* child you are!" Brenda's sweetness never appeared as if it was work for her—she really was *that* happy all the time!—and that made me angry.

"Get mad at me!" I shouted. "When I yell at you, you're supposed to get mad! Those are the rules!"

"Is that how you play the married game?" Brenda asked. "Fun!"

I brought books home from the school library, read them aloud to Brenda, and asked her to read them aloud to me. The two of us listened to our own voices transporting us to the boundless worlds we imagined. In a corner of Brenda's living room, I cleaned out Brenda's Easy-Bake, then we played library. She would ask me, the librarian, for books, and I would help her find them.

Once, I brought over a small bag of flour. "We can use this to cook," I said. I didn't tell Brenda how I threw a public tantrum, and earned a rare Gonzalo butt tap-spanking, to get Dolores to buy it.

"It doesn't say 'Maseca,'" Brenda said.

"It's American," I said. "It's better."

"American?" Brenda asked.

"Yeah, it's what we are," I said. "You and me, we were born here. Somos americanas. You were born here?"

"Sí, but not my momma," Brenda said.

"Doesn't matter. You're American. Don't forget that," I said, already sounding like my mamá. "Also, if you eat McDonald's, you're super American. We have to do that, too."

"Today?" Brenda asked.

"No, we have to work for it first. Those are the rules. We can read for a while and then get McDonald's as a reward. I did some chores for Mrs. Yanes and I can buy us food."

I walked Brenda to the Arroyo Seco branch, more of a hoarder's house than a library. It was filled with out-of-date science books and months-old newspapers. I sat us at a broken corner table and split the books and papers between us.

"I learn English for school this way," I told Brenda. "Then I go to McDonald's once a month to practice it."

"By yourself?" Brenda asked.

"I'm not supposed to eat fast food before dinner," I said. "I don't order much. French fries and an apple pie. Today we'll order double fries, since they're too good to share."

At McDonald's, I heaved open a large glass door for Brenda. "It's cold in here!" she said, and her body shivered while we waited to order. "Let me speak English," I said. I was nervous ordering for someone else, but recited the words inside my head like a prayer.

"I want two small french fries," I said, "one apple pie, and a large Coke. We are staying here to eat."

"Ta bien, hablo español," a young server said.

I stared at the busy workers until I found a young white man in a crisp blue short-sleeve shirt with a silver pen in his breast pocket and waved him over.

"Excuse me," I said. "This one spoke in Spanish when I ordered in English. Please fire her."

He laughed and said, "We don't fire people for making our customers feel welcome. But we're happy to serve you. Have a great day!"

I carried our tray of food to a cool plastic table and set Brenda's portions in front of her.

"Don't eat the fries too fast," I said. "You'll get tummy sick."

"I wanna come back here every day."

"You can't or you'll get gordita," I said. "But ask your mom to take you for breakfast. That's the only time they serve hash browns. Those are better than the fries. She could like it here, too."

"Better than fries? I'm gonna ask her until she does!" Brenda said. "Let's come back tomorrow! Like amigas americanas!"

"We can't eat here every day," I said.

"Please!" Brenda said. "My mom will treat us both before she goes to work."

I sighed. I thought, Podrías ser mi hermanita. *You could be my little sister.* It felt too weird to say aloud.

I never said I would meet her, just shrugged my shoulders. Maybe a nod. Nothing more.

"Fun!" Brenda said.

The next morning, a middle-aged man in a car watched me walk across the restaurant parking lot. He had a bowl haircut and was reading a comic book while he ate a sandwich, taking small, methodical bites. He scratched at his face with the hand holding his food, getting crumbs on his chin.

I stopped at the playground by the front doors and gripped a hamburger ride-on spring toy.

The man smiled, nodded at the McDonald's, and mouthed, "Go in," his tongue full of chewed bread.

I couldn't see if Brenda and her mother were inside, but something felt wrong. When he reached over to his glove compartment, I ran home.

I opened my front door, thinking of what to say to Brenda about why I didn't show up. An hour passed. Then two more. I set down my book and crust-free mustard sandwich, staring back and forth down the long outdoor corridors. I fiddled with the holes in the screen door. I played hopscotch, alone.

Brenda and her mother had gone to McDonald's for breakfast. Like I told her to. I would later recognize the man I saw in the car from the television reports. He was an unemployed correctional officer who, sometime after I left, walked into the restaurant wearing a stolen police uniform with a duffel bag holding several guns and six hundred rounds of ammunition. In a conspiracy-laden journal entry discovered later in a storage unit, he wrote, "I was a patriotic American. Society had their chance."

Brenda was shot five times. Twenty-two others, including Brenda's mother, were murdered. Nineteen of them were Mexican American,

and fifteen of those were children. He allowed white parents and
their kids to leave while he reloaded.

I'm not here for you today, he said.

Grief and wailing swelled through my building like floodwater,
pouring through our apartment's paper-thin walls. I watched the
local news every night, where I heard the massacre's details recited
on a loop. I don't know why I did this. Maybe I thought they had
gotten Brenda's death wrong and the news would change. But why
would it change? Not once had I heard Brenda's or her mother's
name on the news, didn't see pictures of their faces. I never learned
how five separate bullets—a bullet seemed such a big thing—could
fit inside Brenda's tiny body.

Gonzalo asked Dolores, "¿Por qué la dejas ver esas porquerías?
Las noticias la van a volver loca."

"Ni las entiende," my mamá said. "She's fine."

The McDonald's was razed. In its place, a field partially enclosed
by chain-link-mesh fencing, which became an ofrenda of flowers,
photographs, candles, and mounds of stuffed animals. Plans for a
stone memorial were considered for months, but scrapped when
the head of the local bar owners association said at a televised city
council meeting, "I'm boycotting this unless we only put the real
Americans on there."

Soon, I couldn't sleep, and demanded we go to the site.

"¿Por qué?" Dolores asked. "I didn't even know you liked her."

Ducking through a gaping hole in the fence, I walked amid the
ofrendas laid in the patches of scratchy, ankle-crawling weeds. Dolores, stingy with public displays of affection, clutched my hand,
but I slipped out of reach. I tried to imagine, amid the dirt mounds
and valleys, where they found Brenda's body. Her hands were like
teacups, her hips no bigger than starlings. Where had she been frozen in time? Was it here, by these piles of trash bags, where Brenda
collapsed and fell? I was searching for something I could find there
that would let me cry and hated myself that I hadn't yet. A part
of me had been stolen and I didn't know where to find it or how
to get it back.

Why didn't I go inside to warn Brenda? I don't know. I wish I had. I found, tucked underneath a novena candle, a crumpled page from a Bible. Proverbs 10:7—*The memory of the just is blessed, but the name of the wicked shall rot.* I didn't believe this. I saw Brenda's murderer's goofy Sears family portrait every news hour, heard the consolation he was offered in sympathetic editorials and interviews with his wife and three kids.

"How terrible for his family," a newscaster said.

Two days before my parents moved us to our first house, I found outside my front door Brenda's Easy-Bake Oven wrapped in a trash bag. After several revolting attempts, one of which almost choked my father, Gonzalo, I baked a palatable cake, which I left at the ofrenda site by a framed picture of the Virgin Mary. On the cake, written in large, crusty blue frosting: *Hi, B.*

When we finished moving, Dolores opened the front door to flush out the dust. While she was in the kitchen, I locked the door. I never went to sleep without double-checking the locks again.

In a short time, I became our home's self-appointed safety monitor. "Checking the locks every night," my mamá screamed. "¡Esto no es trabajo para una niña! You don't think we can protect you?"

"No, Mamá," I said. "That's my job now."

I said earlier that I had no bad memories at all. This is why. It wasn't a bad memory because I learned the right lessons from it. Brenda saved me from becoming someone who would stand out, a person who would call attention to themselves. I nourished this idea like a flame, retreating further into myself and my books. By sixth grade, I tested into a gifted junior high school program. The summer weekend before school began, I went on an overnight "Meet your new classmates" trip to Joshua Tree National Park. My mamá signed the permission slip, which disappointed me.

"Pierdes el tiempo con los libros," she said. "You cannot become like everyone else by being alone."

It was four hours on a bus without air-conditioning. Thirty-eight students traveled to see the "Queen of the Night," a once-in-a-year night-blooming cereus.

"It means 'cactus,'" Mrs. Reál said.

Why don't they call it a cactus, then? I thought, then bit my upper lip. I hated when things I learned in school had more than one word for them.

That night was the first I slept away from home. I skipped the sunset class walk around Indian Cove to sulk inside a campground barracks tent, preoccupied with why Debbie Lang had borrowed my compact mirror at our sack lunch and hadn't returned it. I dozed off—how long I didn't know—then heard Mrs. Reál shout.

"Come outside," she said. "The queens are blooming. Hurry, come and see."

White elephantine flower bulbs crackled under a bath of thrumming moonlight. Their flower buds secreted a rank, heady smell. The children considered the flowers, then gradually ignored them. They ran in circles through a patch of lavender beavertails, nipping at each other like eager pups.

On a side trail, I saw Debbie sitting atop a high, pale, craggy boulder on a hill, surrounded by razor-sharp yucca plants and a thin creek of brackish water. Her bright blond hair caught the sun and floated a ringed halo above her head, as if she were already regarding this moment from someplace in her future, in a spectacular pink mansion by the sea. I knew you could see danger approaching in a house that size, imagine danger's satisfying fall from its smooth bright abalone perimeter walls into a murky shallow moat below. I wanted that blond halo, too. I already knew, even then, it had an ability to bestow on its wearer an unbreachable entitlement and privilege.

I picked up a rock and held it in my hand. It was gray and odd-shaped, like an ice cube held under a water faucet. I hurled it with force at Debbie. It just missed, landing near her sneakers, but she got spooked and moved. This feeling inside, I understood, was strength.

"Gracias, B," I whispered.

Sorting through the newspaper clippings, I found an article that showed postage stamp–size photographs of every victim of the massacre. Three rows down, four heads across, was Brenda. Her smile showed her missing front tooth. I rubbed her face and thought, *Okay, here they come, the tears I have been waiting for.*

They didn't come.

I put the articles away, double-checked the front door locks, turned on a night-light for Mel, and went to sleep.

Four

Over the following days, each morning before I made coffee and watched Mel kick and toss herself awake, I checked the wall. Was it gone? Or was Brenda there, sitting on its ledge, swinging feet that didn't touch the ground? I waved at a few neighbors, but given the distance my house was from theirs, I was never sure whether I could be seen.

I had a fleeting moment of dread that Alex wouldn't show for that Saturday's pickup, since I had asked for Mel's band document that would make her transfer to Leland final. I imagined Mel's face pressed against her bedroom window, waiting for her no-show dad.

He arrived at nine a.m. sharp and parked down the block, walking onto my front lawn on a path that went around and completely ignored the wall. Was he oblivious or did he simply not see it? I didn't ask him about the wall because I didn't want him to think I was crazy, then weaponize that thought to get Mel back in his house.

Alex handed Mel a small plush rooster, some barrettes for her hair, and gave me her band paperwork in an official-looking envelope.

"Thank you," I said, "but you didn't need to buy her new things. She'll expect them every visit."

"These were left behind," he said.

"Thank you, Daddy!" Mel squealed.

Alex lingered, shuffling his feet. Was he expecting something?

None of us knew what to do next. I had never invited him inside our house. In that early-morning air, standing on our modest front porch, it was hard to grasp those memories of Alex that had led me to love him for years. I could hear how he laughed at a movie, or remember how he squeezed my hand during a blood draw. Those memories were inside me—they hadn't gone anywhere—but had been reshelved. I didn't know how to access them. I didn't want to be rude, but I wasn't in the mood to invite Alex in and show him around.

"Mel, get your lunch box," I said. "I can get you a cup of coffee to go, if you want," I told Alex.

He skimmed the property, then stared right in the wall's direction. With its metal flakes, it was a shimmering puce, the glint from it like a wink. Impossible to miss. Alex said nothing about it.

"I'm fine," he said. "Mel finally settled in her new school?"

"She likes it," I said. "Made a couple friends, I think. Everything okay with you?"

"I guess," he said.

"Good," I said. Our intimacies depleted, we stood in silence, two strangers waiting for the child we created to set us free. When Mel came outside, she was wearing Alex's new barrettes.

"Okay, bye, Mommy!" she said, and ran into Alex's arms. They walked around the wall, Alex ignoring the stone footpath to the street, again oblivious to the fact that the wall hadn't existed a few days ago. My ex-husband did obliviousness so well.

From my kitchen window, drinking a cup of coffee, I watched Alex and Mel drive away, bringing my focus back to the wall. As if it sensed I was thinking about it, the phone rang. It was a man named Tim from Unity Builders. He said he'd gotten a call—"several calls, actually"—about a wall that had been built on my property without my knowledge or approval. Tim said he didn't have time to visit my house because of a backlog of Prop 3–related work, but could do a phoner right now if I had time.

"You want to explain what happened?" he asked.

"I'll try," I said. "I've lived in this house for three months, woke up one morning, and there was a large wall outside blocking the front of my house."

"Okay," he said. "By blocking do you mean you are obstructed by it? You can't get in or out of your house?"

"No, I can leave my house freely," I said.

"Okay," Tim said. "So this isn't a safety hazard."

"I mean, no, not really," I said. I sensed his growing incredulousness and my inability to explain what was happening. "But it's blocking the view from my house to the street."

"You can't see outside of your home?"

"No, no, that's not it," I said. "I mean, I have to walk a long way around it when I didn't have to before. And my daughter," I said, then stopped. How could I tell Tim that my daughter said it was growing? What man would believe a woman telling him about something he couldn't see with his own eyes?

"So you can also walk around the wall, too," Tim said.

"I can," I said, "but my daughter. She's tried climbing it and she's too young for that."

"How high is the wall?" he asked.

"About four feet," I said. "And Mel's nine years old. She could fall off it."

"Can you use your camera on your phone and show me?"

I held the phone like some kind of scanning device up and around the wall from several different angles.

"I'm not seeing anything," he said. "Your screen is black. How about taking some pictures?"

I took about twenty different shots and texted them.

Predictably, Tim said, "Your photos aren't opening."

"I've never had a problem with this phone," I said.

"How about you describe what you see, then?" he asked. I explained the wall's dimensions, composition, its thousands of tiny metal shards scattered throughout. Enough specific details to make me sound like a sincere witness, or a lunatic.

"And you're saying this happened overnight?" he asked.

"One day it wasn't here, the next day it was," I said.

"Never heard that one before," Tim said. "Can you wobble the wall? Does it give at all when you push it?"

For sincerity's sake, I set my phone atop the wall's ledge and leaned on it with my whole body.

"Nothing," I said.

I heard what sounded like tapping on a keyboard. "What you're telling me," he said, "is literally impossible." The prep and backfill alone for a wall as long and big as I described, he continued, would take several days at least. It could not have been constructed overnight. It would've been done in stages. If it hadn't, the wall would have collapsed or sunk on its own because nothing in that wall would have had time to set. The most obvious explanation, he said, is that I had confused my property with another when I was house hunting. This, he assured me, happened frequently with new homeowners.

"I have been living at this house for several months," I said. "I'm not confused."

"I understand, ma'am," Tim said, in a way that meant he didn't understand at all. "I mean, renovation projects sometimes build over one another. Perhaps this wall was excavated when some utility company did some work in the area. I'm spitballing here because what you're describing is not possible, and I can't see what you're looking at."

"Sure," I said. "But, it's there. I can see it."

Tim paused, as if reading the silence on my end. "It's peculiar," he said, "but it's definitely not the weirdest thing I've ever heard. There're many people who'd pay good money for, and really appreciate, the retaining wall you're describing." I had never considered that a wall could please the senses.

"So you're saying I'm stuck with this thing?" I asked.

"You could hire someone to drill past the bedrock outside your home. Maybe you'd find something that, I don't know, pushed that stone out of the ground. It's also possible the soil could swell over time, meaning the foundation would come loose and it'd fall over on its own in a few years."

"Years?" I asked.

"If you're lucky," he said. "But to figure that out now, you'd need a lot of time, money, and a crew that isn't committed to another job."

"I guess the next step is to get some other contractors' opinions about this," I said.

Tim's voice tensed, bristling like a cat's tail. "Since Prop 3 passed, every crew I know has waiting lists nine to twelve months out. And anyone who knows what they're doing will tell you the same thing." Men hate having their expertise challenged and will go to any length to make you feel stupid for doing it.

"I have to live with it," I said.

He took my helplessness as his cue. "At this property," he said. "Yes, ma'am." Then he wished me luck. It sounded like a curse. And maybe it was. Whether it was the Proposition 3 construction boom or bad luck, I wasn't able to find another contractor who had time to inspect the wall. One man claimed he stopped by when I was out running errands, but wouldn't return. When I asked why, he sounded spooked. "Lady," he said, "sometimes crazy things just *happen*."

Inside the house, the bay window had framed a bright shale sun over a concrete horizon. Something was askew, though. What was visible of my lawn and the street beyond the wall was different. The view was off by a couple inches, perhaps more, but I noticed. I spilled some coffee on my clean counter as I tried looking at the wall through my phone. The wall's specks glinted in the phone's viewfinder, scrambling its image.

There was less of my view than when I woke up. It happened while Tim and I were talking, right in front of me.

The wall rose.

The wall *grew*.

Oh, I remember thinking.

This wasn't an actual "Oh my God" moment. Not yet.

Five

I saw the first wristband scanners at FARM.

That was fast, I thought.

Bored employees nodded in unison as a manager quick-drew a scanning gun from its cloth holster. "Slide the band face in front of this part of the gun, point it at the customer, then, *gotcha!*" he said, and laughed. "Like you're scanning an item." His dutiful employees echoed his laughter.

Over the next days, the machines materialized everywhere, in all areas of my daily life: gas stations, grocery stores, and every football stadium–size chain store where I bought Mel's clothes and her favorite cereal.

When I got home with Mel from after-school, two men I didn't recognize were walking along the wall with their dog, who sniffed at it every few steps. The men looked straight ahead, neither of them acknowledging what their dog was sniffing at. I was surprised to see people walking so close to my house. I wasn't sure at first if they were real.

"Hi there!" the taller man said, and offered his hand. "I'm Todd, and this is my husband, James."

I stood there for a moment, eyes blinking. I hadn't prepared myself to, at last, talk to someone right outside my home. That eye flutter also betrayed someone processing information they weren't expecting. *Did he say husband?* I recognized that turning-the-lights-on-in-a-dark-room blink well because I saw it in women's eyes when they asked about Mel. Yes, *she* is my child. Yes, *I'm* her mother.

"I don't think we've seen you around," Todd said. "What's your name?"

When meeting anyone new, I say my name the way I pronounced it in my head, enunciating vowels the "American way": not *I* as in "eh," but *I* as in "Eye can see." Unrolled, firm, immovable *r*. No hissed out *s*, floating away like a weather balloon into the land of zz's. Eye-ris. Not Eeee-rheh-suzz. *Almost sounds like Inés*, I could hear Serena say.

In junior high, when time and hormones changed my body, a fact that I neither adored nor despised ("Good!" Dolores told me. "Keep that up the rest of your life"), my seventh-grade teacher Mrs. McIntyre's tongue kept tripping on my first name during homeroom roll call. Inés became Eye-Neez, then Eye-Nice, Eye-Ness-Say, and then, one random morning, "How about I call you Iris?"

I liked how that sounded. *Iris.* I didn't want to make any trouble, nor did I want undue attention, since Mrs. McIntyre would keep mispronouncing my name, and I would keep hanging my head in shame.

On my first day of eighth grade, I counted the names down to mine during attendance. I heard that pause as Mr. Byrd tried to fish my name out of his mouth.

I raised my hand and said, "Just call me Iris," and shrugged my shoulders, an apology for embarrassing my teacher. When I told my parents about the name change, they shrugged their shoulders, too, exhausted from their jobs, their early-morning commutes to work, and my new "Oops, a baby!" sister, Serena, a twelve-year gap between the two of us. Of course, my parents gave me the Mexican name first, instead of what they thought was a white-passing name to my baby sister, though as Serena Williams got popular, my sister said her teachers seemed more and more confused: *What are your parents' names? Do you celebrate Kwanzaa? Would you like to do a report for the class on Martin Luther King?*

The sonics of smoothing the rough edges of my old first name down transformed me from Inés Soto—*Eee-nay-zee Sha-toh*—into Eye-ris So-toe. Teachers could now pronounce both my first and last name correctly and loved saying both names together. There was an awkward transition of name correcting and reintroductions, but soon there was nobody left who didn't know me by Iris, no one who cared enough to remind me I went by another name, and nobody to use my maiden name when I got married. I was divorced now, sure, but I wanted to make the right impression in this neighborhood.

"My name is Iris," I said. "Iris Prince."

"Wow, what a name!" Todd said. "Well, welcome, Iris! This rascal here is Daisy. I'm sorry we didn't meet sooner, but James and I have been so busy with work, it's like we forget we live here. We were in Italy for some much-needed vacation."

"Were you in the Lake Como area?" I asked, flexing my watched-dozens-of-walking-tours-of-Italy-videos experience.

"God no, we don't have that kind of money," James said. "But we'd love to hear about your travels there."

"Sure," I said. "I'd like that."

Todd and James knelt down to Mel's height. "And who's this?" James asked.

"Say hello to our new neighbors," I said. "It's okay."

"How do you like our street?" James asked.

"My dad doesn't live here," Mel said.

"How lovely she is!" Todd said, hiding his double eye blink better than I did. "It's a great place for a family, which you all clearly are! And the rest of the neighbors, they're great. Oh! And Rebekah! She's at the top of the block. She's great! She's Luh-tee-nah," he said, his voice trailing off, as if initiating me in a secret club.

"Latina?" I asked. "Oh," I said. My eyes double-blinked again. His husband caught me.

"Todd, jeez," James said, exasperated.

"That was stupid," he said. "I'm sorry."

"It's fine," I said.

"No, you're being kind. I mean, she's, you know, but so what? I just wanted you to know what kind of neighborhood you live in."

"Wrap it up, Todd," James said.

"Really, it's fine," I said. "I'm an adult, and I know what you meant. I love Latinas!"

"Can you train my husband, please?" James said. We shared a collective laugh.

As I shook their hands goodbye, their dog tried to raise a hind leg to the wall, then yelped as if jolted by an unseen current, and loped away. Neither Todd nor James acknowledged the wall.

I checked my voicemail. There were several messages from a payment management service asking me to upload my band's identification number immediately. "We can grant you a short grace period during this transition period," the automated voice continued, "but your services will be paused, or ultimately disconnected, until your information is verified."

I grabbed a tape measure inside and noted the wall's height and width on my phone's notepad. Grit stuck to my fingertips. Coarse, like pink sea salt. I could smell its mortar, its earth, what held it together.

Over the wall, warm lights came on in my neighbors' homes and living rooms.

I don't want to leave here, I thought. What would my mamá do?

You were born here, she'd tell me. *That is something you can never lose.*

———

My parents' neighborhood is defined by ironwork. Security gates welded atop front doors with beautiful stained glass inserts. Ornate armored bars drilled over historic bay windows. Black metal grates barred taco truck service windows. Garages with graffiti-blanketed metal shutters lined their exterior walls with shards of broken glass, barbed-wire strands, and random shrapnel. I hated how burglary protection in West Vecino blacked out any shred of color, light. It was a grotesque, visible deterrent, unlike in North Azulia, where a constellation of tiny pulsing red lights and hidden surveillance created an unspoken agreement between owner and trespasser. *We don't have to show you that you don't belong here.* With wealth, I saw that security didn't have to be ugly.

When I lived at Alex's in South Griffy, I would visit my parents twice a week and shop at Emilio's, a local grocery and panadería, since it had much cheaper prices. Plus, my mamá would harass me if I stopped going. *Emilio's wife saw you drive by their store and you didn't even wave hello! You're not too good for that store, you know! Mel's things are so much cheaper than at the gringo stores! Everything I needed for Serena growing up I could get there!*

Through a weird quirk of geography and redistricting, West Vecino was only a sixteen-minute drive from North Azulia, but each of those minutes added to the enormous gulf between them. In West Vecino, words slathered on glass in lurid green, orange, and tomato-colored paint varied from English/Spanish to Spanish. Banda music drifted over wooden fences into backyards with waist-high weeds. Taco trucks and street merchants congregated under billowing rain tarps along the main boulevard. Gunfire crackled at night, nudging me and Alex off the couch after my mamá's dinner and back home.

West Vecino was like my childhood neighborhood years ago. Back then, I could find a comfort in the sights and sounds, seeing and hearing them drift by as I laid down on the plush red felt back seat of Gonzalo's "carrazo" Monte Carlo. At some point, that comfort had transformed into fear, then curdled into almost shame. I was afraid of sitting in a drugstore parking lot, day or night, waiting for Gonzalo to get his ear medicine and bottles of black hair dye. No more trips to the ninety-nine-cent store when a small fire broke out in the school supplies aisle, its flames and toxic white smoke smell ignored by the customers and staff. I couldn't unsee the chaos. Had youth made those sights easier to ignore, or had I lost something essential—something alive—in me that now equated silence with security, and noise with danger?

Sometimes I made the mistake of taking Serena shopping with me.

"These stores aren't for pochas like you," Serena said.

"I enjoy shopping in both places," I told my sister, which was mostly true. "I'm free to do that."

"Why don't you stay shopping in North Azulia?" Serena asked. "You know, 'azulia' is a made-up word. It's how gabachos think Spanish should sound. They Americanize our words with mortar and pestle."

Siblings *think* they're the only ones who know you. All my sister got right was that I suspected I was different from everyone, broken somehow. When Brenda died, my emotions hardened into a mask of grinned silence that hid my true self. It was a cast worn in public places—the carnicería, the panadería, the tienditas on the boulevard—that deflected questions about whether I was "okay" or "fine" or "happy." Nobody noticed I wasn't, not even my parents, who were exhausted from work. I assumed my mask was invisible and working as it should. I could fade into the background of my family's day-to-day life and listen to Dolores's free-flowing conversations, swollen rivers of chisme and laughter. I wondered if my own laugh would one day sound as ripe and unguarded as my mamá's, but it never did, except when I drank wine.

Growing up, I found it harder to slip that mask off. It was a valuable tool in places I was expected to translate for Dolores and Gonzalo, both of whom understood and could speak English, but didn't trust they could get the words right quickly in important conversations. The older I got, the more I had to speak for them in banks, doctors' offices, the DMV. Any space that smelled like bleach, where I had to sit down on a hard chair next to my mamá or father, made my stomach ache, like I was about to take an exam I hadn't prepared for. Except the questions, and the judging facial expressions—eyes that may as well have said, *How embarrassing they are*—from the other side of the large desk never changed. My mask kept these people's accusations, the loud sighs, the exasperated, muttered insults, in a kind of receptacle that couldn't hurt me, and inoculated me from blaming my parents. The mask protected me and, without recognizing it, became who I was.

Eventually, I learned older kids observed two things: poverty and difference. They noted my basic black glasses—*dumb!*—the number of books I voluntarily took home—*dumber!*—but saved their most damning allegations for what I wore. *¡Pinche pantalones de Goodwill! ¡Zapatos chafas de Payless!* They made their insults soar like a chorus. My bullies wore the same "la ninety-nine" combos I did, but their collective families' lack of money was a bond I broke by being smart. Stupidity is entitled. Brains implied shame, and a potential for escape. I kept my books hidden from then on.

During verbal schoolyard arguments, where playing dirty was essential, I realized I could brag about my status as an American citizen to end a fight quickly. I had years of practice repeating "I was born here!" with my parents. Yet the one time I did it on the playground, under a blossoming jacaranda tree, my taunt landed flat.

"So?" I heard back.

"So" was right. Many of my classmates' parents, like mine, were undocumented, as were some of my schoolmates and friends. How could something that out in the open be shameful? In return, I didn't feel guilty for what I said, because there were no consequences for saying it. I heard the words *illegal alien, beaner, spic,* and *wetback* tossed back and forth by the fifth-grade boys like water balloons. Beyond the chain-link fence, those words had an actual heft. I heard them, and the weight they carried, on the street when Gonzalo cut someone off for a parking space—*Fucking wetback!*— or in the nearby park on three-day weekends when it filled with white people who didn't come often and asked aloud, "Why is the park so *crowded?*" The words were the same, but their *sound,* and how my parents reacted to that sound, was different. My friends were firing blanks that pinged off each other. My parents absorbed live rounds. They pinched their shoulders, to pretend they were holding their heads high with pride instead of anger or fear, followed by a sharp intake of breath, to remind themselves to keep their mouths shut.

I didn't want that way of life for myself, or my daughter. So whenever I traveled to places like North Azulia and saw fictional,

bastardized Spanish words scattered everywhere—Paza, Ranchina—
I knew these were geographic markers that really meant *You're safe
here, just as long as you blend in, nice and easy.* There I wouldn't
have to strategize my shopping to certain hours so I wouldn't be
harassed or catcalled by shirtless men who hung out in parking
lots. Serena was too angry to understand why I found life in South
Griffy or West Vecino exhausting, though I could no longer recall
when Serena wasn't angry about something. And why? My sister
was raised in a house (not a garage, and then an apartment, like me),
where our mamá exonerated Serena from a thousand childhood
crimes I would have been punished for. My younger sister's fury was
a luxury, a gift of indulgence from our parents, who were too old to
discipline her properly.

Since moving to my new home, I had to cancel a few family
dinner nights. There was no use inviting my family over because
they would never come. Gonzalo didn't leave the house, Dolores
was too exhausted after work to travel, and my sister wouldn't
come without my parents. In the past twelve years, I had never
missed two family dinners in a row without being sick. When I
canceled my third dinner, Dolores called me less than sixty seconds
after I texted. I picked up the call mid-scream.

"Sí no vienes a cenar, ¡no eres mi hija!"

"Mamá, I'm still your daughter! I'm coming this Saturday,
okay?"

Truth was, I wasn't sure what a family dinner would be without
Alex. I brought him home when I was twenty-five and remember the relieved looks on my parents' faces. *Finally, someone who
will love our unlovable, unlikable, always complaining, impossible to
please daughter.* I wanted to say, *But how did I get that way, Mamá?*

Gonzalo was at ease speaking to Alex, who enjoyed talking to
him because he was much less demanding than his own father or,
I guess, me. Gonzalo spoke with Alex for an hour about TJ dance
clubs Gonzalo went to in his twenties, how my dad wore high-
heeled botas on Saturday nights, and how his friends had nicknamed
him "el Tigre" because he was so smooth with the ladies. I had never

heard these stories. Gonzalo showed Alex faded floppy 1970s photos, including a picture from the day he crossed the border. His lush rayon, butterfly-print long-sleeve shirt made my father look as if he were the subject of a Renaissance painting done on black velvet. Serena would make Gonzalo show those photos whenever she was depressed and needed to laugh.

"Damn, Papá, you looked so paisa!" Serena would say.

"*Super* paisa," I'd agree.

Alex later told me, "Your dad's such a simple man." It took me a few moments to realize he meant this, first, as a compliment to my father and, second, as a question: *What happened to you?*

How can we be related, I wondered, when my father can rest wherever he's at like a house cat, capable of disconnecting from hard decisions and unpleasantness? If there was a wall growing outside his home, he'd laugh, hold his fingers close together like pincers, and say, "Esto es lo poquito que podemos hacer." Perhaps my father's apathy was his secret to happiness.

Dolores's house was on the far side of West Vecino, inaccessible by public transportation or a direct freeway exit. There was a saffron light in the sky at sunset, a curried smog that coated the streets in a nostalgic, tranquil aura, a honeyed 1970s Instamatic glow that obscured how the area changed after dark. When I left Melanie for a sleepover, I gave Dolores one specific instruction: don't let Mel play outside after seven p.m.

"Ay, bájale," Dolores said. "No estamos en una película de narcos." Later, when I'd call to check on Mel, I'd bite my lip as Dolores shouted over the heavy *whump* of a police helicopter hovering above, sirens screaming past.

The loud *clang* and slide bolt *ping* of a black steel security door being unlocked meant I was home. The same doors were on all of Dolores's neighbors' houses along with black security bars on their windows, too. No way in or out.

I came into my mamá's home through the kitchen. Melanie cheek-kissed Dolores, then ran to a closet where a box of her toys and books were kept. I grabbed a Tecate from the fridge and set it by Gonzalo's trembling hand. This was Alex's gesture of deference and care.

"¿Qué quieres?" Dolores asked genuinely. She asked this of anyone who entered our home. What do you want, which meant, *What can I offer you?* "La cena está casi lista."

"Tá bien," I said. I asked Gonzalo, "¿Cómo va el Monterrey game?"

"Meten la pata cada vez que los veo," Gonzalo said.

Here is when Alex and Gonzalo would laugh and clink their beer bottles. I envied his relationship with my father. I wondered if the part of Gonzalo that I could see when my father relaxed and laughed with Alex while they watched fútbol together was gone now. I hated to think that I was taking this away from my father. Or from me. Gonzalo spoke more to Alex than to me these days, using a sticky drawl that, when caught on an English word whose definition didn't satisfy what function he wanted his story to perform, would spill into laughter until his Spanish came out. I wanted to know what it felt like to make my father laugh with me.

I wondered if Gonzalo was not talking to me now because I had taken away his fútbol companion, but even when my father was present, he was rarely there. It was the same affliction I saw in Alex, though I often wondered if I was too demanding to expect a man to be more than present with his wife every day. How did my mom handle that ghostliness for all these years?

Dolores told me one summer afternoon that Gonzalo didn't know his biological father in any meaningful way. He was raised by a man in his village he'd called "el Padrino," a man who loved fútbol and, sometimes, Gonzalo's mother, Dominga, though they had a tempestuous relationship. They'd laugh, they'd drink, they'd date for a few months. Then he drifted away either for work or because he didn't want to keep dodging Dominga's butcher knife. When el Padrino settled down and married someone else, Dominga never forgave him, and el Padrino's childless wife never forgave Gonzalo, it seemed, for existing. El Padrino's wife exiled Gonzalo, who heard from a distant cousin that el Padrino died from falling off the roof of his house, where he used to climb using a rickety ladder at dusk to watch the stars rise. Gonzalo made a pilgrimage to el Padrino's grave, where he saw inscribed on the headstone: MARIDO, COMPAÑERO, GUERRERO. He had to feel the stone to convince himself it didn't say what he knew it should have: Padre. Gonzalo put a small rock over the space where he thought "Father" should be, and never returned to his village.

When did he tell you this? I asked.

Tell? I overheard him say this to Alex, Dolores said.

Alex? Why not you?

Hombres, Dolores said. *Les valemos madre.*

On television, one fútbol game ended. Another began. In the flickering television light, I saw tufts of gray hair where Gonzalo's dye job faded. Each flicker revealed more strands to the point where it seemed my father was aging in front of me.

I didn't know what to say to Gonzalo during these matches. Before his retirement he had little recreation time for himself and I felt it would be rude to attempt a fake conversation during the one thing he enjoyed. I hated these long silences, but my father felt comfortable in them. For years, when Gonzalo came home from work, he went to the couch and his remote control, not his family. It didn't matter whether he had a factory job or, when he was older and had less strength, his custodial jobs. It was a straight line to the honeyed lights of a fridge that dispensed endless Tecates and a television where a game could always be found, day or night. Even when Dolores forced him to punish me, I never took it seriously. One time, to get his attention, I grabbed the remote control and ran around our tiny living room with it. Dolores couldn't find her chanclas to swing at my butt. Gonzalo grabbed his pant loops and threatened to take his belt to me. I dropped the remote and laughed, dancing around him as if his legs were maypoles. He gave me a kiss, grabbed the remote, and sent me outside. My sister, Serena, grew up seeing how unsuccessful I was and learned how to placate my father's needs before asking for what she wanted in return. I wished I had learned to be that direct.

On the stove were large, old aluminum cooking pots that Dolores used instead of the fancy cookware Alex and I bought her for Christmas years ago. She cleaned them with a shredded sponge and a small plastic container of dirty wash water next to the faucet. I used to empty out the slimy container until Dolores presented me with that month's water bill. The dishes, I know, are drying in the dishwasher rack, as my mamá had never once turned the machine on. (Alex had warned me not to buy it.) Watching Dolores make dinner, I saw no recognizable imprint in my own cooking. I calculated sugars, fat contents, and artificial flavoring necessary to reproduce something my mamá cooked in an effortless dance from memory.

Six days a week Dolores drove two hours each way to the same industrial custodial chemical complex she'd worked at for twenty-seven years, then came home, disinfected her clothes from that rancid chemical smell, cleaned the house, and cooked dinner with at least fifty percent materials from scratch. She did this every night while raising me and Serena.

Why did I require emulsifiers, cardboard baking trays, sauces squeezed out of foil packets to make "just add water" tamales? I peeled out the strands of synthetic sweet-smelling dough, plopped them into a pan of lukewarm water, watched as they ballooned up like string cheese, then removed the warm clumps, slit them open with a (provided) slicing knifette, then turned that knifette into a spatula and smeared the pre-bagged cheese and meat slurry across the dough, folded the tops down, and ¡listo!, ¡tamales! My plastic cooking utensil splintered when I cut across the result. I thought less about what my mamá cooked—which ranged from good (pozole, chilaquiles) to ruining-my-taste-for-it-when-eaten-anywhere-else incredible (enchiladas, tamales, and frijoles refritos simmered with chorizo, a style I hadn't ever come close to emulating)—and inhaled the elements of ingredients that warmed my nostrils and triggered nostalgic endorphins of childhood: wet flour, lard, fresh tomatoes, chopped onions, cilantro. Whatever stress I felt ebbed away, for the moment.

Fútbol halftime meant we could eat. "¿Esperamos a Serena?" I asked.

"No, no queremos morir de hambre. Sit down y coman," my mamá said. "¿Cómo le va a Melanie en la escuela?"

"She's doing fine," I said, and made two plates. Our dinnertime was in shifts: first a plate for Gonzalo—men eat first in this house—then a smaller plate for Melanie in her playroom. I had to remember not to make a plate for Alex.

"¿Qué significa 'fine'?" Dolores asked.

"The teachers say Melanie has a bright future."

"Decían lo mismo about you," Dolores said. "Entiendes perfectamente."

Yes, I knew. Those words—"bright future"—drove Dolores crazy. *Oíste los maestros,* Dolores had told me. *Try harder.* I thought this was initially my mamá misunderstanding the English words. When I became a mother myself, I realized Dolores understood the condescension, the pity, the demeaning tone, the implied patronization, the gentle hand already positioned to cushion each of my expected falls and predicted setbacks, even when they never came. "Bright future" meant "current Mexican girl loser."

"Mamá, do you have my birth certificate?" I asked. Gonzalo raised his head away from the game, curious.

"Sí, somewhere," Dolores said. "¿Por qué?"

Before I could answer, Serena flung open the security gate and in one fluid, practiced motion, sat at the table, doling out a full plate of food in one hand, while the other scrolled her phone. I *hated* that phone.

"Mamá, you hear what happened with the national anthem?" Serena said.

"¿Lo perdieron los gabachos?" Dolores asked.

"No, they didn't lose it. They suspended some college basketball players who didn't put their hands over their hearts to protest police brutality." This, I knew, would become an argument if I said what I truly felt. Stories like this—which spewed out in an endless torrent from her fucking phone—had created so much distance between us that almost nothing of who I thought was my sister remained. We were obligatory siblings. Every day she shared some new story from somewhere we didn't live or would never visit and turned it into an emotional litmus test about how we really felt about race, or gender, or equality. What did it matter what I felt? Why was I expected to do anything about these issues at all?

I *really* hated that phone. But I hated silence more.

"I just don't understand what the big deal is," I said aloud. "If the players put their hands over their hearts, they can play and won't risk their scholarships. They only have to follow the rules. Right?"

"It's not in the rules to pose that way," Serena said.

"Because everybody already knows you have to do that," I said. "We did that every day in school and never had a choice."

"All the tiny gringa cheerleaders and players already put their hands over their heart. The Black players clasp their hands behind their back. You could ask why, but I guess you'd rather be a good American—more concerned about where a Black man's hands are than what happens to his body. ¿Verdad?"

Truth, I thought. Truth was something my sister loved to rub people's noses in. Serena made her truth oler a mierda. She got me so mad sometimes I was able to find my Spanish, hidden like an unfavored toy in the back of a closet. Alex and I had agreed that, despite our lack of Spanish primacy, we should raise Melanie bilingual. This was a much more important decision than whether Melanie should be raised to believe in God or eat meat (both her choice, when she was ready). Our plan was for Mel to speak Spanish when prompted at school, to my parents, and to Spanish speakers who proved they could switch to English. If someone other than Dolores and Gonzalo spoke to her only in Spanish, she was to reply in English. "This rule isn't for tus abuelos," I told Melanie. "But don't help someone be huevón. I mean, lazy." I spat out "lazy" as an expletive. It was a denigration, a personal offense, something I reserved for people who disappointed me most, like Serena.

When Serena was sixteen, she wanted to be a lawyer. She insisted I call her "abogada" and loved shouting, "Objection!" covering my face in spittle. I gave Serena an LSAT prep book as a high school graduation gift, since it's never too early to start. When Serena bombed her practice test junior year in college, she said, "Law school is no place for brown people."

"Stop using your race as an excuse for not working hard," I said.

"I didn't major in whiteness in college como tú," Serena said.

"Too bad your skin color flunked you on the final! God, I hate you, Inés."

The words—*hate, Inés*—seemed to surprise her as much as they did me, like a fish that had swum out of Serena's mouth and thwapped between us. We stared at a space on Dolores's brown linoleum kitchen floor, our nostrils flush with grease smell.

It was easier to track what we couldn't talk about instead of what we could. Gone was the Serena who joked about how chinos couldn't drive. Now even weather was on the "don't discuss" list, as was fast-food chicken sandwiches and raccoons. I affixed a SUPPORT YOUR LOCAL POLICE sticker on my car and was treated to an hour-long diatribe about racial bias and judicial incarceration.

"I don't judge a whole group by a few bad apples," I said.

"Doesn't one bad apple spoil the whole bunch?" Serena asked.

"Smart-ass," I said.

"Pocha," Serena said.

"¿Por qué you two siempre se están chingando?" Dolores said. "¡Malditas hijas como ustedes son las 'bad apples'!"

I couldn't keep track of Serena's activism stances. Who had time for limitless outrage when Melanie spilled her cranberry juice pouch on her Sunday sneakers? Once, Serena picked up a box of red laminated cards at an immigration rights center for undocumented people to hand over to a police officer if they were stopped. On the card: "I do not wish to speak with you, answer your questions, or sign or hand you my document, based on my Fifth Amendment rights under the United States Constitution. I choose to exercise my constitutional rights." On its back, the same information in Spanish. Serena splashed the cards across her social media pages, then gave me a stack and said she'd hand out five hundred of those cards by week's end. Dolores found all of Serena's cards stuffed in a paper bag under her bed.

No matter how hard I tried, I couldn't resist confronting my sister's version of *truth*.

"Weren't you mad about the bands last week?" I asked.

"That's why I'm late for dinner! That guy with the junkyard still had a ton of those stupid lawn signs in his yard. The election's been over for months, so I knocked them all down."

"You're lucky the police didn't catch you. He has a right to his signs on his property."

Serena laughed. "You won't be happy until todos seamos vendidos. When they come to put us on the trucks, Iris will take out her little clipboard and put herself in charge. You're on welfare? On the truck! You do drugs? Get on the truck! You're a cholo? Adiós, mofo! Oh, you married a gabacho? You can stay with me!"

"Stop pretending you know me," I said. "Mamá, can't you tell your daughter something?"

"Es verdad que te gustan los clipboards," Dolores said.

"Papá, ¿quién va ganando?" Serena asked.

"Nostros no," he said. "¿Quieres ver el próximo partido?"

"Maybe later," Serena said, and flicked her screen. Gonzalo had long stopped asking me to watch games with him, but he always held out hope that Serena would join him. My sister held her very presence over our heads like a threat. At any moment, an urgent message from her phone could send her out of the house for an hour, or overnight. She held that phone in a series of defensive boxing postures—block, parry, evade—to divert and deflect conversation. Stories used to be a staple in our home. We sat around, gossiped, laughed, and listened to each other. Now, with dinner over, my sister went to her phone, my mamá, Mel, and I to the dishes, and my father to the game.

"Mamá," I asked, "did you ever have to alter your documents to work here?"

"Alter?" she asked.

"You know," I whispered. "Pretend."

"No, no seas loca. Nobody ever asked for anything. ¿Por qué haces una pregunta tan tonta?"

"I don't know," I said. "Just thinking about things. You remember Brenda?"

"Who's Brenda?" Serena asked.

"¿Tu amiga de grade school?" Dolores asked. "¿A la que mataron en el McDonald's? Ay, sí, sí. You hated her, no?"

"Inés had a friend who someone killed?" Serena asked, using my old name. "Why didn't you mention her?"

"Same reason you call me 'Inés' instead of my actual name," I said. "Mamá, do you remember what happened to Brenda's family?" I thought learning their fate might explain why I saw Brenda on the wall.

"No, no sé," Dolores said. "Acabó mudándose al desierto. Brenda era tan joven. Ella me recordaba a Angelita."

"Uncle Enrique's kid?" Serena asked. I didn't know she was listening.

"Sí, tiene una niña, Angelita," Dolores said. My memory about Brenda now became my mamá's story. I enjoyed how my uncertainty braided our camaraderie. Dolores was our family's best storyteller. Her voice had a firm determination that my own voice lacked when I asked Melanie to pay attention.

My mamá's words rushed over me in a soothing balm, but my Spanish was out of practice. I had to work hard to process them, gathering them up like loose marbles, and translate them into English. Uncle Enrique, my mamá said, was visiting his sick mother, Perla, in another town and asked a cousin to watch her. One day Angelita wandered from the rancho and fell down a ravine. Angelita was dead, but there was no way to reach him, and he wouldn't be back for a few days. The cousin raced off to bring him back home. People from the town put ice-cold bottles of Coke and Fanta under Angelita's bed for days to preserve her body. When Enrique came back and saw Angelita, he went crazy. Ran barefoot for miles. Nobody knew where he was going. They captured him in the middle of the night, wrapped him up in bundles of cornstalks, and took him to the mental hospital in Guadalajara.

"They put el tío in a tortilla!" Serena said.

I touched Melanie's head, which in the heat of this story felt warm to the touch. I imagined a dark purple night sky and full moon, my uncle Enrique's body shape sliding through the stalks in a cornfield, the sound a scratchy hiss, then him shrieking out pieces of his lungs, attracting birds to feast on his innards, tendrils of corn silk swallowing him into blackness. Losing a child must feel that way.

"Did that really happen?" Serena asked.

"Sí, tu padre lo vio todo."

"Papá, tell us!" Serena said.

"You saw all this, Papá?" I asked.

This was the rare occurrence when Serena, my mamá, and I agreed on something. I wanted my father to turn away from his game to join our conversation. Soccer was an ever-constant joy for him and a distancing aura from everyone else. I remembered once when México scored a goal in a World Cup game. Seeing my father's spirit was a revelation. He was engaged, present, in a way he never was for checking my schoolwork, or helping with chores, or day-to-day parenting. Gonzalo seemed happier in that moment on the couch, Tecate in hand, than when I put Melanie in his lap and said, "Meet your nieta." When that goal was scored, I heard cheers from houses far down the street, a silent majority unafraid to pierce their collective invisibility, together, shouting, ¡Que viva, México! It was stunning to realize Gonzalo was part of that community. I couldn't take that away from him. Yet he had a family, too. What would he say?

"No, no vi nada," Gonzalo said.

Serena and Dolores razzed him, but this felt like an honest answer. My father didn't deny the story. He's not that kind of man. His mind—then, or now—was somewhere else.

Gonzalo closed the conversation down. Serena returned to her phone. I knew there were no more stories to share tonight. These days, my family shared brief, mutually agreed upon moments of togetherness followed by long periods of emotional detachment and separation. At least nobody commented on Alex's absence, an unspoken covenant that what had happened was too raw, too new, to tease me about. Serena was, I'm sure, given a moratorium that she would honor until she got mad enough not to. I wondered, while packing up Mel's toys, if Serena sensed how delicate the compact was that kept us together as a family. Was it only the physical house that united us? I once was afraid of this house, of its sudden cold spots and perpetual darkness even during hot summer days. Sometimes, I saw what I thought was a little girl running past my open door. I wasn't worried Brenda had come to possess me. I thought it was another version of myself that had split off at some point. The part of me that didn't hold my nose when I used la letrina outdoors, without running water, at Gonzalo's mother's house in México. I had cried, spooked by a scorpion crawling across the dirt floor, and wouldn't stop crying until we left Abuela's and checked into a motel. I remembered seeing a movie called *The Thing* years ago at a drive-in, since converted into a naco swap meet I didn't shop at anymore. An alien from outer space absorbed people and you couldn't tell who the imitation was and who was left that was real. A character said, *If I was a perfect imitation, how would you know it wasn't me?* But how, I shuddered, would *he* know he wasn't him? I could be absorbed, taken over, and not even remember which version was me. If I saw this other version of me, could *I* acknowledge her? What would *that* Iris want?

"¿Estás dormida?" Dolores said, rousing me. "Aquí tienes tu certificado de nacimiento."

"Oh, thanks," I said. "I think I need this."

"¿Para qué?"

"No importa. I should take Melanie home."

"Why do you need the certificate?" Gonzalo asked, his head turned away from the game. "Your mom asked you that."

I was stunned. Serena had put down her phone, anticipating something.

"Papá, it's nothing. I promise," I said, and lowered my head, trying to think of an excuse that wouldn't worry them. "I need it for Mel's school. They're doing a class project."

"Okay," Gonzalo said. "She should be proud you were born here."

"She is," I said. "I'll see you soon."

Mel was asleep in the short minutes it took to get home. My headlights caught the metal flakes embedded in the wall, then cast their light over the windowpanes and grilles on my bay window frame. Seeing those flakes made my whole body shiver. I was cold and dry-mouthed.

The lights should have stopped at the fourth row of vertical glass panes. Instead, they stopped at the fifth row. Around the wall was disturbed clay, damp to the touch. In the air, the faint scent of compost and excavated earth.

The wall *rose*.

The wall was *growing*.

Six

One Saturday, after a quick shopping trip at FARM—quick being an hour—I assembled festive paper bags of travel-size white wine bottles, assorted fruits, and blue light lawn bulbs. Unlike blue lights meant to discourage drug use in public places, these bulbs honored law enforcement.

Others here thought the way I did. I was in the right place. It was time to meet my neighbors.

While I handed out the bags, Mel offered a written invitation for Sunday coffee and pasteles from Dolores's panadería. Some things are too unfamiliar (meaning ethnic) for new "nice neighborhood" neighbors. Baked sweets aren't one of them.

Three people said they would come: Todd (his husband was busy), Stephanie, and Rebekah Parra. She lived in the Le Roman model home, the largest house on our cul-de-sac. Rebekah invited me into the vestibule for a friendly chat. Her living room was sanitized with framed inspirational-quote wall art and a color palette of tan or crème. No bright colors, no crosses, no Our Lady of Guadalupe candles or Santa Muerte statues, nothing to give her neighbors or visitors an opening to ask an endless litany of "What's this?" questions, followed by the inevitable "Fascinatings." (I learned this the hard way with Alex's parents.) There, on a stand outside a bathroom, the same Clothesline Linen fragrance candle I had in mine. Next to it, a small decorative box holding a set of keys, and a jar of farmers' market beeswax. Marble—*not* granite—kitchen counters. A cell phone docking bay with speakers streamed NPR.

It was a smart, well-protected arrangement. Nothing to lead you to believe Rebekah was Latina aside from her last name.

"Your home is lovely," I said. "Perfect, really."

"Thank you, Iris," she said, and touched my elbow. "I'm very much looking forward to coffee with you on Sunday."

In my mind, this coffee meet, if planned right, could become a ritual. Sophisticated, invitation-only conversations over curated, subscription-only whole beans, each cup ground by hand with a crank grinder Alex had purchased for me one Christmas, poured into a special service set that took me five weeks of research to buy, then went unused until now.

I thought, then overthought, how the event would be arranged. Table set or not set? Coffee standing by or made one at a time while the others waited? I enjoyed planning for all the variables of my guests' needs to make it appear as if I'd given it no thought at all. I was attempting to meticulously create a casual event.

When the morning arrived, I kept an eye out the bay window to see if my neighbors would stop at the wall, marvel at it as if it were a new and valued—appreciated—addition to the community. They arrived while my back was turned, setting the table. I slid a vintage table out of a side closet in a single magician's arm motion. I could hear the comforting approbation in their "Mmms" as Rebekah sat first. She was dressed in a conservative but fashionable pantsuit, complemented by two intertwined gold necklaces, and a simple but what I knew was expensive silver bracelet.

I thought, *I like her style.*

I served a fresh pot of coffee on my one nice kitchen towel with cats dancing around the Eiffel Tower between an assortment of colored mugs, a sugar bowl with wooden tongs, and four different kinds of milk. From this angle, over my neighbors' heads, I couldn't see the wall. Instead, an unblemished sky, and trees bending in a soft wind.

Finally, I thought. *This is my home.*

My neighbors cut the silence slurping their coffees. It was a grating sound. They knew each other well, but were waiting for me to speak first. I felt the weight of the wall—how nobody mentioned it as they walked in—and its shadow pressing against my chest. I had researched books and serious current events to discuss. Instead, I chickened out.

"Has anybody noticed that dark van parked away from the streetlights?" I asked, fabricating the vehicle.

"A van?" Todd asked. "How 1970s. Exciting!"

"Good eyes on you, Eye-ris," Stephanie said, and winked. "Don't worry, I'm not flirting with you."

"She flirts with everybody," Rebekah said.

I liked these people. Instantly, I yielded to gossipy neighborhood chismes and vicious rumormongering. Our gossip followed predictable patterns: nobody had heard about whatever action someone was "guilty" of, but once mentioned, the group attained instantaneous total recall of corroborating evidence. An unknown car spotted twice in the same week meant someone was having an affair. Overgrown lawns signaled junk-hoarding, drug-addicted owners. Mess and menace went hand in hand.

"This was a gorgeous idea, Iris," Rebekah said. "We're so glad you're here. Let's do this again?" The group nodded their assent.

Soon, I was invited to a broad range of activities that escalated in frequency and intimacy: a Shopping Mall Saturday, a Book Club Tuesday, and frequent scented candle gift exchanges. I handed out spice and candy packets that I bought at the Mexican supermarket near my mamá's home. My neighbors didn't recoil at these goodies' "foreignness" the way most of my white colleagues had at work (*Do I . . . eat this?*), but found the concept of an entire Mexican supermarket unimaginable. "It's all Mexican things," Stephanie said, "but anyone can go there? You don't need to speak Spanish? *Fascinating.*"

In between these days, Alex texted sometimes, asking if I wanted to grab coffee or lunch. But I had learned to live without him *while I was with him* for so long that doing so without his actual body wasn't a problem. It was easier for him to just not be there. And with each of these neighbor-bonding moments, I felt a deeper sense of community, purpose, and belonging.

One night, I walked out to the wall and stared at Rebekah's house, as if it were high up on a golden hill, for a good hour. I held on to the wall and whispered, *That is the life I want.*

I felt my body shudder. Or was it the wall?

I watched the wall every day—how could I not?—but it hadn't risen in a while, making it less of a priority. Each day, the wall's steady, unchanging familiarity became a bizarre, reliable comfort. I'd stand next to it sometimes, searching for sensory clues. I brushed my hands across its rough, graveled stone, felt the chalky residue on my fingertips, held it to my nose. The quiet in the wall's shadow was peaceful, not the way I experienced "quiet" growing up in my neighborhood. There, quiet was noisy, too.

I didn't hate the wall, exactly. It wasn't an eyesore, nor had it raised any questions from my neighbors, which I found odd, but aesthetically, aside from it being made of thick limestone, it almost fit on the cul-de-sac. No other houses had retaining walls, but if they did, they'd probably resemble this one. Also, I had other issues to focus on: work, daily meal plans for Mel and me, grocery shopping. Hell, saving money for Mel's college fund was a more pressing matter. Our lives—*my* life—couldn't stop for a wall. I simply wondered why it was there.

I told Melanie to avoid it, but over the days my resolve softened as it grew kid-irresistible.

"Can I play with it?" Melanie asked.

"How do you play with a wall?" I asked.

"¡Mira!" Melanie ran around it in circles, raced to and from it. Then, one morning, Melanie hoisted herself up on its ledge and leapt over the wall, disappearing behind it.

I shouted her name.

"Here I am!" Mel said, popping up. "It's scratchy, but I beat it!"

As my days passed, so overfilled with work, Mel, grocery shopping, Mel, cooking, and Mel, I grew accustomed to seeing the wall. I hated that I had simply accepted this thing whose presence I couldn't explain, but seeing it when I got home was familiar, reliable. Almost like a co-parent. Under some late-afternoon suns its surface, from a distance, was a crisp golden hue, like apple skin. Other evenings its color was an almost perfect blend with a hazy horizon. Seeing it when I rounded that last corner into the cul-de-sac became a part of my daily routine. Spotting the wall meant I was home.

In my vulnerable moments, I was tempted to crowdsource online opinions about it. I trusted anonymous reviews, granting the nameless and faceless a grace to not be biased, but had no confidence in finding help from friends I actually knew across my various, mostly dormant social media pages. Faint acquaintances felt comfortable expressing things in the most intense way possible. It felt like a personal responsibility to accuse someone of, well, something, at least once; otherwise, how could you say you were an engaged parent? Often, when I blocked out a rare two-glasses-of-white-wine-on-the-couch afternoon, I watched posts happen in real time. It was hypnotic, watching the vitriol unfold, like going to an aquarium and watching water splash against the tank, then recede, each return wave bringing back more detritus, more people to hate, exclude, erase.

I didn't have the energy to stay in a heightened panic about the wall. I tried willing myself to actually believe the wall *had* been there when I moved in and was almost to the point where I thought it was true. Who was I to say otherwise?

About a month and a half after the wall first appeared, Rebekah invited me to a neighborhood party at her home. Mel and I held hands as we walked through Rebekah's three-and-a-half-thousand-square-foot, five-bedroom, four-bathroom home that I couldn't possibly afford if I divided myself into a dozen me's.

Assembled on pristine marble countertops were rows of wine and liquor bottles that seemed to replenish themselves, while an arcade of crockpots simmered tamale flavors identified with hand-stenciled signs on tiny wire mounts: CHICKEN, ROAST PORK, POTATO AND BRIE. We adjourned outdoors, behind the master living room, into an extraordinary backyard and garden anchored by palm trees. I was raised going to parties decorated with homemade and ninety-nine-cent store decorations, with loud sound system speakers connected to old record players playing banda music at a distorted volume. You sat in folding chairs scattered amid piles of dog shit underneath white tents bought at a swap meet, while aluminum trays with Sterno burners were loaded with steaming, delicious tamales right next to the cabinet of unsecured and uncapped insecticides that you'd have to slap kids' hands to stay out of.

Rebekah motioned me over to an anchored patio table with Todd, Stephanie, and their respective husbands. Everyone wore lit gold bands around their wrists. I dropped Mel off at an oversize bench where children were eating and coloring.

Rebekah shook her band. "You like? I wished they came in purple!" Her crowd politely laughed along. "Did you get yours?" Rebekah asked me.

"Not yet," I said. "I've been so busy with everything."

"Don't wait on it, Iris," Stephanie said. "They make all the stuff you hate to do so much easier. And restaurants are giving discounts."

"Because they're good for the environment, right?" Todd said. "I'm glad to see businesses finally being responsible community citizens."

"You guys sound like the commercials," I said.

"I hope we're more fun than that!" Rebekah said. The crowd laughed politely again.

Rebekah's husband, Steven—whose appearance landed somewhere between "unremarkable" and "forgettable"—asked, "Iris, do you need an extra seat for your partner?"

Todd and Stephanie stared at their food. Rebekah squeezed her husband's forearm, whispered something in his ear. He nodded, shook my hand, then slumped away like a dismissed game show contestant.

"I'm sorry, he doesn't, you know, *think*," Rebekah said. "Sit next to me. Please."

"I hadn't thought much about Alex until now, I guess."

Rebekah stared at me, wondering, it seemed, if I was going to bring her inner circle's "party within a party" down. That's when I realized I belonged here—was accepted as a friend. No, better than a friend. A *regular*. I had an obligation not to ruin Rebekah's party.

"But I'm so happy to have such beautiful, hardworking neighbors," I said. "Like you."

"To neighbors, and to Iris!" Rebekah said, raising a plastic flute. Our neighbors followed. I drank from my glass, which Stephanie had overfilled. Had my rank in the group risen?

Rebekah leaned in and said, "I knew it was the right thing to choose you, chica."

"To be friends?" I asked.

"For the neighborhood."

"Oh," I said. "What do you mean?"

"It's not an accident you're here," Rebekah said. "I saw what was happening over there, at your home. We chose you."

Chose? Like sci-fi, creepy neighbors from Mars chose? Or Twilight Zone *chose?* That thought, and the wine, made me flush. I heard Mel laughing with a group of children. What was Rebekah saying?

"I saw some chuntis walking in the front yard of your place when it was for sale," Rebekah said.

"You can see that far?" I asked, curious.

She didn't answer, instead explaining that she asked Todd to use an app on his phone to instruct his house's stereo to play a loud, belligerent, hectoring English-language talk radio show from his window. "Tedious," Rebekah said, "but they make some good points." When an African American family with three teenagers toured the house, she asked Todd's husband to put the Mexican dance party standard "La Chona" on repeat, loud.

"They never came back," Rebekah said, "so I guess some Blacks must have some unresolved cultural issues with us, too, right? You can't teach bad people how to make good decisions."

"Oh," I said.

"That's why I love these," Rebekah said, fingering her band.

"Nobody has to hide anymore. I can't wait to see your band, Iris. After all, you belong here, hermana."

Hermana, eh?

It was past eleven when we got home and I tucked a sleeping Mel into bed. From the bay window, I tippy-toed to see Rebekah's house over the wall. I was becoming convinced—paranoid, really—that unless I got a band, I had no future in this new world. I'd lose the one friend I'd made since college.

Her name was Gertie. One night, she showed me how she intended to fix her birth records to apply for an additional year of study in college using my scanner, some white-out, and a dull ballpoint pen.

"Don't use my stuff," I said. "You'll go to jail if you get caught and I'll be an accessory."

"God, how square are you?" she said. "Come here, you might learn something."

"Don't drag me into anything you're doing," I said, then pretended not to watch over her shoulder.

Gertie was a light-skinned international student from Nicaragua and my best friend. Before orientation weekend, I rented a flimsy-walled ground-floor hovel a bus ride's distance from my college campus to cut the two-plus-hour commute from home. Next to the water heater, I found a ten-pound bag of glitter and a family of dead rats. In the local supermarket, I looked for the tortilla aisle and found an international foods display that jammed salsa next to "Oriental" fish sauce. When I took out the trash, I crunched on used syringes.

I considered myself a consensus builder and felt comfortable appealing to my landlord for help. He felt differently, ignoring my calls and messages, and driving off in his tar-black Hummer when he saw me. When I cornered him, I asked if he could change the exterior bulbs in the complex to blue lights. I read that made it harder for drug users to find their veins.

"You think light bulbs will stop a junkie?" he said, and laughed. "You're a troublemaker. I don't listen to troublemakers."

I changed each bulb in the complex myself. My landlord retaliated by billing me eleven hundred dollars. I moved in with Gertie before the end of winter break.

I liked hanging out with Gertie. For her, conversation came easily. She said things with confidence and could make me laugh. "Let's try that new bar off campus. The women there got the clear skin and the big, proud booties!"

I took comfort knowing ours would be a temporary connection. We worked well within the confines of a college schedule and we needed each other for emotional ballast. Gertie curbed my weekday homesickness, and I tried to quell Gert's insecurities with what I considered tough love.

"Doesn't it bother you that *only* a young güera can be the voice of our generation?" Gertie asked.

"Where do you get this stuff?" I asked.

"White people are different when they think they're alone. I take notes. We can bust them all!"

"I can't waste time," I said, "being mad about everything you're angry about."

"One day, I'm gonna write a story about you," Gertie said.

"Fine," I said, "just don't make me out to be a racist."

Gertie would tell me we were the victims of trying to occupy two different, nonexclusive worlds. One at college, where we ate garden burgers and politely answered dumbass questions like "Does your family sell weed?" Then, at home on the weekends, we could speak Spanish to our families, and eat real, hearty, life-affirming home-cooked foods without being maligned.

"We need multiple personalities to deal with los güeros!" Gertie would say. "Don't you miss Sunday menudo?"

"I eat pancakes with syrup on the weekends," I said. "My mom hates tripe. Makes us both sick. Stop making my life out to be either-or. I don't have to choose."

My mamá never preached a rigid identity of who I was supposed to be. She simply informed me what I needed to do to be accepted by Americans. The rest was up to me.

"You don't believe that, do you, Eye?" Gertie asked. "Show me where you grew up."

She let me drive her car. The apartment complex I'd lived in with Dolores and Gonzalo, before Serena, was gone. There was a chain-link fence around the remains of the demolished buildings, which had come down without me having the satisfaction of watching it happen. A banner said SHOPPING EXPERIENCE COMING SOON! I couldn't remember ever seeing "coming soon" on a sign growing up. There was never any sense of excitement that anything would come soon, or change, or had ever been something else aside from abandoned stores with greasy blacked-out windows and piss-soaked entryways that tore your eyes up.

We walked the neighborhood. Next to where my old apartment building had stood was a new-to-me strip mall. I walked into a concrete-floor art gallery for street artists and fingered a carousel rack for Mexican "artesanía tradicional" light switch covers, twelve dollars each.

Down the block was a coffee roaster in the old ninety-nine-cent storefront. Next to it, a craft beer bar, formerly the hair salon where Dolores took me once a month to get the same badly copied Dora the Explorer haircut. I wondered what happened to Blanca, who gave me those dumb haircuts. Did she flee the neighborhood, too? Had her vanishing been sudden, or was it like filling up a bathtub, drowning the holdouts with the sight of things they could never afford? We walked farther and saw the rest of the avenue hadn't gentrified or changed at all, stuck in a naco time warp of junk store tienditas, auto parts shops, off-brand furniture stores, and storefront churches, *exactly* the way I remembered it as a child. There's a whole life of people who exist right past the line gentrifiers refuse to walk. That line shifts and changes, but it never goes away.

The beer bar was the dividing gentrification line, so we walked inside and, after scanning an overhead chalkboard menu, ordered a pair of "locally brewed Latinx" pilsners called Brownberry Beret. Gertie ranted about my "lost culture" while I listened to the earnest bartenders speak to their customers about respecting the neighborhood's residents and the community's values.

I'm so glad, one of them said, changing out a keg, that the entire street hadn't changed, that there were still places here the way it used to be back then. That was important.

Drinking my pilsner, I wanted to say how dangerous this place was for an eight-year-old girl. How many times I had been propositioned by gross old men in large cars saying, "Vamos a dar un paseo," or grabby obreros stumbling from bars at three p.m. as I walked home from school. Back then, being here *sucked*, and I resented white people, or crazy MEChAs, or Gertie, telling me I had to appreciate their idea of authentic-ness. Who was more authentic to *my life* than me, anyway? I adored the dispensary with the two-gram watermelon-flavored CBD gummies and the coffee shops serving six-dollar oat milk lattes and wished I could have grown up in this version of my old neighborhood instead, all the while knowing my family could never afford to live in a place like this was now.

Do you want another one of those? the bartender asked me.

Why not, I said. *I'm not ready to go home yet.*

Junior year, Gertie joined MEChA. She changed, and by that I mean I changed around her. Our friendship felt like shortness of breath. I tried to reconcile what Gertie told me to look out for. The loss of who I really was.

One day, I sat in my customary back-row classroom seat, hand raised, not being called on. I stopped raising my hand, which seemed to suit everyone—students and professor alike—just fine. I watched white women speak whether their hands were raised or not. Then it hit me. It wasn't how white women looked, I thought, but how they behaved. They acted as if they were *first*. First to have an idea, first to speak, first in line, *regardless*. I thought if I behaved "white"—that is, if I positioned myself *first*—other white people who by their own admission didn't "see race" wouldn't see mine, either. I was invited to enough parties and mixers where I was the only Mexican woman and saw how white women didn't know what to "do" with my presence. I saw white guys' boundless capability (and horniness) to fetishize me. If I followed a white woman's example, perhaps I could claim some of that power for myself. This moment radicalized me, but not the way Gertie intended.

One night, Gertie came home with a megaphone. She grabbed a sleeping bag and packed a roller suitcase.

"It's four a.m.," I said. "What's happening?"

"We're taking over the quad," she said. "I won't be here for a few days."

"What do you mean, 'take over'?"

"Occupy," she said. "We're making a camp."

"For how long?"

"Until we get what we want," she said. "I'm not asking if you want to come."

"Oh," I said. "Take a jacket. It's cold outside."

"Sí, mamá."

"You want me to stop by later and bring you something? Water, food?"

"We're fine," Gertie said. "I won't ask you to inconvenience yourself."

"What does that mean?" I asked.

"You're only proud of what you're not."

Later, from a distance, I checked out the protest, a minimal campsite of a half dozen tents erected in the center of the cobblestone quad. A redhead with a "tribal" bicep tattoo said, "What do *they* want *this* time?"

I watched as Gertie shouted into a megaphone, demanding a Latino Studies program. "Man, so many sleeping tents out there," a Mexican guy in a crew cut said to the redhead, striking up a conversation. "Damn, that's *ghetto*."

I walked away, embarrassed not for her but for myself. Selfishly, I feared this would bring undue attention to me. Since I didn't overtly identify as Mexican in college, it didn't. I pretended the op-eds in the college newspaper about sending ICE to the quad weren't about me. *I wasn't making a scene or calling attention to myself. I didn't ask for anything more than I was given. I didn't want them to make me visible.* Couldn't Gertie understand how vulnerable that made me, how any unexpected visibility would tempt me to drop out and disappear?

Before my shame hardened and calcified, I was walking through the rest of the unconcerned campus, over green, perpendicular trimmed lawns, amid the quiet brick and limestone courtyards flush with armorial decorations and old, relocated elm trees. Spaces that made me feel special, privileged, accomplished. Welcomed. For the rest of the week, I walked a new path to class that took me twenty minutes out of my way.

I found a new group of Mexican friends. We bonded over our mutual discomfort about MEChA and having to explain to new white people we met on campus, "No, I'm not *that* kind of Mexican." This answer either disappointed or relieved the person asking. If it relieved them, I answered what I felt were, to me, much less annoying questions: *Do you know someone in a cartel? Why do you speak Spanish and not Mexican? Where do you eat when Taco Bell's closed?*

When MEChA called for a student walkout to support a "reconquista" of the football stadium, Gertie asked me for help papering the campus with flyers. I was sitting with a white-passing Mexican friend named Brian.

"MEChA's been doing hunger strikes," he said, "so the frats set up barbecues downwind. The whole place smells like hamburgers."

"That's awful!" I said, and laughed.

"It's not funny, pendejos," Gertie said. "Some of those kids could die."

Brian said, "Hunger-striking because someone's in prison, or so braceros can get health care, is one thing. They're doing it for a Latino Studies major. Why risk your health for that?"

"So you fools could know something about yourselves," Gertie said. "God, nobody hates a Mexican more than a Mexican American."

A week before graduation, I learned that my GPA had earned me summa cum laude, but a clerical error meant I'd be listed as magna cum laude in the official commencement program.

"You have such a bright future," a dean said in an exhausted voice. "Next Sunday, this won't matter," he said, and offered me an Altoid.

"If I was chino," I complained to Gertie, "they'd reprint the programs overnight."

"That kind of thing doesn't matter to anyone," Gertie said.

"My parents deserve to see my name in the right place," I said. "I worked for this and was cheated!"

"You got a break," Gertie said. "You told me your SAT scores. You went to a much better college than you deserve. Why do you think that happened? The fake Ballet Folklórico program you were 'vice president' of in high school? The fund-raising trip to build a school in Guatemala where you sat on the beach and took pictures? You're only a Mexican when you're showing off to white people."

"Stop telling me what kind of Mexican you think I am!" I shouted. "You're worse than a 'curious' white man!"

"You're only proud of what you're not," Gertie said.

I lost contact with Gertie when the semester ended. When I decided, years later, to find her on a social media site after my second glass of wine, Gertie was now Kristine, an executive at a large overseas bank, married to a white man from Brussels with the same job description as hers. Reading her older posts, she had grown tired of her skin color making her a "suspect" ally and grown disillusioned in the same ways I had, which comforted me. Her bio read: "I don't see color. Tells it like it is."

I said to the screen, *Good for you, Gert.*

In the garage I found my old scanner from college in the next-to-last moving box. I laid flat my birth certificate, and ran a chewed pen hard and fast on wet cardboard. Using white-out, I blotted my parents' birth places—"México"—and replaced them. Then I found the least fake-looking birth certificate template online, created a document for my mother, opened a link on the state's upload-proof-of-citizenship site, and hoped these poor forgeries would be enough to qualify me for a band.

I wasn't doing this only for me. I was doing this for my daughter. For a safe, secure place she could call home, and so she wouldn't be embarrassed whenever I had to prove something I already knew. This was to clarify ownership for everything I had worked for, and the stability for her to work for what she wanted, too. I didn't consider this breaking the law. I wasn't chasing anything I didn't already have when the rules flipped on me. I had a right to be left alone until, one morning, I didn't. All I was doing was getting that right back.

I was clearing up a misunderstanding.

I fell asleep at the computer for a few hours. Waking up around dawn, I took one last pass at my files, then uploaded my forged documents. I was proud of how convincing they looked. I went to check on Mel. She was already up, drawing on a butcher sheet.

"Look, Mommy!" she said. "My hands!"

"There's two sets of handprints on this," I said. "Are both yours?"

"Nah, that's your hands!" Mel said. "Don't you recognize them?"

"These hands are too small to be mine," I said.

"They're from when you were little, like me!" Mel said.

"Why's one of the fingers much longer than the others?"

"Because they're pointing," Mel said.

"Yeah? Where to?"

I stared out Mel's window. It was morning, but the view was covered in shadow.

Mel followed me outside. The wall was almost five feet high. I strained to set my elbows atop it.

Mel spotted the shoes lying by the wall first. "Mommy, look!"

A pair of tiny, kid-size chanclas, coated with clay, smelling of long buried soil.

"Those aren't mine," Mel said.

In the distance, I saw a faint light bounding along the top of the wall.

"Honey, go inside. Mommy needs to do something."

"What?" Mel asked.

I knelt by the wall, holding the tiny chanclas in my hands. They smelled of cut grass and sulfur, a resurrected wildfire. On the wall's stone facade, I felt on my palms hideous images carved in cool limestone undulate and breathe.

How do you tell your child, I don't know?

Seven

I thought that morning about Karina saying that white people need metrics to believe you. So after breakfast, I found a tape measure and noted the wall's height, length, and width, recording these numbers in a phone app. Then I grabbed and poked and prodded all along the wall to see if I could feel some—*any*—kind of activity or movement. I did the same thing in sixth grade when I planted a young sapling outside my elementary school and touched it after school for hours every day until Dolores yelled that going outside to play didn't mean hugging the damn trees.

I measured the wall that evening before dinner, the next morning, and the morning after, too. No changes in feet, inches, or even millimeters, but no matter. I *knew* what was happening. Before Mel woke up, I changed into black sweatpants and a too-thin, bright pink pajama top hoodie and fondled the wall for clues in pitch-blackness. I was guided by a strapped headlamp I'd purchased at a doomsday hardware store from a kindly old man who smelled like rancid paint. Five minutes wasn't enough to inspect the various contours and angles of the wall before work. I rose earlier and added ten more, then fifteen on top of that.

In a week, I was up before sunrise, teeth chattering while my skin broke out in prickly, cold-induced rashes. I slapped the wall's gritty, rambling stone facade, shredding my fingertips and knuckles down to calluses probing for clues, insight, or any kind of detectable change. After work, in the suburban gloaming, I surveilled the limited, framed world outside my large bay window, checking if the wall rose the way my neighbors would check, and recheck, on a "strange" car parked across their street. Why was this wall here? What did it want?

I gave my neighbors enormous credit for not calling the police to report what to them could have easily been construed as suspicious behavior. It was probably my hoodie that told them it was me. When I thought about it more, though, if I spotted someone with a flashlight outside Todd's house, I would call the police. Had they been tricked by social media Serenas discouraging people from calling the police for minor infractions? That's not how I felt. Hadn't I heard for the past twenty-plus years *If you see something, say something*? Didn't anyone feel my house, my daughter, *me*, was worthy of protection? Did anyone see me?

Why *hadn't* someone called the cops on me?

No, wait . . . *What the hell was I thinking?*

Why couldn't I *stop* thinking?

Early Saturday morning, Alex texted that he was under the weather and couldn't make Mel's weekend pickup. He hadn't missed a single visit in the past two months. I was inclined to let it go until Mel padded over in stockinged feet asking, "When can we go home?"

"We are home," I said. "This home is ours. Mine and yours."

"Daddy's home," she said. "I want Daddy's home. Can I ask him when he comes over today?"

I wasn't going to let my daughter go crazy over her father missing a weekend.

"Get dressed, mija," I said.

Promotional signs—WE'RE ON THE BAND!—were posted throughout the North Azulia farmers' market. I liked the idea of a farmers' market more than the actual marketplace itself. Every food item seemed overpriced, parking was impossible, and I forget (even when I remember to toss them in the car) to bring cloth totes, meaning a fifteen-cent upcharge for plastic bags. I left with a handful of political activism flyers whose causes I would never have time to engage. I stashed them in the glove compartment, since the nearby trash cans were for recycled plastics. Tacked onto the market were a string of arts and crafts booths, with a parade of food trucks and carts whose vendors enthusiastically asked for and scanned bands, since it meant they didn't have to pay a convenience fee for processing purchases.

We stopped at a Mexican folk art booth. I wanted a small candle, but couldn't find anything without a saint's portrait or that coordinated with our new house's furniture-showroom color scheme of crème, eggshell, or near-white. Serena told me that folk art could affect a house's appraisal value in an effort to rally me to her cause that institutional racism exists everywhere—instead, it confirmed I should keep shopping at Target. I just wanted something that wouldn't stand out. Melanie fingered a T-post of handmade wristbands.

"Be careful, Mel," I said.

A lady wearing a series of interlocking macramé bracelets said, "Ta bien, my things are kidproof." I stranger-grinned, but disliked when adults contradicted what I told Mel she could or couldn't do.

"The nice lady said you could touch if you want," I said, "but please don't pick anything up."

Melanie reached for a purple bracelet with a screaming tiger on it. The lady wrapped it around Melanie's wrist. "¡Qué bonito!"

"Mommy, can I have this? She says I look pretty in it."

I winced. *Pretty.* "Maybe next time," I said. "Please take it off." Melanie tugged at the bracelet and put it in my palm. I tried attaching it back to the T-post, but couldn't figure out the clasp. I was distracted for maybe ten seconds.

Mel wasn't beside me. Whenever I couldn't spot Mel in public, if I counted to five, I would find her. At "four" I saw her hiding behind a rack of hats and purses at an adjacent booth, where she was reading a card.

"Why did you lose me, Mommy?" Mel asked, and laughed.

"What is that?" I asked.

Melanie handed me a prayer card of Santo Toribio Romo González. On its back, "Oración por el refugiado."

"Why do you have this?" I asked.

"She gave it to me," Melanie said.

I stared at a blond woman with long hair, in knee-high, leather-braided cowboy boots, wearing a turquoise squash blossom necklace.

"How come you gave my daughter this card?"

"Did you read it?" the woman asked.

"We don't need this," I said, and slapped the card on the table between them.

"I'm sorry, I wasn't trying to offend you," she said. "It's a prayer for all viajeros."

"We aren't going anywhere. We're . . ." I said, and paused, confused. "Americans."

I walked the length of the market, saying little, frustrated I'd lost my patience. Past a chain-link fence was a paleta cart. The paletero's presence here surprised me. After a sweeping crackdown on street vendors, only carts or trucks that paid a steep permit tax were allowed to sell inside the farmers' market. Yet children here clustered around his cart, just like I did as a child. It was ninety degrees and unusually humid for this time of year, but he wore a dark flannel checkerboard long-sleeve shirt, Wrangler jeans, an oversize silver belt buckle, a straw cowboy hat, and black boots. He chimed bells that were hooked on the cart's handlebar, dripping fat sweat beads that fizzed on the hot sidewalk. How had he walked on these wide North Azulia boulevards that had no sidewalks? How did he get here?

"Mommy, I want a lime paleta!" Melanie said.

Lime, too, was my favorite flavor. When I went to my white friend Tricia's birthday party in eighth grade, I asked for a lime paleta. Tricia said, "We don't have any Mexican food in my house."

Inside the roped-off food court was an "artisanal" shaved malted ice truck selling various fruit mixes in a sugar cone.

"They have ice cream over here," I said.

"No, Mommy, I want paletas!"

"We can share a cone," I said. "Come on."

After waiting behind three customers, each with specific requests, fixes, and alterations for their order, I asked for a coconut ice cream.

"You have to be more specific," she said. "Take a look at the board." Once I "optimized" my order with an oat milk drizzle and a boysenberry paste, the cone was eleven dollars, including a preset twenty percent gratuity. Melanie dug into her ice cream heartily because it was ice cream, but in the heat, it soaked through the recycled newspaper wrapper around the sugar cone.

"You like it?" I asked Mel.

"It's too sweet," she said.

I tried hard to convince myself, through several bland swallows, that the cone was the better choice. Through a trick of memory, I imagined the snappy bite of a lime paleta on my palate. When I looked for the paletero on the way out, he was gone.

On the drive home, Mel was drawing on thick paper I kept in the car to entertain her when she was out of tablet time for the day. "What are you drawing?" I asked.

"It's a secret," Mel said. "So I won't get lost again!"

"Honey, you didn't get lost. You were hiding."

"Uh-uh! Did you know where I was when I was hiding?"

"For a moment, no," I said.

"Then you lost me!" she said. "Daddy never loses me."

Dad would need to be here to lose you.

"Okay," I said.

We pulled into the driveway. Melanie collected her drawings and stomped inside the house. I breathed deep, reminding myself to take an extra moment before facing Melanie's moodiness. I checked around Melanie's seat to see if she'd left anything behind. *I bet that prayer card is back here,* I thought. *It'll pop up as some kind of reminder, or a punishment I'm going to get later. Like the damn razors.*

I felt around under the seat. Nothing. In the driver's seat, my eyes drifted to the wall, as if it had asked me a question.

I don't want to feel this way. I didn't do anything wrong.

That night, an insomniac anxiety kept me up past three a.m. I ignored a text from Alex asking how Mel and I spent our day together and resisted the temptation to reply with a link to the song "Cat's in the Cradle." Poising the lit headlamp over my forehead, I aimed the light through the bay window out at the wall while I scrolled through my phone, reviewing important notes I wrote myself throughout the day: "Don't eat a cupcake for the next eight days" and "Remember you hate her," though I couldn't remember who her was.

A shadow passed in front of an end table lamp. I gasped in shock.

"Mommy," she said, "are you okay?" Melanie stood there, rubbing her arms.

"I'm fine, sweetie," I said, shining my headlight in Mel's face. She winced.

"Are you going somewhere?" she asked.

I snapped off the light. "No, honey. I was checking on something."

"You can see the wall from my room," Mel said.

"Oh," I said. *How long had Mel known I was watching the wall?*

"Can you stay by my window until I go back to sleep?" she asked.

We went back to Mel's bedroom. I pressed my lit headlight against her window, illuminating the wall, which appeared to ripple in the dark. I watched the blackness, nearly asleep on my feet, until it became a memory of the waters around Key West, the last place Alex and I traveled together, to work on our marriage. We had a few long walks at sunset, away from the young, happy reverie on Duval Street, trying to keep our footing on narrow, jagged, sun-pummeled streets, dodging cars and mopeds. Our conversations about what each of us wanted out of life seemed to ebb and flow with no end or agreement. He wanted to go back to the way things were before Mel—sleeping until noon on weekends, ordering pizza three nights a week, not acting like we were parents who couldn't do anything fun in our lives.

"But we *are* parents," I said.

"I never wanted to be one," he said. "You said you wanted a child. You never said I had to want one, too."

We reached a thin border of shoreline between the island and the water. Out there, past the thick blackness of a tarnished silver night, were passing clusters of lights from cruise ships. I thought, *Would life be better if I was on that ship with Melanie?*

Our battered three-hundred-dollar-a-night motel room was across from a church. I had insomnia my first night there and in the late hours between ten p.m. and three a.m., a pickup truck with an attached camper stopped in the parking lot. Other times, a lone car would slowly circle the lot. I wondered if either of these drivers were serial killers. Which one had come to a parking lot at three a.m., saw my desk light on and thought, *One more body for the road,* then realized they'd parked by a church? What changed their minds? Did God absolve them, then help them drive onward?

When Alex and I stopped our walks, I sat by the one bench on the docks not next to a trash can but fitted with a security armrest in its middle so people couldn't sleep on it. It was a meeting place for sunset cruises. Alex asked how seeing the sunset on the ocean for two hundred dollars would differ from seeing it for free on the dock, and while I had reached that point in a marriage where being on my own was preferable to companionship, I still couldn't work up the courage to do something I really wanted to do, alone.

I watched the crowds gather and board. White-bearded, potbellied men wearing Punisher shirts whose designs mangled and defaced the American flag—black stripes; frayed, melting, tattered edges; swapped-out stars for a gun's crosshairs—symbols that graphically represented the exact mix of citizenry they accepted and acknowledged as American. Young white women in impractical heels and high school reunion dresses. Families whose toddlers scampered across the wet deck up to the catamaran's railings. Old couples who claimed their seats early only to have to finger jab and angrily move over when someone boarded at the last minute. Each of these groups danced against the rhythm of each other's movements. Then the boat lurched out to sea and this large group of people that had never met before were jostled together and cheered in a collective yawp. I couldn't remember when I saw a group that large expressing collective agreement, let alone joy. A strong breeze carried a briny saltwater smell, and I felt something rise in me.

On my last day in Key West, there was a dark, green, overcast sky over the water. At the dock a sunset cruise departed. I thought, at first, *I'm happy I didn't do this, because if I had I would have picked today and the experience would have been ruined*, but that part of me that thrilled watching boats disembark rose again. I wanted to know how it felt to set sail into those dark clouds on the horizon, into that rough sea, my phone in my purse, not cocked and loaded for selfies I wouldn't look at tomorrow, feeling the spray lash my face, not holding the handrail, plunging into the weather that was out there waiting for me.

Back at the motel room, instead of packing, I stared out the window and wondered what a moonlight three a.m. walk across the church parking lot would feel like, to drift through patches of moist, warm air. Dangerous and exhilarating.

I could walk away and disappear. *But Mel . . .*

My headlight slipped, hitting Mel's windowsill. Through the billowing ether, I saw prison-bar shadows, dark slat-like silhouettes divvying up the ground. There's a cut in my memory, a blank spot where that time should be, and I was back in my half-empty bed. No alarm clock because it was Sunday.

Again, the front door was unlocked. I could tell by the morning light it was a few minutes past sunrise, but from the vestibule, the bay window was shrouded in darkness. Was it overcast today? Weather forecast was for a sunny day, like all the days here.

The wall had grown. It was at least ten feet high, maybe taller. It was as if the wall had made the house and the property recede from the rest of the cul-de-sac and my neighbors' homes. The wall cast a large, cold shadow over my lawn, the porch, and much of my house.

I shivered in the early-morning sun. "Hello?" I said. How hidden was I from the neighborhood? Could anyone see me?

Once, Alex sent me a video about a small Italian town on the shore of Lake Como. Layered into the valley of a steep mountain, the town's residents get no direct sun for five months and are known by locals in neighboring towns as "shadow crazy." They see a sharp borderline on the mountainside where the sunlight stops and know that it is day, but cannot feel its warmth on their faces, living in a daylight darkness.

It was not morning yet. I heard birds in trees, somewhere. The neighbors' yard lights hadn't shut off yet, casting a mountain range of shadows on the other side of the wall that I couldn't see, a distant horizon of community I would have to trust still existed.

"Is anybody there?" I shouted.

My voice—altered, flecked with a hazy accent—*Was it mine?*—echoed back at me.

Eight

After bitter coffee and a damp microwaved breakfast that made me feel less awake than I did when I got out of bed, I searched for home improvement centers. I had to do *something*. What, though? How could I research online when I didn't know what I was looking for? Dig around the wall's foundation and destabilize it? Paint and camouflage it? The ideas sounded absurd, but so was a wall that appeared out of nowhere and was now standing ten feet high. Would the wall stop if I did nothing? I couldn't wait any longer.

In the living room, Melanie "talked" to an automated entertainment kiosk that Alex had been excited about for three days, then lost interest. It almost sounded like a real, give-and-take conversation. I couldn't decode the machine's muffled, gentle replies, its voice not male or female, but heard Melanie saying "lost" in a loop.

"Mel, get dressed," I said. "Mommy has errands to run." Mel didn't move. "What were you talking to the machine about?" I asked.

"I'm learning how far things are from each other so I can draw a map."

"Why are you doing that?" I asked.

"Because I don't want to get lost again."

"Honey, I told you, you weren't lost. You were hiding. You walked away from me when I told you to always stay by my side in public."

"I felt like I was lost," she said, drawing on her paper.

I wanted to curl Melanie's words back into a lesson about staying close to Mom. I felt a shiver on my shoulders and decided against it.

"Mom made a mistake," I said. "I'm sorry. It won't happen again."

"Uh-huh," Melanie said.

"Because you're going to stay close to Mommy from now on, right?" *Damn, couldn't resist.*

"No, Mommy!" Mel said. "I'm going to be a cartographer! I didn't want to get lost again, so I knew I needed a map, so I asked the machine who makes maps, and the machine said it's a cartographer, so I'm going to be one now."

"You've been busy out here."

"Uh-huh! Did you know it's forty-nine thousand, six hundred and seventy-seven steps from here to school?"

"No, I didn't," I said. "Making a map's a good idea. If you come with me to the store, you can count the steps in person."

Uncertain, Melanie asked, "Can I take my paper and pencils with me, too?"

"Sure. Keep track of things for both of us." I squatted at eye level with Melanie. "I don't want to get lost, either," I said, and hugged her. She went limp, but I didn't stop until Mel hugged back.

"Okay," Mel said. "Mommies can't lie, you know."

My GPS found a home improvement center in North Azulia. I had browsed cavernous halls of mega-size aisles of wood, plastic, metal, cleaners, and tools with Alex when he bought "spite" holiday gifts solely to infuriate Kevin. I never thought a man could feel threatened by an electric air inflator (*There's nothing wrong with my lungs!*), but there was no shortage of ways for men to demonstrate their hate for their fathers.

It was disguised as an English manor house, which explained why I hadn't seen it on my drive to and from work. Greenhouse glass covered an enormous wing of items and supplies in the patio and garden section. Pallets of soils, mixes, pebbles, and manures were stacked many shelves high. Melanie ran ahead and played with lawn ornament decorations, activating sound chips in plush animals by squeezing bear, dog, and tiger paws.

"Stay where Mommy can see you, please!" I said.

I knew about rocks from Alex's townhouse, but I hadn't had a chance to learn much about actual living things in a garden. I read online that *clay-rich soil destabilizes objects*. Did that mean I needed organic soil? Premium topsoil? No-float mulch? Would redwood-colored rubber nuggets help? With an eye on Melanie, I approached an older, balding man in a bright green smock.

"I need clay-rich soil," I said, enunciating the words with a confident inflection.

"Okay, what kind of garden situation do you have?" he asked.

"Situation?"

"What are you trying to grow?"

"I'm not growing anything right now," I said. "It's the soil I need."

"If you tell me what you're trying to plant, I can tell you what kind of soil will work best for you."

"I'm trying to take something down," I said.

"With soil?" he asked. His eyes fluttered to my bare wrist. I wasn't used to a man's eyes drifting there. *Uh-oh, bomb makers can use fertilizer to make explosives, can't they? What was he thinking about me?*

"I want to fill a hole," I said. "I need clay-rich soil to fill holes. In my garden. For trees."

He led me to a pallet of twenty-pound bags. I called Melanie over. "Help Mommy hold the cart, okay?"

"Those bags are heavy, ma'am," he said. "Tell me how many you want and I'll load them up for you."

"Four, I think," I said.

"How are you today?" he asked Melanie. "Aren't you a pretty girl!" Mel smiled at me.

Pretty, I thought. If he asked a question, I knew what came next. The comments about Melanie—what Alex called "compliments"— started when she was three or four. Alex's mother, Cynthia, saw Melanie and said, "I'm surprised she isn't duskier." Cynthia sounded disappointed. When Alex was with me, this kind of interrogation vanished, the same way I was never catcalled in a grocery store parking lot unless I was alone. I tried explaining this to Alex and he stared at me, oblivious.

"Are you and your daughter from here?" the man asked, bag on shoulder.

"Born and raised," I said. He dropped a bag into a cart, hoisted another off a pallet. *Two. Come on, let me go on with my day. I don't need help with strings attached.*

"Isn't that something. How about your parents?"

"Can't get more 'here' than them!" I said. Another bag whomped in the cart. *Hurry up, hurry up.*

My life is full of endless moments like this. Over time, they add up to so many lost seconds, minutes, hours—and the experiences I would have had in those moments—that I will never get back. I learned in college and in my life afterward that people will not accept a simple one- or two-word answer about who I am.

"Have you ever done one of those, you know, DNA tests?" he asked, and grabbed a third bag. "I bet your results would be fascinating."

I had wondered if Alex would be resilient enough to handle the pressures of being a father to what I thought the world would see as a biracial child. I never imagined I would be examined instead. I learned, as Melanie aged, it was my job, not my husband's, to engage, deflect, and avoid many such "bad" conversationalists, who asked me about my own ethnic origins, or if I tested my DNA. I had nothing to hide about my daughter, but I hated how much time I had to waste with politeness every day, like I was somebody famous, to act out a courtesy to strangers who wouldn't extend it in return because, as Alex said, they were "just curious." They were never just curious. They were box checkers. Which box did I belong in?

"Some guys are bad at making conversation," Alex said. "Stop seeing the worst in people."

It took me months to learn the best way to walk away from unearned follow-up questions. "I need to take care of my *child*" worked with women. "My *husband* is waiting for us" finished conversations with men. Emphasizing *I* never worked for me.

"My husband is waiting for us," I said.

"Okay, that should do it," the man said and walked away. Three out of four bags.

I yanked the fourth bag and heaved it into the cart. I also carted buckets, outdoor gardening gloves, and wood- and fiberglass-handled shovels. I wanted to at least *appear* to others that I belonged here.

Signs above the registers said GET ON THE BAND—TODAY! Checkout divided into two distinct lines, one with mainly older white women, the other with mostly brown workmen in baseball caps, thick-soled work shoes, and double-layer wool socks, clothes that Gonzalo wore before he retired. There wasn't any clear signage to mark who stood in what line. People saw who was in front of them and self-selected into respective queues. A manager noticed a Latino man follow three other brown-skinned men into a single line and said, "Both lines are open."

The man said, "I thought this was where you wanted me to go."

"No, no!" the manager replied. "Any line you want!"

The men were asked at the registers if they had wristbands. These interactions were hostile, with checkpoint-like efficiency, the cashier's voice inflected the way you would accuse a child of lying. The women were asked energetically, but many insisted on presenting their bands on their own, waving them in the cashier's face, while some threw mild fits when it took several scans before the machine read the band face. It was an absurd, confusing process.

My cashier gingerly scanned each woman's band at a distance, careful not to touch them. Many of the women held pocketbooks or purses worth hundreds, no, thousands of dollars. It made sense why they wore bands and wouldn't want to dig into these bags for their wallets. The beveled grain of grapefruit-dyed leather, the buffed shine of their gold latches and clasps, the double stitching around the bags' seams. I hated that I knew how much these bags cost, but I had spent hours envying and caressing them in department stores. How could these women take these bags everywhere, to a *home supplies store*, and not worry about losing them? My current middle-class salary and budget meant it'd take me about twelve hundred hours, without any emergency expenses, to save up for and buy one of those bags, which, with their price tag, would come an accompanying paranoia of never being able to let the bag out of my sight or let Mel anywhere near it.

I laid my items on the conveyor belt. Leaning over to grab a divider, my cashier hooked my wrist in a swift, firm motion, and reached for her scanning gun.

It took a second to process her hand on my body. I hated unexpected touch. The cashier's movements seemed so natural and comfortable for her. Cashiers had more trouble helping me tap my credit card to pay than this one did corralling my wrist.

"I don't have a band," I said.

"You don't?" the cashier said.

"No, I'm paying with a debit card."

She let my wrist go. "People have been asking me to scan, not scan. I get on autopilot."

Her apology felt reasonable until I realized she hadn't said she was sorry. I autofilled that in for her. I could hear Serena's voice over my own benefit of the doubt: *The güeras asked to be scanned and look how delicate she was. She grabs your wrist, and forces you to be scanned, like the obreros in the other line.*

Why did I let Serena into my head like this? I knew Serena's voice was, in fact, my mamá's voice. *Esto es lo que pasa when you go to the white stores. Where you don't belong. Why do you want the things not meant for you?*

It was an honest mistake, I thought.

No mistake, I could hear Serena say. *Se le ven las orejas al lobo.*

"Sign the screen for me, please," the cashier said, "and push whether you want a receipt of our transaction."

I signed an X on the screen—trembling on the upstroke, furious on the down.

Casting my house in a milky, frigid shadow, the wall was too high to scale without a ladder. I waved frantically whenever I saw passing neighbors, like I was lost in a lifeboat. I expected Rebekah, Todd—anyone at all—to exclaim, "What's happening here?" and see if Mel and I were okay. They politely waved at a spot behind me, almost as if they were waving at an echo of where they thought I was. I tried knocking on their doors at various times of the day, but for some reason there was never anyone home, or no one there to answer. Weren't suburban neighbors supposed to be nosy? Why were they minding their own business?

Couldn't they see the wall?

On Wednesday, Alex asked if I would like to have dinner Friday night. I hadn't spoken to him since he missed Mel's day last week.

"You're inviting me out the night before you're picking Mel up on Saturday?" I asked. "You know how sleazy that sounds."

"It's not like that," Alex said. He explained that he knew how much I liked fideo and thought I'd want to try it out. Why didn't he put this much energy into nurturing my joy when we were together?

"Sounds like a maybe-date," I said. "We're divorced. Please respect my boundaries."

I heard his familiar exasperated sigh. "I just thought it would be nice for us to catch up."

"You've known me for almost twenty years. What do we need to catch up on? Focus on your daughter, not me. You missed your day with Mel."

"She's already forgiven me," he said, confident, and right. "You haven't. But I appreciate you not speaking ill of me," he said, earnest. "I know, and can tell. Thanks."

"Yeah, well," I said. "Look, I really need to go."

"What can I do for us to spend some time together?" he blurted out. "You always said, 'Tell me what you want,' right? I'm telling you I'd like to spend some time with you. How can I make that happen?"

"Bring Esteban," I said. Esteban was Alex's sole work acquaintance. I encouraged Alex to hang out with Esteban because I thought Alex saw him as a surrogate father figure. Or maybe I imagined Esteban as the father I wanted my own to be, the kind of dad he could have been if I'd been a son. It was almost miraculous the way Gonzalo became a different, easier man to be around when he hung out with Alex. His shoulders unclasped, his posture straightened, his face wrinkles—caked on with stress—dissolved. Alex was looking for a father in older men, too, the way I was. He saw that in Esteban when he started his job, but they had drifted apart in the way work colleagues do when you bond too fast.

"Why him?" Alex asked.

"Three's a great number for a divorced couple." I heard that exasperated sigh again.

"Okay," Alex said. "I'll text you the address."

I was charmed, a bit. Angry, too, but I liked seeing that old sense of initiative in him. I heard the old pre-baby, pre-adrift, "before" Alex in that phone call. Was it nostalgia? I hadn't had a chance to consider Alex much because the prospect of him recognizing he needed to change, or find his way back to who I thought he was, seemed impossible. I had learned patience and accommodation were key to a successful marriage, but insight into what my husband wanted was a struggle. He took stands on things that didn't matter to me, and avoided making decisions if there was any chance of an unsatisfactory outcome.

Any thoughts on what you want for dinner?

Whatever's easiest to make.

What do you want to do this weekend?

Whatever you think is fine with me, he said. He'd said the same thing about having a child, though I didn't realize until it was too late he didn't mean that.

I was thinking we could watch that new reality show tonight.

That garbage, are you serious? What about that classic android sci-fi movie I've been trying to show you for years? Why don't I ever get a vote in anything?

Alex took fandom—borrowed thoughts and words—seriously.

As he slid and calcified into his mid-thirties and grew bored with people who feigned a basic understanding of what he did for a living, fandom was his defining characteristic. He had such a broad range of pop culture references it was hard to know where his own thoughts ended and ghost-quoting others began. Alex would pontificate on topics such as immigration or drug addiction only insofar as he could relate those themes to television episodes. He passed off, as his own thoughts, lines from his favorite movies or documentaries—for God's sake, he had *favorite documentaries*. He passive-aggressively played me these shows without remembering (or caring) that I noticed his insights on death or spiritual fulfillment weren't his own, but platitudes from the movie with a computer-generated genie. Or he bolstered his own opinions, some of which I genuinely found startling and revelatory, by saying he heard this discussed in a specific program he watched, only to see said documentary and discover that nothing of Alex's argument could be found. He invented the attributions, but needed the cover of having learned them from another source. Alex had no opinions unless someone expressed an opinion of their own first. He was in dire need of an outlet, direction, a passion, and I got tired of waiting around for him to realize he was missing it. Perhaps my leaving helped him find one. I hoped it would.

I dropped Mel at Dolores's, then drove to a tequila and fideo restaurant in a gentrified three-block stretch of West Vecino. Alex and Esteban were balanced atop micro-barstools tethered to a wobbly end table. I was giddy to join them, maybe even a touch nervous. I wanted to see Alex's playful side again, which used to be visible on his second drink. There was no chance the wall would come up in conversation because Esteban brought entire conversations with him.

I didn't recognize Alex in a collared shirt, dark necktie, and slacks. Also new: his band, which emitted a haloed glow around his wrist.

"Mi amor!" Esteban said, and bear-hugged me. A waitress asked if we wanted to pay with the billing info on our bands and both Es-

teban and Alex readily agreed. I wasn't as impressed by this function as the men were. Alex mouthed that he would cover me when
Esteban wasn't looking. She returned with a tequila for Esteban,
a fancy citrus cocktail for me, and a club soda and lime for Alex
(not a good sign).

"What could be better than hanging out with my compas drinking some good chelas?" Esteban asked. "If my dad saw how much
I was paying for fideo tonight, he'd say, 'Ah, the gringos got you,
too!'" If Esteban knew we were separated, he didn't show it.

"The price is reasonable for what they serve," Alex said.

"Easy, vaquero," Esteban said. "I haven't even started to embarrass you! Wait until they bring the mezcal. Tonight, you can
elongate your *o*'s and rediscover that gorgeous Mexican accent you
drop around los güeros!"

"I don't," Alex said, then stopped himself. *God, he's trying to
avoid the letter* o. "That's a lie."

"Alex, he's teasing," I said. Uncomfortable, I finished my drink
too fast.

"Ta bien," Esteban said. "Alex's been cranky at work for weeks
now. Our supervisor, Dennis, mistook him for me again, for, I don't
know, the thousandth time, even though I'm a foot taller and fifty
pounds heavier. I keep telling him, 'I'm the good-looking, barrel-
aged mexicano!'" Esteban's raspy laugh shook the table. "Not that I
wouldn't mind being the güero who gets to mistake a dark-skinned
indio like me for you."

"You want to be a white guy?" Alex asked. "I'm surprised to hear
you say that."

"I'm not talking about becoming one of those light-skinned
Nazi 'para mejorar la raza' assholes," Esteban said. "But I'm a ruco.
I don't want the hassle anymore. That's why I got one of these as
soon as they opened the portal." He waved his band up and down,
its glow like a firefly's.

"What does the band have to do with anything?" Alex said.
"They're a device for convenience and safety. When we get Mel's
band, there's an app that will let us see her wherever she is."

"Really?" I asked. "That would have been handy at the farmers' market." I hadn't realized I'd slipped up, but Alex did.

"Why, what happened?"

"Nothing," I said. "Mel thought she was lost, but it was like five seconds and it turned out she was hiding. Since then, she's been drawing maps."

"Why didn't you tell me any of this?" Alex asked.

"Tell you?" Esteban asked. "What man doesn't know what goes on in his own house?"

Alex and I exchanged nods and eyeblinks. *I'll cover for us if you drop the questions.* Somehow, Alex always understood what I was thinking whenever the potential for him to be publicly embarrassed arose.

"We've both been busy at work," I replied.

"Get your stories straight!" Esteban said, and laughed. "If they keep your kid safe, que Dios los bendiga. But that's a bonus. Just leave me alone. White men don't need extra shit to be left alone, but the rest of us do. Women need whistles, African Americans, Latinos, even the chinos need cameras. That's why I love this thing. They can see who I am, leave me alone, and bother the next guy. You don't need this shit, Alex, but I stand out. Güeros disbelieve brown people too much for me not to take this seriously."

"That's going too far," Alex said. "I don't believe any of that."

"Wait," I said, "I want to hear what you mean." Alex puffed and shifted his body, then remembered he could Humpty Dumpty off his tiny barstool if he so much as breathed wrong.

"Look, what I hate most is disbelief," Esteban said. "The worst thing about being a Mexican around white people is having to explain things over and over again. They listen, but they don't *believe.* Alex probably forgot, but we got acquainted over *Star Wars.* My abuela took me, on the bus, to the Mann's Chinese on Hollywood Boulevard. Four days after it opened, four days after her birthday. I was twelve years old. Ten a.m. Sunday showing. She sacrificed Jesús for Chewie!" Esteban gave the sign of the cross. I liked Esteban and wished his sense of outspokenness would rub off on Alex.

"El boletero said, 'We have two seats in the front row and *that's it.*' We sat with our heads bent way back for two hours. My abuela fell asleep and her neck must have killed her, but I was hooked. Super *Star Wars* fan invented that day. Now, if I was an old white guy, there'd be reverence. Awe. Respect. *What was it like? What do you remember?* But when I tell these waiting-weeks-in-a-line-for-opening-day nerds I'm an OG fan, they go, 'You're lying! *Star Wars* didn't open in Spanish. How did you understand what Obi-Wan was saying?' Ha! The Force is universal, pendejos! But Alex believed me right off the bat. We Chicanos know each other. We don't support one another like we should, but we *know* each other. Good, the drinks are here. ¡Salud!"

Alex was quiet through dinner. While we ate, my thoughts returned to a young Esteban, staring up at a massive movie screen, awestruck, and how he's tried to connect that pure, magic moment to people over the years that have disappointed and denied him his own reality because he was the wrong kind of misfit, the wrong kind of outsider or, perhaps, as a darker-skinned Mexican, the wrong kind of person of color.

Finishing our meal, and two drinks in, I felt I was on the verge of understanding something significant about my identity, something I have tried to return to in rare, fleeting moments since college when, troubled by excruciating strokes of fear and anxiety, I paused what I was doing to examine the source of panic that led me to ask, again and again, *Who am I?* I wondered if Alex felt the same way.

"God, I'm sorry about that," Alex said, walking me to my car. "Esteban was insufferable tonight. Never having drinks with him again."

The moment was over. Deflated. Alex had not changed.

At my car, I said, "Mel has an overnight bag at Mamá's. If you want to pick her up now instead of coming over tomorrow morning, I'm okay with that. She would love an extra night with you." I then remembered the wall and didn't want Alex to see it. But I also didn't want him to not see it. "I can pick Mel up from your house on Sunday morning. Save you a trip."

"I can't," Alex said. "I have to be somewhere early tomorrow morning. But I'll pick her up at your house at nine a.m." Switching topics, he added, "Mel should get her band ASAP."

"You have somewhere to be before you pick up Mel? On a Saturday morning? Is that why you missed Mel's date last week?"

"I'll be on time, promise," he said. "When do you want to schedule Mel's band? It would really help keep track of her now that it's just . . . you."

"I don't need help," I said. "She wasn't lost. But since when do you have to do something that early on a weekend?"

"Since you moved out."

"Okay, never mind," I said, and slammed my car door too hard. His life wasn't mine to manage anymore. He was right to push back, and I was right to drop it.

I *couldn't* forget it, though. When I got to Dolores's, Gonzalo was asleep in his musty recliner by the television. My mamá was reading a book in English. She had done this for years to keep her skills sharp, even though her workplace, her grocery store, and her home were Spanish-language dominant.

"Mel went mimis?" I asked.

"Sí, early," Dolores said. "¿Estás bien?"

"Why?" I asked.

"You have a look," Dolores said.

My mamá saw through me. If she knew, she would say, *¿Estás loca?* Maybe, but I *had* to know.

"I don't want to wake Mel up," I said. "Can I sleep here on the pullout?"

Nine

My cell phone alarm chimed at a quarter to three in the morning. I was a troubled sleeper in Dolores's house, too, and woke before the buzzer, rubbing flakes of jagged sleep from my eyes. Melanie was watching me from the doorway.

"Mel, go to sleep," I said. "Stop being a creep."

As Melanie stepped back, her feet made a cracking noise. Then I saw her feet weren't touching the ground.

That's not Melanie.

Brenda?

"You're doing something silly," she whispered. "Fun!"

I found my car keys and clutched them in my fist like brass knuckles. Brenda ran down the corridor into Serena's bedroom—who rarely used it anymore—where Melanie slept. I almost slid and fell in my stockinged feet running after her.

Inside, Mel was asleep.

"Now I have to walk back through this scary house alone," I whispered to Melanie. "Unless you want to protect me?" Melanie snored, didn't move.

I changed into a sweatshirt and pants, shivering. I thought about what it meant to see Brenda here, but I wasn't deterred from my plan. Walking out the back door, I heard the ground crunch. In the cell phone light was a wide trail of pink plastic flakes.

I parked at an obscured alley turn outside Alex's townhouse. I didn't have to wait long. His car left at quarter to four. I'm not sure why I followed him, but I wanted an answer to the question:

Who was I married to for such a long part of my life? I felt owed this part of Alex's life.

I knew the route he drove. The moon illuminated the road, which appeared to levitate in the light. What was unfamiliar were clusters of DON'T TREAD ON ME and golden ring BAND flags mounted on neighbors' porches. They floated like ghost sheets, a collective signal in the blackness. Had they been there before, or were they in the garages where I spent a hundred different barbecues with geographic acquaintances, boxed away and tucked in a dark, dusty corner, waiting for a crucial moment to be unsheathed? Did they coordinate their purchases? When did they install the accompanying flag brackets on their porches without me noticing? Stopping at a familiar all-stop intersection, I saw a thirty-foot flagpole I hadn't noticed before, its mounted UNITY MEANS ONE BAND take on an American flag creaking in a gentle night breeze, the *squeak, squeak, squeak* noises sounding like the tune "Three Blind Mice" forced through the bellows of a haunted house.

Alex drove to a church parking lot, where a dozen men and women, none of whom I recognized, handed out donuts and Styrofoam cups of what I knew was terrible coffee. How many bad decisions in this world were made by people drinking terrible coffee? They had cardboard signs, stacks of flyers, and held lighted sticks that could be backyard patio torches or, knowing Alex, *Star Wars* lightsabers. If it weren't for the time of morning, they could be prepping for a bake sale. Amid the predawn action, I expected to see a happier, more animated version of Alex. That would be a relief. I wanted some proof this secret activity was fulfilling him in some way, something that explained the rift I felt between us.

A man I didn't know got in Alex's car. They cruised without headlights through West Vecino. Each took turns photographing small shops and businesses with Spanish signage, planted laminated placards on isolated traffic islands, stapled flyers on telephone poles, and deposited plastic baggies on front lawns and, in several rushed cases, doorsteps. Watching my forty-something ex-husband hobble-jog to a stranger's house was almost piteous. When Alex's car disappeared, I scampered across a damp lawn and snatched his deposited baggie to examine when I got home.

He drove in broad compass-like arcs for almost an hour before dropping his passenger off back at the church. *Such dedication, but to what?* Around sunrise Alex branched off to his house, while I drove the vacant streets back to Dolores's. I left my driver's-side window open to stay awake, listening to the ominous metronome clicks of traffic lights and walk signals. I was confused, sleep deprived, and afraid. Did I want to know what this side of Alex contained?

Dolores was making coffee. "Oí algo cuando estabas fuera," she said.

"Did you see—" I said, thinking of Brenda, then thought better of it. "Why are you up?"

"¿Qué madre es capaz de dormir cuando su hija se ha ido? ¿Quieres un café?" Dolores offered.

"Yeah, I need the bathroom first."

I locked the door, turned on the exhaust fan, and ran hot water from the faucet. Inside Alex's "happy pack" was a pair of kid's-size Tootsie Rolls, a large granite rock with a spray-painted "ring" on it, and a flyer. Drawings of haloed bands were set as top and bottom ornaments. I smoothed the paper on my leg and read:

"We are your silent neighbors! Invaders unwelcome! Nowhere in the civilized world are a country's rightful citizens asked to give too much to those that deserve nothing. It's time for We, the People, to decide who is—and who is not—an American. You're in our country now—you have to respect us! Fight the invasion, West Vecino: Be Safe, Not Sorry! Sincerely, Patriotic Americans."

I heard Brenda's voice: *Can Inés come out and play?*

What welled up inside me was anger, betrayal. *How*, I wondered, *did Alex get this far gone?* I swatted away Serena's comments like mosquitoes. *You did not "tell me so." This is not the end result of how we—I—have lived my life. It's not, it's not, it's not!*

I sat in my mamá's kitchen, repressing my disgust and anger, nauseated. Through Dolores's white lace curtains, I saw dawn creeping across the backyard. I checked my email. My fraudulent band application had been rejected via an automated email sent last night. No reason or explanation was given, but I would not be allowed to file a new application for at least six months.

"¿Mejor, mija?" Dolores asked.

"Fine, Mamá," I said. "Everything's fine."

"'Fine,' eh?" she said.

I finished my coffee. "Yep," I said. "I have a bright future." I kissed my mamá's forehead, then got Mel up and told her it was time for us to go home.

I woke up hearing the front door slam. The early-morning stakeout meant I overslept and missed my alarm. Alex had been on time for his Saturday morning pickup with Mel, who had let me sleep in.

I hated the feeling of missing her leave. She must have run out with her overnight bag, squealing with joy as she leapt into her father's arms. I didn't want what I learned that morning to affect Alex's relationship with his daughter. I didn't think it had to, but that would depend on me keeping my ex-husband's secrets. I wasn't happy about that. That wasn't my job anymore.

I was used to seeing my ex-husband arrive as a stranger to whom I had little emotional connection. But how had he missed the wall? Had he walked around it, oblivious to its new height or that the front of my house was cloaked in murk and darkness on a bright sunny day?

I walked past the wall, halfway down the street. Its hue throbbed in the morning light, its metal shards rising like hot sewing needles out of the stone that could resemble the twinkle you see when you look at a town from a distance. Walking about three hundred yards away, the wall just about obscured my house from view altogether. The street-facing side picked up the mountains in the distance and created an artificial blended horizon line, a mirage that was visually pleasing in color and appearance.

From the cul-de-sac, you didn't see a wall or my house at all. You saw a horizon.

The wall seemed to teeter and lean, as if it would collapse onto the house. Its limestone skin was now puckered and bubbled, with alligator-skin cracks and undulating wrinkles that ran like varicose veins across its length and width. A ghastly, awful, broken web of rock, marbled like flesh that rippled when I touched it.

Staring at the wall, I whispered, "Fuck you."

"A mommy can't talk like that," a young, twitchy voice said. "Those are the rules."

Brenda was walking along the top of the wall. I followed her.

"I thought . . . I don't know what I thought. Am I crazy?"

"Nah, Inés," she said. "You're safe now!"

"Do you know why this is happening to me?" I asked.

"Of course! It happened to me, too. But you ran away from it."

"Is someone going to harm Mel?"

"You really are silly!" Brenda said. "We're trying to warn you."

"Who's we? Have you been talking to my daughter at night?" I asked. "She spends all her time drawing these crazy maps."

"Mel's trying to get you home."

"How?" I asked. "What am I supposed to do?"

"Just follow the rules, Inés!" Brenda jumped over the wall. I ran to its end a good thirty seconds away. Of course, she was gone.

In her absence, a ringing sound emanated from the wall. The wall was cool, its surface polished stone. I leaned my ear against it, felt limestone flakes litter my hair. High above, the rustle of palm tree fronds, its sound as if whispers were on fire. Something from the wall grazed my wrist. Like fingertips. Its touch was terrifying, and felt like the cashier's at the home supplies store.

I remembered my untouched supplies. The fiberglass-handled shovel was the lightest.

I tapped at the wall's base on the side facing my house, scratching at the hard, inflexible ground around it. Then I pumped the shovel into the dirt and dug a meaty clump of earth. I stood my weight on the shovel and squirted out another clod of soil. It was hard work. After stacking about five dozen small mounds in a row, I exchanged the fiberglass shovel for the wooden-handled one.

The wind died, the palm trees wilted. The sun made my head hot and my hair dampened with lemon-ginger-scented shampoo sweat. Digging was like taking short breaths, and I could hear the soil sigh as I dug into it. There was something lurid about the smell of dirt once it was out of the ground. The exposed ground reeked of warm, fetid rot. With my shovel tip I sifted through loose nails, washers, and an oxidized Indian Head penny. The debris encouraged me to keep digging, as if this trash would reveal some kind of clue.

I worked at it all day. It was empty, mind-and-body-voiding work. By sunset, I had filled many buckets, which I wheelbarrowed away, and poured the clay-rich bagged soil into the leftover holes. After dinner, I collapsed into bed.

The following morning, I rose early, and drank three cups of disgusting instant coffee. I filled more buckets with the old soil, creating a berm, then added more purchased soil at the wall's base to try and destabilize it. My scented sweat plopped heavy into the earth when I smacked the wall's concrete foundation with my shovel tip. It was a teeth-on-edge sound, like cleaving chicken gristle off a bone.

I swung at the wall's base with the shovel, like an axe. It made a hideous, panging echo. I swung again and heard a chip. A piece of the shovel had broken off, its shard stuck in the dirt. Inspecting the shovel, it was as if the metal had been bitten off.

I dragged the shovel tip around the wall's base to scrape away as much soil as I could. Then I swung the shovel again, hard.

Sparks flew, and the force knocked me backward on my ass, a clanging sound ringing in the air. I crawled back to it on my knees, scooping handfuls of dirt next to the wall into neat molehills, as if I were trying to burrow underneath. I flushed my arms deep, deeper in the dirt, until I was down to my shoulders.

"Come on," I said. "What the hell are you!" I shouted.

Melanie asked, "What are you doing, Mommy?"

I spun around. "When did you get home?" I asked.

"Just now," Melanie said. "You didn't hear us?"

I hadn't heard Alex's car drive up or leave. How long had I been out here? I stared at the long berm of dirt I'd accumulated near the driveway. I was covered with soil, sweat, and grime. Had I accomplished anything?

"Did your dad say anything when he dropped you off?" I asked.

"He said he loved me and he loved you and wanted to see us soon."

"That's it? He didn't ask about this?" I said, and put my hands on the wall.

"He was checking his phone," Mel said. "Was I supposed to ask him?"

"No, honey," I said. "I just wondered if he said anything."

"He said that he loved you, Mommy. Didn't you hear me say that?"

"Yes, I did, sweetheart," I said, and pulled Mel close to me.

"There's a lot of dirt on you, Mommy."

"We don't care about dirt," I said.

"We don't?" Melanie asked.

"No, we're women," I said.

"Are you trying to fix the wall?" she asked.

"Yes, honey," I said. "But Mommy isn't sure how."

"Maybe we can paint it?" she asked.

"That's a great idea!" I said.

"Yeah? I need my maps!" Mel shouted.

"Okay," I said, "but first take these shovels and put them in the closet by the front door, please. Then change into sweats and a T-shirt, then come back outside."

I found scrubbing brushes under the kitchen sink and spread out an old, monstrous black velvet comforter (a high school graduation gift from when Dolores bought black velvet comforters as gifts for *everyone*) with an intense space wolf howling in front of the Milky Way galaxy. Mel unrolled a large butcher paper drawing in colored pencil that looked like, well, something. We sat in the wall's shadow, which felt humid and cold.

Along with Desert Taupe, we had cans of Mexican Cake and Pink Moon. None of the colors blended with the graying limestone wall. I have no artistic ability and had no intention to paint figures, shapes, or a mural like I saw in my neighborhood growing up, but I wanted evidence of my attempts to change what I saw outside my window to be more than huge, desiccated mounds of earth.

"Mel, fill a bucket with water, then add a little soap. Not too much."

We dipped the scrubbers into the soap bucket and scoured our side of the wall—the side we saw every day from the bay window—with brisk up-and-down motions. I found the *whish* sound satisfying, almost trancelike.

"Which color should we try first?" I asked.

"Pink," Melanie said.

Pink Moon wasn't pink, but blood orange. Mel dipped her brush into the can. "Pick a spot first," I said, "then brush up, then down, in slow strokes. Then paint what you want to draw."

"I'll start in the corner down here," Melanie said, "because I'm small."

Her paint brightened the limestone to an almost neon hue. I knelt in one of the dirt holes I'd dug out and brushed upward as high as I could reach, about six feet. I wondered if the next time I looked out the kitchen window the paint could fool me into thinking I was staring off at some vivid desert horizon.

I last painted a wall when I was sixteen, outside my family's old house. Taggers hit us once or twice a month with large, jagged, indecipherable piecemeal black and red numbers and lettering. Dolores bought cans of paint and brushes, but neither she nor Gonzalo had a free moment. One Saturday morning, before I went to the library, I painted over the gang names. I was proud of my work, bragging to my parents about how clean and perfect it looked. They exchanged "Don't say anything" glances and smiled. On Sunday, the letters were back, larger, and covered the length of our wall. With Serena watching behind our front door security gate, I painted over them again.

A group of teenagers on a stoop across the street drank beer and laughed at me.

One of them shouted, *¡La van a grafitear mañana, pendeja!*
Let me help, Serena said, but couldn't unlatch the security gate.
Stay inside, I said. *I gave you a book to finish.*

I painted over the tags. Monday morning, they were back, with the word "DUMBITCH" in huge black letters. When I got back from school, I heaved the remaining paint at the wall in large splash patterns. The wall stayed that way.

I set my brush on the velvet spread. The paint stains got lost in the awesome ugliness of the comforter. I saw that, in one corner on the wall, Melanie had painted a nascent row of pink crosses.

"What are those?" I asked.

"I don't know," Melanie said, "but they're for you."

We painted until evening, when I sent Mel inside to wash up for dinner. I scratched at the pink crosses, about two dozen of them in a row, like a cemetery. When I stood up, I saw on the wall's upper corner, high above where either Mel or I could reach, a paint-smeared kid's-size pink handprint. It wasn't there before. It was as if someone grabbed the wall for support before walking inside my house.

I brought out a dining room chair to the wall, stepped atop it, and, arching up as high as I could on my toes, fit my hand in the print. From down below it looked like a kid's handprint. I fit my hand inside it. A perfect match.

The print pushed my hand back, searing my palm with an ice-cold layer of blisters.

I clung to the top of the wall so I wouldn't fall off, my legs and feet dangling. I tried to scream for help, but holding on to the wall meant I couldn't.

"Go home," a voice said.

Can anyone see me? Is there anyone out there who would be-lieve me?

Ten

After picking Mel up from school on Monday, I drove to Dolores's for dinner. I wasn't looking forward to going back home, since I would sit at that bay window all night and stare at the wall. What hideous images would be there waiting for me? Would Mel's cemetery have grown since I last checked? More floating handprints in a limestone sky?

Breathing wall skin would have been preferable to waiting around for my sister, who was almost two hours late. Serena and my mamá had a fight over the weekend, and my mom didn't want to eat dinner until my sister came home and Mamá knew she was "safe."

"She's not sixteen anymore," I said. "Why should we and your granddaughter starve because of her?"

"Ay, stop your drama!" Dolores said. "Family eats together."

Serena rolled in like a fucking rock star, without an apology. I'd already had three Diet Cokes, which had amped me up for an argument.

I set place settings in the house's family order of eating: Gonzalo, Alex, myself, Serena, Melanie, and, last, Dolores. It took me a moment to again realize we didn't need Alex's plate. It used to bother me setting my mom's plate last, but she refused to eat even when served first and would let her food get cold anyway.

"We were waiting for you," I said to Serena. "You could have told us where you were."

"Mamá knew where I was," she said. "I told her not to wait."

"Families eat together," I said. "Tell her what you just said."

"Ay, what's in you today?" Dolores said to me.

"It's disrespectful to be late for a dinner you cooked."

"Mamá cooks everyday 'cause she likes it. She'd cook whether I was late or not."

"That doesn't make it right," I said.

"You gonna cook for us instead?" Serena said. "Huevos con weenies isn't a real dinner!"

"Fine, how about we go out to eat?" I asked, shocked at my own suggestion. I realized that I didn't want to fight with my sister, or discuss the wall, or Alex, or a growing accumulation of weird experiences about the bands. I'd had a total of four dinners out in restaurants with my mamá, all after funerals for old primos I had never met.

"If we go out, nobody has to eat my terrible food, and Mamá can have a day off. What do you say?" I braced for my mamá's gale force of excuses: *Too expensive, too far from home, too greasy, too fatty, too much food on the plate, too American.*

To my surprise, Serena endorsed the idea. "Nada de cocina, nada de platos, comemos fuera. You deserve it. We'll take you." I knew "we" meant I would pay for Serena's meal, too, but thought the gesture to my mom was worth it.

"Let's go somewhere nice," I said.

"Ew, 'nice' means one of those white restaurants in North Az where they look at us like we're animals," Serena said.

"They don't look at *us*," I said, "they looked at *you* that one and only time I took you, because you laughed at that blond girl in the lobster bib who fell off the barstool."

"Everyone could see her chones! You laughed, too!"

"Ay, ¡basta!" Dolores said.

"Watch out, Mel, Abuela's getting the chancla!" Serena said.

"We aren't fighting," I said.

"Not us sisters! We *love* each other! ¿Verdad, Papá?" Serena asked.

Gonzalo said, "Más comida," nudging Dolores to serve him.

"What about Papá?" Dolores asked. "How will he eat?"

"We'll bring him something back," I said. "You still like the burger place, right, Papá?"

"Eh, it's fine," he said. "You go, have fun."

"See, Papá wants you out of the house, too!" Serena said.

Dolores sighed. "Okay," she said, "pero dejen de pelear."

Six of the "nice" restaurants in the North Azulia area were owned by a single conglomerate started by a reality cooking show runner-up. Serena shared an article that had accused the winner, a middle-aged white man, of cultural appropriation, as each of his start-ups was an upscale-chain version of an ethnic cuisine: Thai, Chinese, Indian, Mexican. I ignored that narrative because I didn't have time to parse restaurants' troubling backstories, much as I didn't want to buy products with philosophies or origin myths, mostly out of fear I couldn't afford them. I had tried most of the places for after-work drink functions and appreciated how easy it was to pronounce the dishes, how palatable and photogenic they were when they arrived, and how strong the "regionally inspired" cocktails were. What was the problem?

The Mexican restaurant was out, as Dolores and Serena would collapse into loud hysterics over the endless ways the gringo-fied restaurant overcharged for food they could get in West Vecino at a quarter the cost. ¿Te cobran por chips and salsa? (I admit that bothers me, too.) I settled on the Mediterranean-inspired Peeta. An exhaustive reading of online reviews explained it as "the exotic crown jewel in North Azulia fine dining" and its unfamiliar cuisine would encourage us to try something new. The restaurant was atop a manufactured hill overlooking a freeway exchange. Alex and I had drunk white wine spritzers on their patio, which lulled me into imagining that the whoosh of endless traffic was the Hawaiian surf.

That Saturday morning, Mel was amiss during Alex's pickup. He had knocked on the front door twice and she still wasn't ready to go.

"Mommy, I can't find my maps! Help me!"

"Check under your bed," I said. The third set of knocks were loud, impatient. "I need to let your dad in."

I invited Alex inside our now-always-cold, always-in-darkness house, but he stood on the porch. He was covered in complete darkness under the wall's shadow. Certainly he would say something about the wall, but, like Mel said when he last dropped her off, he was engrossed in his phone and never turned his back. It was a test of my will to see how long I could go without asking him about the wall. If he hadn't said anything, then he must not have been able to see it. But Mel and I could see it—what did that say about us? Or him?

"Can we decide on a date to get Mel's band?" he asked me.

"While you're on your phone?" I asked.

"I'm on the scheduling website," he said. "Is Mel okay?"

"Yeah, she can't find something."

"What is it? Did she leave it at my house?"

"No, I don't think so," I said, reminding him again of the distance between us. "She's been drawing these maps. I told you about them, remember?"

"Maps? To where?"

"I don't know."

"They're probably in her room," Alex said.

"She's looking for them now."

"No, I mean *her* room."

"Her room's *here*," I said. "I don't know why you can't acknowledge that."

"Because she has things stashed between two houses. She's getting confused the longer this goes on."

"Goes on?" I asked. "This isn't temporary. You—" I stopped myself. *Don't bring up what you saw until you know exactly how you feel about it.*

"Mel!" I shouted. "Daddy says the maps are at his place."

Mel ran outside with her weekend bag. "Thanks, Daddy, for saving us!"

Thanks, Mel.

That night, on the drive to Peeta, I pressed SCAN on the radio and caught Juan Gabriel's "Amor eterno." Growing up, I heard this song through a tinny AM radio on Dolores's kitchen windowsill, where it played while she washed dishes. She sang along with joy and no self-consciousness. An indescribable ache came over me when I listened to my mamá's favorite songs. They felt connected to some long-ago piece of my own self, someone I know I used to be—or could have become—but I wasn't moved by the words the way my mamá was and I didn't understand why. It reminded me there's still this irreconcilable, inexplicable distance between me and Dolores, even though I lived my life following her rules and becoming exactly who I thought my mamá wanted me to be, a hardworking success, dependent on nobody, especially a man. In a flash, I felt one step away from shame. I snapped off the radio and closed my windows.

I was nervous because my mamá hated English-speaking restaurants. *No me siento yo misma aquí,* Dolores said in an Italian trattoria I took her to after a day of mall shopping. *I don't feel like myself in here.* My mamá didn't used to think or feel this way. She considered going to "American" places a treat. We dressed up and had to mind more than our manners. "Behave, and be quiet," she said. "Give them a reason to see us." Something had shifted in her, though. The older I got, the more she withdrew from her "American" life. I wanted this time to be different. *Please,* I thought, *let me have one nice night out with my family. Let me have a few hours of peace with my sister. Let me feel like a human being again for a short while.*

Peeta was a cavernous in-the-round space that both absorbed and amplified sound. I waited for Serena and Dolores on a varnished bench with fake hieroglyphics, drowning in a cacophony of laughter and conversation. I was proud I could carve out part of my monthly budget to indulge in a place that would serve Dolores the way I felt she should be served. Restaurants where the water glasses weren't dirty, or I didn't have to steal bundled silverware from a nearby table.

I met Dolores and Serena outside the restaurant. Valets expertly managed the endless parade of cars, bands aglow around their wrists. Serena's navy-blue dress and tan espadrilles were from her college graduation, while Dolores's mauve blouse and dark pants were from a prima's wedding last spring. They had arrived in their best outfits, which made me happy. It was going to be a great night.

A discreet sign on the heavy glass front door said WE WELCOME THE BAND! with an icon of a gold halo floating around a wrist. I almost missed it until Dolores pointed it out.

"Mija," Dolores said to me, "quieren esas bandas aquí. Deberíamos ir a otro lugar."

"No, Mamá, it says 'Welcome,'" I said. "It doesn't say they're required. That's not for us, anyway. We're fine."

My mother laughed. "Ha! ¡Son necesarias para nosotras!"

"Mamá's right," Serena said. "They'll say, 'Oh, we don't have your table,' make us wait all night, then stick us in a corner just before they close."

"No, they wouldn't do that. I came here with Alex and it was fine."

"You're here with us," Serena said. "Alex isn't here to protect you." My sister maintained that Alex's lightness gave me "privilege," a word she used (and misspelled in her texts) all the time. When Alex, Serena, and I used to hang out in public together, she'd see white women compliment my jewelry, my outfits, and mistake me for Persian, Armenian, or Indian. Sometimes I corrected them, but sometimes I let them enjoy whatever mystical backstory they conjured up for me. What was the harm? That night, dining with my mother and sister, I understood Serena was saying that, standing next to them, I would be seen differently.

"Ve a comer," Dolores said. "Serena y yo vamos a comer a casa."

"Mamá, the whole point is that we take *you* out to eat," I said.

"Yeah, but somewhere *she* wants to go," Serena said. "Mamá's never even heard of this place. ¿Verdad?"

"No, no," my mamá said, "pero, 'ta bien, 'ta bien."

"She's just being polite," Serena said. "Don't force her to go to a place she doesn't want to."

"Just give this place a chance!" I said. "Can I treat my mamá out to a nice meal for one night?"

Dolores said, "Serena, basta. Vamos."

I volunteered my name to the hostess for our 6:45 p.m. reservation. After some discussion with a waiter, she cordially explained
that they had one high-top corner table for two that was ready,
far in the back ("We could squeeze in an extra chair, or one of you
could stand"), or it would be a few minutes more for our patio
table, a request from my reservation. The high top's chairs were
too high for Mamá to sit comfortably, so I said we'd wait.

"No problem," I said.

I explained to my mother and Serena what happened. Serena
laughed.

"I heard you up there," she said. "You sounded like you were
apologizing we're eating here."

"I was being polite," I said.

Serena took pictures of the circular dining room decorated
with taupe and white curtains, with candles on each table. Dolores
shrunk into herself on the bench, wrapping her oversize tote bag's
purse straps around her arms.

"Ay, ¡hace frío!" she said, and shivered.

Serena geared up for another rant, when we were told our
table was ready. "Looks like being polite works," I said to her.

Our patio view was a threaded knot of clogged freeway in-
terchanges under a smoggy balsamic haze. I relaxed, knowing
Serena's boisterous, sometimes-too-loud-for-indoor-white-spaces
laugh would dissipate, and not carry into a neighboring booth. She
has only been *shushed* in white spaces—but that is *her* fault.

"Mom, you can put your bag on the chair next to me," I said.
"It's nice, huh?"

"Demasiado bueno para mí," Dolores said.

Serena grabbed the cocktail menu. "We need drinks," she said.

"Ay, no gastes todo el dinero de tu hermana," Dolores said.

"No, it's okay," I said. "Why don't you get a drink, too?"

"¿Estás segura?"

"It's a celebration."

"¿Por qué festejamos?" Dolores asked.

I didn't know. There wasn't a specific milestone to honor, no age-heavy birthday or graduation. Even living on my own after wanting to leave my unsuccessful marriage for years didn't feel worthy of celebrating.

"Us being together," I said. "Doing this."

"She's drunk already!" Serena said. "La borracha had something before we got here!"

A Mexican-American busboy whose name tag read LOGAN filled our water glasses. His pitcher clinked on a decorative centerpiece.

"Glad we aren't the only mexicanos in here," Serena said.

"Why do you always see things like that?" I asked.

"No, tu hermana tiene razón, miren," Dolores said. "Shh, no les digan a los gabachos que estamos aquí."

"I bet 'Logan' sees when he comes to work," Serena said.

"No, es su apodo," Dolores said. "Se llama José."

Logan set a bread basket next to Dolores, a sign I saw as respect and nodded thank you. Serena said, "Logan, ¿güey, te gustan los gabachos de aquí?"

Spanish was a code key Serena used to unlock conversations with Mexican waitstaff. I thought she did it to get better service, which she usually did, but Serena told me, "I like speaking Spanish." In some venues she could have lengthy Spanish-only conversations with servers. I told her to do this only when no other staff members were around, as I saw it pissed off white waitresses or managers something terrible. It confirmed these employees' belief that every time they hear Spanish, they're being talked about in a language they cannot understand. (I mean, *kinda*, but just when they're acting like *real* assholes . . .) Serena and I disagreed on most things, but even I knew nothing brought out a white person's insecurity more than a simple conversation in a language they chose not to learn in high school.

Logan glanced over both shoulders. "Your server will be right with you," he said in a flawless, unaccented English, then smirked, raising his eyebrows.

Serena's laugh boomeranged across the patio, but outdoors its sound wasn't embarrassing, destined to turn heads that said our table didn't belong. It was a joyous whoop, a laugh that sprang laughs out of others, in particular our mamá. I was grateful for my sister's laugh here. Her obliviousness—the lack of awareness that someone could make her feel she didn't belong here, or anywhere, really—relaxed Dolores, helped her settle into her chair.

How did my mamá and sister do this? It wasn't how I saw myself in these spaces, a visitor with a guest pass, a privilege that could be revoked if you broke the rules. No loud laughter or conversation, no sneakers with dress clothes, and no cheap tipping if I wanted to return to that restaurant. Nothing that let a white person create a stereotype around me or my behavior: *Do* all *Mexican women shout like that? Are* all *Mexicans bad tippers?* It was a heavy weight of expectations to carry around in public spaces that once led to Serena's admonition that I was two types of person.

Don't you mean two types of people? I asked.

No, person, Serena said. *One's more herself at home, and the other's too uptight around white people. They break their own rules you say we have to follow. If you're trying to be güera, you can break the rules, too, and it won't matter. Right?*

I'm not trying to be white, I said. I simply didn't want to call attention to myself. Blend in, nice and easy. *I just want to be like everyone else.* What was wrong with that?

Serena and Dolores laughed together, clinking their water glasses. Everyone was relaxed, which meant I could relax. I took selfies with Dolores and chatted about the drinks list—"Oooh, they have tequila! How *Mediterranean!*" Serena said. Simply being together in this space, a restaurant unlike anything Dolores or Serena would choose themselves, felt like victory.

Nobody's said anything to offend one another, no one's disappointed about the service, or complaining about the check. Here on this patio, with my mamá and sister, was a moment of total possibility. *Why can't life always be like this?* I would remember to ask, when the drinks arrived, that Serena take a picture of the way we looked, our smiles, outfits, and makeup, a warm breeze skipping across our table, ruffling our hair just so. Then I would post the photo and offer it as evidence of something—one thing—we did together as a group that I arranged and made happen. Perhaps this could open the door for the much-longed-for family trip we could share. Who cares if I had to pay for the memory of all of us being together?

Here it is, I thought, *our happy moment*.

"Where's our server?" Serena asked. "Haven't you been here before?"

"For drinks," I said. "Usually it doesn't take this long."

"You dragged us here," Serena said. "Politely get their attention, chop!" She laughed and told Dolores a dirty joke in Spanish.

"They should be here any minute," I said, uncomfortable.

A blonde with an indeterminate bronze tan who announced herself as Arielle at another table was serving the entire patio. I didn't want to gesture, but after twenty minutes I raised an arm and waved, several times. Arielle then walked over with a surveying-an-accident gait, as if she was making a determination about what she was going to say to us.

"We're thirsty!" Serena said. "Mamá, pídele tu chela."

"I'll have a frozen peach margarita," Dolores said. She rarely spoke English in public, but I was always surprised how confident she sounded when she did.

"I need to see your bands, please," Arielle said.

"We're over twenty-one," I said. "Get your driver's licenses out for her."

"Mom's way over twenty-one!" Serena said. Dolores play-tapped Serena's arm.

Arielle handed my license back in a practiced gesture without looking at it.

"Did you see our announcement on our social media page?" Arielle asked. "For the convenience of our customers, we are now a 'band-only' establishment."

I glanced around their patio. Not a band on any wrist in sight.

"Well, we're customers," I said. "This isn't convenient for us."

"I'm sorry, but I don't make our policy," Arielle said in a tone that was both accommodating and wholly indifferent. "Perhaps one of you left your band in your car?"

I couldn't decide in that moment what, exactly, was happening. Was this a misunderstanding? *We're not causing a scene. That's a relief, I guess.*

Serena pulled out her phone. "Your site says, 'You can now pay with a band,' but you still accept cash and cards."

"Oh, I'll tell them to correct that, thanks," Arielle said. "Again, I can't place an order for this table unless one of you has a band."

There was a quiet pause at the table. I heard couples and groups on the packed outdoor patio talking, laughing, and shouting above the din of the clogged freeways below. *Where are their bands?*

"Vamos, hijas," Dolores said. Serena bowed her head. I scraped my chair hard getting up.

Arielle said, "You're welcome to come back as soon as you have those bands, okay?"

Inside was a deafening roar, a surge of kitchen noise and boisterous, drunken chatter. Navigating the tented booths, the sunset through the enormous floor-to-ceiling windows, offering an in-the-round view of jagged, blurry mountains on one side, dry valleys of brush on the other, I felt a rising lump in my throat, and a hot flush on my cheeks.

Arielle was so pleasant in how she denied us service, the way you turned away a child whining for ice cream. It was almost kind. What was the cause? I replayed Arielle's conversation, analyzing clues about what specific thing caused her to require something from us that was optional. Our exchange lasted two minutes. Had I triggered it by flagging Arielle over? Had Serena been too noisy? I was relieved we didn't cause a commotion—that would have mortified me—but that was in part due to my not knowing what I should be causing a scene about. People weren't asked to leave places or refused service unless somebody did something wrong. The sign outside said: WE WELCOME THE BAND! That was an invitation, not an order.

What was I missing?

Dolores and Serena had already left the restaurant. I hesitated before going outside. My sister was—*ugh*—right, inadvertently. How could I face Mamá? I had forced her to go to a place she had no interest in. I was deeply ashamed and embarrassed.

But this wasn't my fault. Somebody else must be to blame.

When I caught up with them at the valet stand, Dolores and Serena were hugging each other and laughing, as if they were somehow drunk on the drinks we weren't served. Serena cracked jokes with the valets while she waited for her car. I stumbled forth to embrace my sister and my mother. Serena stepped out of my reach, and corralled Dolores with her.

"I don't understand what happened," I said, too mortified to apologize. Too proud to admit I was wrong.

"Eh, ¿qué esperabas?" Dolores asked.

"Typical North Az," Serena said. "Who cares?"

"Can we go somewhere else?" I asked. "I'll take us wherever you want to go."

"We're gonna get takeout near our house," Serena said.

"No vuelvas aquí," Dolores said, getting into the car.

"Mamá, it was one person," I said. "And maybe she was doing what she'd been told. I'm going to find their website and complain."

"Okay, escríbeles," Dolores said. "Then, no vuelvas. No es para nosotros."

I felt queasy as they drove away. I was breathing fast and couldn't stand up. I leaned against a textured masonry rock wall, trying to push my fingers in between the gaps in the rocks to hold on for support, but the wall was a facade. Its fake dry stack wall was fiberglass. My fingers slipped and I had to hoist my upper body up by gripping onto the wall's ledge. It felt as if it was collapsing away from me. I was unstable, nauseous.

When my car arrived, I grabbed the valet's hand in a clench, then drove to a side of the lot overlooking the hill and the restaurant's long spiral driveway. I could see the concentric, almost perfect figure eights of North Azulia's neighborhoods, and the endless parcel-size pockets of green space spread out like place mats around a dining room table. Formidable rows of elder trees divided the north from the messy spilt-milk sprawl of West Vecino. Driving on the roads below, I never noticed the trees—with their surprising abundance of evergreens—arranged in such an unnaturally natural line, defining pockets of houses and development to one side in North Azulia, away from the barren lots, smeared flat tar paper rooftops, and an absence of green in West Vecino.

In a strong dry wind, the leaves flickered and bristled, dolloping flecks of reflected sunlight into the sky.

I opened a social media account on my phone, unsure if this was where I wanted to discuss my feelings or seek some kind of answer, but I didn't know who or where else I could turn for immediate counsel, wisdom, or release. I didn't want to feel alone in this moment. The first update was from Alex's father, Kevin, who I hadn't unfollowed, posted months ago, before I left Alex and moved out: "If you've nothing to hide, you've nothing to fear."

I had "liked" that comment.

Alex texted a photo of him and Melanie grinning and flexing their biceps, his activated band fastened tight around Mel's wrist. It was shocking to see it on her tiny arm.

Made Mel's appointment for tomorrow at One-Shop near you, he wrote. *Can you take her?*

I enlarged the picture and rubbed where the band and Melanie's wrist met. Its halo-like light hovered around her wrist.

My tears stunned me. I was angry and ashamed by the fierce, sudden wave of emotion.

Ta bien, Mamá. No one here to see me cry.

Band looks great! I texted, wiping my eyes. *No problem.*

Eleven

Approaching the One-Shop Supercenter was like landing at a large airport, followed by a slow taxi to a gleaming futuristic terminal. There was a dedicated freeway exit for the store, an endless, barren drive on Industrial Road Number Four past the now defunct and fenced-off One-Shop Major Center that was replaced by the One-Shop Mega Center, which was then replaced by the Supercenter, then an expanse of road shimmer rising from the concrete parking lot. Sunday afternoons meant accelerating and stopping to avoid distracted cars that swerved into nonexistent spots. It was a maddening several-minute waltz to park before, at last, we disembarked into a bubbled, climate-controlled hum.

"Go get a cart, Mel," I said.

"I wanna push!" Melanie said.

"Okay, but stay with Mom, please. I need to see you at all times."

Melanie and I had a routine, having shopped here without Alex, who called One-Shops "caverns of exploitation." *For once your husband's right*, Serena told me. "I need groceries," I'd said, "not a lecture."

While I let Mel push our cart, I saw other mothers judgmentally side-eyeing me, as if Mel was play-shopping like their kids: running around untethered, pushing toy strollers, heads bowed to their screens, talking back, and shoving their parents to get attention. She didn't play with the cart like a toy. I believe children needed jobs and Mel took pushing seriously. Dolores made me fetch items throughout the store when I was young, but I hated being "the dog" when I couldn't find something, or an item was too high on a shelf and I had to jump up to toss it to the ground.

One-Shop was endcapped and dressed for perpetual summertime year-round with wooden pallets of One-Shop Soda and One-Shop Suntan Lotion arranged in Lego-block stacks by the entrance. I enjoyed One-Shop trips, a scandalous thought I wouldn't dare say aloud or online. For me, there was a sense of order and routine that made my time feel valued. I enjoyed the stores' convenient enormity and consistent, predicable layouts regardless of location. Someone had done the thinking for me, which in the day-to-day matters of house maintenance and childcare was what I wanted after a day of work and raising Melanie. Its familiarity felt like help.

My first One-Shop visit came after Gonzalo had been sent to the tiendita for shampoo and returned with a bottle of Downy fabric softener.

"¿No leíste la label?" Dolores asked, furious.

"Mira la niña," he said and pointed to a kid on the bottle, her head wrapped in a towel. "She washed her hair, no?"

From then on, Gonzalo lost his grocery shopping privileges, and Dolores drove the family to One-Shop. Back then, the closest branch was near a military base. I saw on many bumper stickers what I would later be taught was the Confederate flag. The sharp heat stung my eyes as we walked across a blistering-hot blacktop until I could feel a flood of air-conditioning rush out of the store, making my arm hair bristle and stand. Dolores stopped me before I could reach the cool inside.

"Behave yourself," she said. "Don't give anyone a reason to notice you. I can't help you in here."

A One-Shop trip was followed by a trip to Emilio's, our local tiendita with frozen-food coolers leaking pig's blood and the automatic sliding doors you had to push open, since they caught on the black rubber mat underneath. Over time, One-Shop's international section expanded from a single two-foot area of narrow shelf space to an entire aisle, then split again into a Hispanic foods aisle.

Soon, Dolores could find La Costeña refried beans with chicharrón, Maseca flour, Cacique cheese, Embasa tomatillos, Badia adobo seasoning, multiple flavors of Jarritos soda, Ibarra sweet chocolate tablets, Gansito pastelitos, and dusty bags of irresistible saladitos. Flour and corn tortillas from the Hispanic foods section were integrated into half the breads aisle, culminating in a signage change to TORTILLAS/WRAPS/BREADS. When I was old enough to shop for my family, there were more brands and varieties of salsas than pasta sauce, thus no need for a separate trip to Emilio's.

Our shopping trips began in the pharmacy section. There, I asked Melanie for a bottle of sunscreen. With nobody watching, I pumped a dollop in my hands and rubbed it slowly between my fingers. I liked the sweet buttery scent, the smell of my high school "invitation-only" swimming pool parties. The school bus trip on the freeway was so long I developed a severe form of motion sickness, which morphed into an eating disorder. In four weeks, I lost fifteen pounds and fell into a group of superficial acquaintances. Their alpha was Lena, a popular athletic light-skinned Mexican from Albuquerque. My overheated male teachers called Lena "radiant."

"Iris, huh?" Lena said. "I love your name."

Wow, I thought. *Radiant.*

"We're gonna be friends," Lena said. "But you need to pale up."

I was invited to Lena's house for an overnight. In my home, I slept next to Serena's plastic-and-pee-smelling mattress in a sliver of our living room. Lena had her own bedroom with an accompanying bathroom. It had a golden claw-foot bathtub, and no grocery store paper bag in the corner stuffed with shit-smeared toilet paper. (Our house had what Gonzalo called "Mexican pipes.") Lena's home was straight from the pages of my Baby-Sitters Club books. I loved the stories and their "mythic" setting of Stoneybrook, Connecticut. In my mind, it was a heavenly town stocked with evergreen trees and plentiful, friendly cats. The sidewalk-less streets were lined with two- to three-story homes whose neighbors socialized via picnics, galas, soirees, and an endless cycle of costume and holiday parties. I fantasized about my own room in Stoneybrook. I would have my own closet—nothing shared inside—and endless bookshelves. I could sleep in late on my unshared queen-size bed without my mom storming in at four a.m. because Serena peed the mattress again.

That room was Lena's room. This was a *real* home.

"You should make a list of what you want from a husband," Lena said. "If a man can't afford marble kitchen counters when he buys you a home, you don't need him."

Lena raided her mother's cosmetics and applied foundation to un-shade my face, drinking Diet Dr Pepper until sunup. I liked smelling her mother's six-hundred-dollar jar of face cream made with oyster pearls. "That won't help us," Lena said. "You're beyond 'medium,' but not 'native.' 'Espresso,' maybe? We want you a shade like 'exotic.'"

I saw in Lena a genuineness to help me. After each pale-up session, I peered hard in the mirror, let my eyes go cross, then literally saw my rounded cheekbones disappear, my full lips deflate, my rich "espresso" skin color and upper-lip hair fade. There, with a hair flip, I could be Jennifer Aniston, or grab an imaginary microphone and become Posh Spice (my favorite).

"See, you're not dark now," Lena said. "You totally don't look Mexican."

I heard this as a compliment. A lighter-skinned girl was there, in the mirror. It was myself, *me*. Lena helped me discover a truth I knew but could never articulate. A white-skinned woman has value. I simply had to de-emphasize all the other parts that made me Inés. Speak less—but not forget, of course—Spanish, wear neutral- or bright-colored clothes that flattered and de-accentuated my skin tone, avoid hoop earrings and Mexican-looking and -sounding friends, deploy exoticness only when it was expected and could be appreciated in small, nonthreatening doses.

My friendship with Lena ended when I asked if Lena's father could drive me to Lena's friend's house, where there was a pool party.

"My dad's not a *chauffeur*," she said.

I knew, without asking, that I would never see Lena's bedroom again, we would no longer socialize, and I would lose access to Lena's social circle. It didn't matter. I knew how to make white friends. I tried teaching these specific, micro-lessons to Serena, but she had transformed from a gurgling, squalling baby into a spoiled tantrum thrower whenever I'd rub that sweet coconut-smelling sunscreen on her plump cheeks.

"Mel, let's put a dab on you," I said now, rubbing her arms and shoulders. She shivered with laughter at the cold lotion.

Next, greeting cards. Dolores loved receiving them from Mel any time of year. I took the high shelves, while Mel looked at cards slotted near my knees. She found one next to a white woman standing next to RELIGIOUS/INSPIRATIONAL.

"How about this for Abuelita?" Mel asked. The woman leaned down and said, "I'm guessing that isn't for *your* abuelita!"

I was not a Mexican mother who treated my daughter's lightness as an accomplishment or a prize for this very reason.

"Mel," I said, "don't talk to strangers." The woman glared at my wrist and reached for her purse, as if she was about to cell phone record our interaction. I set the card down and walked us away.

In the center of this enormous shopping venue was a halo-shaped, neon-ringed hub with large signage: GET ON THE BAND HERE! I stopped at the appointed time Alex reserved and was asked to sit in an uncomfortable chair. Mel busied herself in a play area, where kid-friendly videos of children wearing the band talked on tethered screens about what you could and couldn't do with a band: "Show your band to your teacher! Have a parent charge your band at night! Take your band off before a bath!" I was surprised at the abundance of children here and wondered how many had parents who were like me. *Bandless.*

We sat in a kiosk with cubicle partitions and goldenrod carpet. An armed security guard stood next to the processing station. Workers with plastic neck lanyards milled about. Empty clamshell take-out containers were piled on desks. There was a reasonable air of grudging acceptance among us parents in the same way as whenever we were made to wait unreasonable periods of time for minute-length transactions.

After our own unreasonable waiting time, I scanned a code Alex had forwarded me, then escorted Mel into an examination area. She sat on a high-chair extension bench to have her photo taken, then had her thumbprints scanned.

"You're doing great, sweetie," said a young Latina whose name tag read CHRISTINE. She took a cheap plastic band from a plastic baggie under a locked counter, held it under a scanning light, then attached it around Mel's wrist.

"You're all set!" she said, and gave Mel a golden balloon with a ring on it. Mel waved her wrist back and forth and smiled at me with pride. In fact, I *was* proud of her.

"Can Mommy have a balloon?" Mel asked.

"Did you already get your band set up?" Christine asked.

"No balloons for Mommy," I said, faking a laugh.

Melanie asked to push the cart again, but had a hard time holding her balloon and waving her lit band in circles, fascinated by its glow. She ran ahead down a main aisle until we reached the cleaning supplies.

"We're turning here," I said, and pushed the cart down the cleaning products aisle. Up ahead was a precarious arrangement of jumbo "family size" laundry detergent boxes on the highest shelf. Each detergent box must have weighed twenty pounds. I once made the mistake of buying one to save money, but it was impossible to move around or store in my tiny laundry area.

A young woman in a dark jumper tried to reach one of the detergent boxes that were pyramid-stacked on the shelf's edge. She had climbed atop a pallet of hand sanitizer for height and was gripping the shelf for support. Her balance was wobbly. I wanted to help her grab the soap box, but didn't know how to approach her.

The woman grazed one of the box's corners, nudging it to the shelf's edge, then tried to hang on to the shelf for support to knock one of the boxes off it.

"Stand back, Mel," I said. She took that as encouragement to run to the other end of the aisle by the mops and brooms, her gold balloon bobbing as she ran.

"Miss," I asked, "do you need help?"

Melanie was about to leave our aisle. "You're too far away, Mel," I said. "Stop and come back. Right now!"

The woman's feet dangled off the ground—her body frozen for an instant in midair—before I heard a loud metal snap and a popping sound. The shelf collapsed, splintering into large metal pieces that clattered to the ground. Detergent boxes fell in a chain reaction, pounding the concrete floor, their concussive hits like fat whipcracks, echoing in the cavernous space. Explosions of white powder splattered across the aisle, hanging powdery shiitake-shaped clouds of detergent in the air that stung my lips and eyes, the powder coating my eyelashes.

Amid the lingering clouds, I saw the girl in that same dark jumper. It was Brenda.

"Fun!" she said.

I rubbed my eyes. She was gone. So was Melanie, as if my own child, too, was an hallucination. I tried calling out her name, but had breathed in too much detergent.

A gold balloon floated up to the ceiling. Where was Melanie?

From the next aisle, I heard voices soar in confusion and agitation.

What was that?

An explosion?

Gunshots?

What's that white cloud?

Smoke! Bomb! Run!

I tried coughing the soap flakes out of my throat to say, *Stop, it's not smoke, it's not a bomb.* Then I heard a rumble, as if lightning had struck the store. A rising sonic bellow, a thrumming communal chain-reaction scream, leaping from person to person, hopping over aisles, multiplying into shouting that carried throughout the cavernous superstore. The fear was a nonnegotiable reaction, rising in the air with the detergent cloud, as if a crowd had been given permission to unleash their fear.

"Where are you, Mel?" I shouted at last, drowned out by the panic-shrieking that drenched the air.

A voltage electrified the shoppers as they abandoned their carts and staggered to the exits. Their running feet sounded like the rush of a hurricane.

Where was Melanie?

I tried not to panic. I had practiced drills with Mel and Alex about how we would all respond in a catastrophic situation. I just had to follow what I practiced in my worst-case scenarios, but there was a stutter in my memory.

I thought, *Let me count to five.*

One: *Retrace my own steps, or Melanie's?*

Two: *Stay where I am, or go aisle by aisle?*

Three: *Shout Melanie's name?*

Four: *Shout our code word, then Mel's name?*

Five: *What was our code word?*

"Melanie!" I screamed, a fierce, unnatural howl I had never used before or knew I had in me. "Come to Mommy, Melanie! Please!"

Throngs of parents hoisted their own kids by their hands and wrists like laundry sacks or picked them up and cradled them as they ran. Bodies—old, young, out-of-shape men and women— were throttled, shoved, and slammed to the ground. Packs of stampeding shoppers hurdle-hopped over them.

I could barely hear my own voice. The din was like rushing floodwater, one intense roar after the next, gone, then back, sloshing up to my neck, swallowing my calls.

I skimmed each aisle in succession, a blur of potato chips, sodas, car accessories. We had arranged a meeting place if we got separated. . . . Hadn't we? What was the place? The eyeglasses shop? Baked goods? Cashiers? Lost and found? That would make sense, but where *was* lost and found? I couldn't remember the meeting place myself.

An intercom voice echoed in an automated loop: "Your safety is very important to us. Please walk to the nearest exit." I felt an intense virus of panic infect funnels of crowds swirling past. It was stunning how fast this final wave of terror happened, as if it leapt out of my own panic at losing Mel and infected bodies through inhalation, a contact fear. Their screams intensified as other people screamed simply because they heard screaming. The word "bomb" leapfrogged around me. Shoppers hurled full shopping carts directly into aisles congested with people trying to evacuate the store. Rounding one corner, I was lifted off my feet by a tumor of rabid shoppers and almost hurled headfirst into a pallet of flat-screen televisions.

I saw Brenda, quick as a flash, smeared with white powder, ghostly hand imprints around her neck, head, and across her back, running.

Up ahead, an exit. Customers flooded around obliterated pallets, narrating the event in real time on their phones. They held them behind their backs to capture the image of themselves running for their lives.

Where was Melanie?

There was a new wave of anxiety, a sickening stomach-retching fear. What should I do now? Once upon a time, I'd voraciously read stories aloud to Alex in bed about parents separated from their children and gloat.

How do you lose your child? I said.

People get distracted, Alex replied. *It happens.*

That would never happen to me, I said. *I would never be that irresponsible. If you lose a child in a public place you deserve to never see them again.*

"Melanie!" I screamed. "Where are you?"

An arm-in-arm line of employees herded customers out of the store. I had reached the last stage of panic. Calling Alex was a kind of defeat, but I dialed and left a shuddering message to get to the One-Shop, now, the big One-Shop, now, the *new* big One-Shop, now, where he had made the band appointment, because I needed his help, *now*, then ran into the employee arm chain.

"My daughter's missing," I said. "She's somewhere in the store. Please let me go back inside."

"Ma'am, the store has been emptied," a young woman in a bright green vest said. "We need you to leave the store." She sounded concerned and indifferent.

"I'm her mom. My daughter will only come to me. I have to go back in there."

"Ma'am," the woman said, "there was an incident in the store." How old was this woman? Not older than Serena. There was no incident. Someone (a stranger? *Brenda?* . . . No, that was a trick of the eye) dropped detergent. Then someone panicked, who then panicked someone else, until they panicked a crowd, which then panicked crowds of crowds, and now I couldn't find my daughter. How could I explain this to Alex? I lost our daughter because someone dropped a box of soap? This avalanche of people and fear, flooding into the aisles, would have seemed absurd to me weeks ago. Now this wave of trampling, stampeding inhumanity, whose intensity multiplied and swelled like a flood of hornets, felt, somehow, inevitable.

"My daughter's missing," I said. "Help me or arrest me!"

"Ma'am, we have cleared the store," she said. "Please wait outside and follow our instructions."

I wanted to shove past and run into the store. But I hated breaking rules, and that belief nagged at me to stand still. *Follow their directions, that's the best way to be reunited with Melanie.* It felt contrary to my instincts. A real mother would be screaming, being held back by a cluster of muscled security guards, kicking, shouting, causing a scene. I needed to be visible and stand out from the crowd. I should be demanding to speak to someone in charge, but I couldn't see who that would be amid the pandemonium. What I hated more than breaking rules were spectacles, drama, people watching me. I was acting so unlike how I imagined I would in a crisis. Whose fault *was* this?

"I can't believe you won't let me in," I said, stepping away.

"Right over there, behind the white line, thank you," she said. I was held back by one teenager.

I would never do this, I thought, which is exactly what I did.

I walked away—furious, powerless, scared—with my daughter somewhere in the evacuated store.

Police cruisers arrived, their sirens piercing, then cut silent. Officers waved people to and fro in contradictory patterns while they established a perimeter. A police helicopter and a news chopper jousted overhead for airspace. I checked for messages, and redialed Alex, stalking the exits, but no answer. No Mel. I loitered, adrift, skimming pockets of chattering groups to see if Melanie was wandering around, like me, lost. I staggered in a defeated semicircular amble that felt wrong, but I didn't know what else to do.

Over the din, buzzy chimes I misidentified as cell phone rings. I even checked my own phone. Police officers had corralled a caste of young Hispanic One-Shop baggers. They examined their wrists, then scanned those wearing bands with side scanners attached to their gun belts.

Mel had a band. The phone app could track her! I found Mel's profile. A circular gold band refreshed in a circle. It said "SEARCHING FOR WEARER."

While I checked and rechecked my phone, I settled into an orderly queue for a One-Shop employee with a clipboard writing down a list of items left behind in the store: purses, backpacks, phones. I wanted to jump the line, push to the front, and slap the clipboard from his hands. *I have a missing child! Who cares about your backpack?*

I waited politely until it was my turn.

"My daughter is lost in the store," I said.

"We'll page her and do a search," he said. "She may be hiding somewhere. What was she wearing?"

I blanked. Again, I was failing a significant parent test. I kept seeing Brenda instead of my daughter. Then I remembered what Mel was wearing: pink sleeveless blouse, baggy jean shorts, black slip-ons.

"Can you please let me back in there?" I asked. "She'll only come to me."

"We need confirmation the store is safe for our customers and we don't have that yet," he said in a starched, air-dried voice.

"But if it's not safe for us, it's not safe for my daughter. Please let me back in!"

"I can't give you permission," he said, "until the police give us the all clear. I appreciate your patience. I'm sure she's fine."

I was effusive in my gratitude, but could hear Alex's voice say, *He doesn't know if Mel is fine.* I didn't care. I needed this small comfort of someone, even a paid employee, telling me things would be okay.

Soon, the copters skittered away. Police withdrew from the perimeter, but loitered, as police have permission to do, around exit points in the parking lot. I'd read about what other parents did right after a child went missing, about how they stayed focused, remained positive and proactive. It wasn't that way for me. I had to pee, and kept imagining scenarios about Melanie's whereabouts: trampled by the runaway crowd, stuck in one of the frozen-food freezers, locked in an airless storage room. I tried to blot each of those pictures out. Not knowing the whereabouts of my child was a dull flaring throb of nerve pain that grew exponentially each minute I waited.

I checked the phone. No calls from Alex.

The band app: syncing, syncing, syncing.

My phone battery was almost dead.

I walked to the car, at the far end of the lot a quarter mile away, to charge my phone. There, visible from a good distance, was Melanie, standing by the driver's-side door. I ran in a way I hadn't since tenth-grade physical education. I felt a delirious headache of relief washing over any anger I felt about being separated. Seeing Melanie flushed my own punitiveness away. I picked her up and her lavender-scented hair tickled my nose.

"How did you get past me?" I asked.

"The car is our meeting place." It had been the car. Where else would it be but the car? *How did I forget that?* I thought, and wanted to apologize, but my punitiveness returned as fast as it was spooked.

"You shouldn't have left my side," I said, opening the car doors. "Buckle up, please."

The acidic burning taste of detergent lingered on my tongue and lips as my house and the wall slid into view. It had changed, again.

Its contours were transformed, deepened. Its bricks were pock-marked and wrinkled, revealing infinite tableaus of weeping suns, setting into calligraphic waves of dissolving mountains, roiling oceans, and disfigured land. Closer, I saw dismembered bodies, disarticulated limbs undulating as if adrift on a limestone sea. Its brick inhaled and exhaled.

Alex emerged from behind the wall. His band's golden light shimmered around his wrist.

"Daddy!" Mel shouted.

The three of us stood there in the shadow of a wall that Alex didn't acknowledge.

With Mel clinging to his chest, I waited for one simple reason he didn't pick up his phone that made sense. A basic gesture that would ease me through the rest of this hideous day.

"I couldn't believe those messages," he said. "You left Mel in the store? Why?"

Something inside me went numb. My brain felt thick and chewy, like taffy.

"We were separated," I said, my anger stuck in a foggy remission. I didn't push back.

"How did that happen?"

I heard, in Alex's voice, the same tone I would use if he called and said he lost Mel. What story would make sense? A vision of my dead childhood friend started a panic riot? My punishment was now to reenact a play-by-play of what happened, to listen to and process all the ways Alex would have better handled the situation. Now was the worst time to ask him, *Do you see a ten-foot wall behind you?*

"None of this makes sense," he said.

"I'm aware of that," I said. "It doesn't make sense to me explaining it to you."

"How did you find her?" he asked.

"By our car."

"How long did that take?"

"Maybe a half hour."

"She was alone for thirty minutes?" Alex shrieked.

"I thought she was in the store."

"And it never occurred to you to check the meeting place you drilled into both our heads?"

"I never saw her come out," I said. Listening to my answers, I sounded reckless, negligent. I understood Alex's incredulousness and was, frankly, happy to see it. Something had reached him at last. I would accept whatever punishment he felt right.

"I was thinking," he said, words that filled me with a furious dread. Dolores has said, ¿*Cuándo ha sido bueno para una mujer que el hombre piense?*

"Thinking," I said. "Okay."

"Why didn't you use the app to track her?"

"It didn't work," I said. "It was 'syncing.'"

He held up the phone to demonstrate. His phone said "The wearer is 0 feet away."

"I think Mel and I need to talk about this," he said. "At my house. She has a change of clothes there. I'll drop her off at school tomorrow morning."

"Oh," I said. "Okay."

Their bodies dissolved into the band lights around their wrists until they drove away. Then I keeled over, as if I had been punched in the chest, and threw up. I had no fight left in me.

I hadn't bought any groceries at One-Shop, so that night I drove to FARM and wandered the aisles, uncertain, shivering and lost. It had been a long, treacherous kind of day that felt like three or four days. I had no desire to eat and with no dinner to cook for Mel, I didn't have a taste for anything and left the store empty-handed. I used my phone three blocks from my house to remind Alex not to give Mel too much of the chocolate milk he keeps on hand for her, when I saw a police cruiser waiting to turn left into an intersection. In the ten seconds it took the light to change, the cop stared at me, then at my SUV and its front plate, then at me speaking on my cell phone. He doubled back and followed me.

I remembered the single driving lesson Gonzalo had given me when I practiced for my driver's test.

Never give a cop three reasons to turn his head, he said. *Cops won't stop on a double take, but three reasons and you're getting pulled over.*

Ser moreno, my father said, *es la razón número uno.*

You're crazy, papá, I said, and laughed. *Cops don't do that. Besides we're not that dark. That will never, ever be me.*

When those alternating, stunning-as-an-eclipse lights flashed in my mirrors, and I heard the sharp squawk noise, I was one street away from my cul-de-sac. I was desperate to find an alley to turn down, an obstacle to hide my car, but he replayed his squawk noise, louder this time. I flicked on my turn signal and stopped in front of Rebekah's house. I prayed she wasn't home.

I tucked my phone in a cup holder and put my hands at ten and two on the steering wheel. I wasn't afraid; in fact, there was a stomach drop of excitement. I'd have a contrary story to tell Serena! No drama, no confrontation, no viral video in the making where one sees the tail end of a cop losing his patience and not the minutes of abuse he absorbed before the camera started filming. I would be respectful, obey orders, and not ask any challenging questions, receive my ticket, and go on my way.

Officer Jimenez had a firm but polite tone of voice. His indistinguishable face was offset by a nose like wadded ground beef.

"Good evening, ma'am. Do you know why I stopped you today?"

"Yes, sir, I do," I said, emphasizing *sir.* "I was using my cell phone." I motioned with my left hand. "I put the phone away as soon as I saw you."

"That's appreciated, ma'am," he said. "Can I see your license and registration?"

I handed them over. "So you don't have your license transferred to a band?" he asked.

"No, sir," I said. "I haven't had time to get one. I believe there's a grace period to get them."

"We are in that grace period," he said, "but in this county, any state resident not wearing a band during a traffic stop can be detained and examined to confirm their status as a citizen."

"I wasn't aware of that," I said. "I'm sorry, sir. I am a citizen."

"I need you to step out of the car for me."

"Is there another form of ID that I can show you?"

"Ma'am, this is the second time I am asking you to step out of your vehicle."

"Oh," I said. "Okay."

"Watch your step, please," he said. "We don't want an accident."

He directed me to the curb behind my car. His red and blue lights cast me in an alternating darkness. "I'm not arresting you, but you are being detained, as you are not wearing a state-issued band during a traffic stop in this county. I need you to turn around and put your hands behind your back."

"Thank you," I said, though I didn't know why I thanked him or where that impulse came from. My arm motion was automatic, which surprised me. I heard the zippered snap of the thick plastic cuff tie. I tried relaxing my arms, but the tie chafed my wrists in that position. I held my shoulders erect, and at attention, so the tie didn't cut into my skin.

"I need to collect your information," he said. "If you come back clean, you'll be on your way."

"Okay," I said. *Clean. What does that mean? Don't ask any questions, don't complain, don't move, don't breathe, don't breathe and hold it in. . . . Can you take longer breaths? That way you won't move as much. He's a police officer and has the right to question if I belong here. How would he know? But why would he assume I don't belong here? No, don't ask any questions. Don't question anything. What did I tell Melanie, over and over, after all those police officer classroom visits? Cooperate, comply.*

A steady parade-crawl of traffic blew a stinging eyewash of my own hair, street grit, and trash at my face. When I was stuck in traffic and saw the cause was someone in handcuffs, I reveled in the moment, did a little victory dance in my seat and hand-clapped inside my head. *Thought you'd get away with it!* I shouted, singsong. If it was someone white or Asian: *Shame how you threw your life away.* If it was someone African American: *I thought so.* If it was someone brown: *You are always fucking embarrassing us.*

I gulped long painful breaths that spider-walked down my throat. I tried twisting my limbs to re-angle my body.

"Don't move, miss," the officer said.

"I'm trying not to," I said. "I'm moving so I can stand still."

"I need you to refrain from moving and speaking," he said.

Jimenez adjusted my shoulders, arms, and wrists into increasing positions of discomfort and unnaturalness. I didn't see another person on my entire block, but I knew everyone was watching this unfold. Watching me. The thought of being a spectacle for my neighbors was deeply humiliating. The shame of visibility and surveillance caused my eyes to well up. Blinking filled them with tears.

Even though he's not white, don't let the officer see you cry.

I stared into Rebekah's house and saw her privacy blinds flutter. In her endless array of front-porch windows, I saw my own reflection.

I can't believe this, I thought. *I brought this on myself.*

Then, *Am I really defending his right to humiliate me?*

Whenever I moved my arms, my cuff tie snapped me back into an uncomfortable, prone, chest-out, standing-forward position. It was a disorienting, hostile sensation, being unable to move, or wipe my eyes clear, a vertical drowning in panicked gulps. My hair was a flowing, tangled mess. I spat strands out from between my lips. The wind slapped my spit back on my face.

"Okay, turn around," Officer Jimenez said, uncuffing me.

I had been in that position for just a few minutes, but the relief my body felt at being released was euphoric, almost superhuman.

I experienced some kind of endorphin high from moving my arms again.

"You came back fine, but you weren't wearing a band during a traffic stop. Here's your warning," he said, handing me a canary paper slip. "Those bands are easy to set up," he said, his tone now friendly, "and will help keep us both safer next time you're driving around here."

"Thank you, Officer," I said. "I appreciate it."

I felt, once again, that same tidal wave sense of relief and appreciation. Why not offer him gratitude, too? He could have arrested me for any reason—because he *wanted to* would have been enough.

I drove to my house. In that brief distance, my appreciation faded, the way light disappears after dusk. I had broken one rule I knew of, was let off with a warning about another rule I knew nothing about . . . and yet I was stopped, and detained, and cuffed. I couldn't shake off what had happened, and a sudden, determined anger stalked me as I parked the car.

The wall smelled like dank rot, ammonia. And like *home*, which terrified me.

I gripped it tight, its mountain-raised ridges cutting deep into my hands, and felt a shudder underneath my feet. A shrieking bled out of the wall. The noise transformed from vibration, to harmony, to song, to words.

I whispered what I heard, over and over, like an SOS: "El otro lado. El otro lado. El otro lado."

The other side. How could I be repulsed by and drawn to the same thing?

I wanted to sleep in that Monday morning. Instead, my insomnia woke me up around four a.m. My body floundered and tossed in bed through most of an early dawn. A loud, insistent knocking around seven finally got me out of bed.

Rebekah was on my front porch. Her eyes swung like a pendulum from my face to my bandless wrist. I saw the trajectory of her thinking laid bare.

"I'm sorry, I thought you would be up by now," Rebekah said, leering into the hard darkness of my house. We stood under the wall's shadow with the sun completely blocked out over our heads.

"This won't take long," Rebekah said.

"Oh," I said.

"It's about your situation."

"That sounds serious," I said.

"I'm sure you remember that I'm our HOA president, and as such it's my duty to inform you that your property is in violation of our charter. The rules about physical barriers are clear." *At last, someone other than Mel and I can see it.*

"I was wondering when you'd say something," I said. "This has been a nightmare."

"So you agree it's a nuisance," Rebekah said.

"Of course," I said. "I can't sleep, I can't concentrate, I don't know what to do. I've been waiting for someone to help me."

"I'm not here to 'help,'" Rebekah said. "We, all of us, just want it—*you*—to stop."

"You think I'm doing *that?*" I asked, motioning at the wall. This gesture confused her. "Have you ever seen a truck, or a work crew, or heard tools of any kind?"

"I'm trying to be professional here," Rebekah said. "There are community standards each of us must adhere to so our neighborhood *stays* our neighborhood. Work on anyone's property requires a neighborhood certificate of appropriateness. Did you file for a certificate of appropriateness, Iris? Because I haven't seen one."

"I didn't file anything," I said, "because I'm not doing anything."

"What you're *doing*," Rebekah said, "is attracting vermin, deer, and wild animals. You've created a hazardous situation next to your property and that impacts us all."

"Next to?"

Rebekah pointed at the large berm of dirt I'd dug out from the wall.

"I don't know what you do out here in the morning, bobbing with your headlight," Rebekah said. "Frankly, our community ignored this too long. That I take responsibility for because I considered you a friend." I realized, when she said it, this was the first time Rebekah had used that word to describe me—"friend."

"You care about the dirt?" I shouted. I couldn't take her blindness any longer. My flooding anxiety made it much easier to be confrontational. "I'm talking about *that wall* right behind you! Can't you *see?*" I asked, jabbing a finger at Rebekah's head.

"I don't understand," Rebekah said.

"Look!" I shouted, grabbing handfuls of small rocks from beside the porch. "Look! At! That!" I threw the rocks at the wall. Rebekah ducked out of the way. They landed short in the grass without a sound.

"Iris, stop," Rebekah said. "We don't respond with violence in our neighborhood. But I have everything I need. You've agreed it's a nuisance, you didn't file a certificate of appropriateness, and you just attempted to assault us. As HOA president, I'm initiating a lien on your property for dereliction of maintenance and creating a community hazard. We intend to foreclose on this house as soon as possible. Last night—where you were arrested outside my house—was the final straw."

"I wasn't arrested!" I said. "I was detained."

"There's no difference when the outcome is the same," she said. "We're a community that doesn't want 'misunderstandings.' That doesn't happen to good, law-abiding people. I'm sure you can move somewhere where you don't stand out."

"I was born here!" I shouted, and heard the echo of my mamá's voice. "And you're not white! You're Mexican like I am!" I heard the echo of my sister's voice.

"My ancestors are Spaniards," Rebekah said. "I can trace my family back to Galicia."

"Great," I said, "then get your Spanish ass off my porch."

"Iris!" she commanded. "Stop being dramatic."

From the front hall closet I grabbed a shovel and slapped it at Rebekah's feet. It landed with a clang. A moaning echo hung in the air.

"*That* is a wall," I said, and pointed behind her. "I can see it. It's there. It exists. It's real. When you're ready to see it, too, grab one of those and start digging."

I slammed the front door, then heard her steps recede.

It's okay if it's just Mel and me who see it.

It's okay even if I lose this house.

It's okay. We're okay. Everything is okay.

Can I get five minutes of sleep before I have to start my day?

I can't. Time for work.

Twelve

It was an atypical-typical day for me, one I handled well enough on three hours' sleep and the events of the past day: work, Mel, dinner. Just the essentials in my life.

For everyone else: fear. And fear had been busy.

In the twenty-four hours since what had been labeled the "Clean Bomb" incident, an online collective of incensed voices coalesced and emerged into a massive storm of discontent. An initial One-Shop investigation revealed three Mexican-American workers had not performed necessary safety weight-restriction checks on One-Shop shelving units, causing them to collapse. It was also revealed that none of these workers had bands, as One-Shop did not require its employees to have bands to work there.

The voices said, *Coincidence? No!* Had One-Shop required bands to work there, this potential tragedy could have been avoided.

Those of "unverified origin" or the "unbanded," as they were soon called, were flaunting the state's rules and regulations, hiding in plain sight. The unbanded, these voices clarified, were different from the bandless, law-abiding whites who could get a band but chose not to surrender their freedom to the government.

An unbanded potentially sabotaged the store's IT infrastructure, leading to One-Shop supply-chain shortages statewide. Groups of unbanded were targeting the state's largest corporations to attack capitalism and hasten its downfall.

"This was a warning," the voices said. "What if the next time someone is killed because an unbanded didn't do their job or was somewhere they shouldn't be? The unbandeds are not us. Wear your bands and prove you belong here. *Real* proof for *real* Americans. Band Together!"

How had this event become about the bands? I watched, fascinated, as the narrative of what happened cracked into dozens of conspiracies, which spread like a poison gas people rushed to inhale. Something had shifted: the unbandeds were everywhere, like boogeymen, and had to be dealt with, now. People who were able to get bands but resisted them, wary of government overreach, signed up in record numbers as a way to demonstrate their patriotism. The state facilitated and fast-tracked band application access to those with deceased parents and no access to their physical birth certificates, allowing them to apply for temporary band status. Lawsuits about the band's legality, which had been playing out in various stages throughout the state, were all but invalidated when an emergency case that would decide the band's constitutionality one way or the other was turned away by a newly installed supermajority Supreme Court vote.

I wanted to explain, somewhere, to anyone, that there hadn't been an actual bomb, that this wasn't a thwarted terrorist or unbanded (the words were now synonymous) attack, which became the commonly accepted narrative, but there were too many theories and counter-theories online about what had happened. I had no idea how I could be heard and believed. I made a feeble effort on my own social media page to write my narrative, which was discredited with suspicion and hostility. The creeping-shadow dread I experienced walking through an empty parking garage from my high school sales job when I was seventeen was the same feeling I had when I opened my social media account.

"What you actually experienced," someone wrote on my page, "doesn't supersede how I feel." When had my yoga class become a host to discussions about gender fluidity being a Marxist conspiracy to reduce birth rates, and that vaccines caused homosexuality and tooth decay? This was followed by links to a post about how "the unbanded" had tried in the One-Shop attack to infiltrate our water supply via irradiated laundry soap.

As my own bandless days accreted, something changed. I can't say when, exactly. It was like a time-lapse effect from those 1980s music videos I loved watching in college for fun. Something that wasn't there, all of a sudden was. All I know is that it felt different to be an American. Or being an American felt different.

I heard these words, everywhere: *Unbandeds*—you know *them* when you see *them*.

It came first at work, a new daily vocabulary, whispered, then openly spoken by coworkers and then in public spaces. I wondered how long I had been suspected of being one of "them"—because there was no clearer word to describe what I felt. Did they see Melanie as one of "them," too?

I wondered, too: How much of these feelings was I inventing in my head? Did it matter?

I thought, and couldn't stop thinking: Which of these people voted for the bands? I remembered my own vote, how frivolous in retrospect I had been in my decision.

On social media, a relentless march of shrill, jumpy recordings dropped you into momentary snippets of rabid-screaming fury looped to repeat as long as you kept watching. Belligerent entitlement morphed into frothing anger and assault.

"Where's your fucking band you fucking wetback!" a bare-wristed white man shouted at an abuela cowering in a fetal ball on a disabled parking spot while a crowd of people recorded her public berating from multiple angles. Endless videos of brown-skinned bandless men, women, and children confronted, shouted at, wrists grabbed and held up like trophy kills, limbs fractured and broken, bodies physically assaulted, shoved to the ground and camera-phoned.

I inhaled noxious social media for two or three minutes each day before a wrenching kind of sickness, a turbulent nausea, pummeled me. That idle bloat distilled, upon repeat viewings, into a finger-trembling rage, as if I were contracting the anger in these videos by watching them. These attacks were decried and analyzed, then discussed and absolved, until at last there were too many to keep track of as noteworthy. They were as common as fatal freeway collisions—a sad but ultimately unavoidable consequence of people not following the rules.

I observed, as the days passed, that society had reached some kind of unspoken agreement about the bands. They were wielded like a political statement, a patriotic yet wholly optional accessory for white wrists (the bands still never seemed to function in most transactions), and boiling over into a necessity for brown ones. Gas stations, convenience stores, wherever customers want to conduct business in a hurry. NO BAND, NO SERVICE signs were everywhere in North Azulia. YES WE SCAN! and ¡SÍ, SE ESCANEA! stickers popped up on sliding glass business doors and car bumpers.

Shop owners asked young and old abuelos in my skin color range (one or two shades lighter, and every shade darker) for their bands.

Then they asked young women.

Then they asked women who dressed professionally, like me.

Then they asked me, and didn't stop asking, gently but firmly escorting all of us unbanded onto the street: *Thank you for stopping by, have a nice day.*

My paranoia evolved as fast as the social contract had changed. White people—a few with, but mostly without, bands—distanced themselves from me. I developed a new "sense" about not wearing a band in public, fast attuned to the sonics of evaluation: overheard comments at work that faded when I rounded a corner, the way a mouth clicked after a glance or a stare at my wrist, fast steps away when I was spotted in an office corridor, the unnecessary second or third cough in an elevator when it was me and a white person.

I was not accustomed to this new, aggressive, never-ending feeling of being scrutinized. When I'd experienced situations before that I considered "weird" or "angry friendly"—white men race-quizzing me, white women fondling Melanie's face like produce—there had been limits to these interactions. Somehow, in an overnight or two, my social contract had been renegotiated. Politeness vanished.

I practiced reasons that explained why I was bandless—*It was still too soon after the vote, wasn't it? They were supposed to be optional, weren't they? They didn't mean my parents; they didn't mean me*—but realized these explanations required the goodwill of the listener to actually listen. There was no easy counternarrative that sounded believable. You either wore a band or you didn't. The deep-seated conviction I felt that I belonged, my ability to *blend in* because of the rules Dolores taught me as a child, had evaporated. White people saw my bare wrist and they *knew*.

Embers of suspicion blew from rooftop to rooftop, through North Azulia and into surrounding communities like West Vecino. Band-supporting signs and flags (Where had they come from and why were they needed?) reappeared on front lawns and porches months after the election that had decided the result. On drives to and from work, I was sometimes followed by a leathery-faced white man in an oversize black pickup truck with a guttural engine who cruised the area, trailing a large red BAND TOGETHER! flag with a golden band at its center, surrounded by a crown of guns.

Menial jobs became impossible to fill, meaning there were rolling shortages of nearly everything. Medical supplies and prescriptions were impossible to keep in stock. Two- to three-hour waits at fast-food restaurants were common. Supermarket aisles were barren, with no regular deliveries of produce, milk, eggs, and meat. Prices for fresh fruits and vegetables skyrocketed as experts predicted tons of unharvested crops would rot in fields. There was no steady supply of loaders to unload items from trucks or planes, and no drivers to move things from one city to the next. In a country that prides itself on mass and volume, the question was asked again and again: *Why is this happening?*

Rumors abounded that our company's management association would require bands to enter the workplace. I dug into my

closet for hardly worn, long-sleeve cardigans and blouses, temporary work-arounds that in a perpetually warm climate aroused suspicion. I prepared for potential confrontations by over-prepping
my identification papers, the way I would going to the airport. In
lieu of a band, did I have at least three forms of ID: driver's license,
credit cards, health-care cards? I still hadn't updated my utility bills
with my band information (Mel's band didn't work as a stopgap—
the accounts required someone eighteen years or older) and was
worried that any day now I would lose service to every utility si-
multaneously. These physical cards and papers so necessary to live
our lives and so prized at any bureaucratic depot for processing
identities now seemed worthless, but I held on to them in the hope
that nostalgia for the world that once was would save me. I changed
my grocery shopping schedule to when I figured stores would be
their emptiest. I saw other bandless there, too, checking my wrist
and nodding in what I assumed was solidarity. I tried to say with my
eyes, *I am not like you, okay? I followed the rules. I do not condone you.*

At work, each conversation was a dreaded game of chicken
where, at any moment, talk pivoted from silence to accusation.
Like storm clouds rolling in, it happened in stages. First, the silence,
then the head nod at my wrist, followed by the lean in, and, at last,
like a child whispering that someone touched them in a private
place: *Did you forget your band?*

A simple trip to the grocery store became an exercise in holding my breath. Anyone was a potential body snatcher. Perhaps
the checkout woman who spoke in patriotic clichés? Or the fifty-
something bagger in the checkered long-sleeve shirt whose band
I never saw, but always had a stick of cinnamon Big Red chewing
gum for Melanie at the ready? Once, a man smiled at me while I
got out of my car and watched me walk across the parking lot. I
grabbed at my wrist for a band that was of course not there, and
rubbed my forearms, shivering in the perfect afternoon weather.
The experience unsettled me so much that I waited an extra fifteen minutes in the store before leaving with my groceries.

Each night after Mel went to bed, I scrolled through online

reports, distilled by rumor and anecdote into a fact-slurry. End-less stories about Mexican-American unbandeds being arrested and indefinitely detained on spurious charges throughout the state. Children at public schools across the region were denied access to their classrooms because they weren't wearing bands; packs of vigilante parents "arrested" droves of Mexican-American elementary school children and filmed it on their phones (older kids were tougher targets, as they fought back). There were plenty of ensconced planned communities like North Azulia, often teth-ered at an inconvenient geographic Siamese hip to a city like West Vecino, that passed new city laws and ordinances, using the bands to "refresh their demographics" and keep the unbanded out of se-lected public spaces known for "illicit activity." At a One-Shop store somewhere farther south, in an area "known for crime and racial discord," eleven Mexican-American men, women, and chil-dren simply "vanished" right out of the store—surveillance caught them coming in but never going out.

Each night after picking up Mel from after-care was a race home to stare out my window at the ten-foot-plus-high wall growing in front of my house, and a diminishing view of the world. The grass in its shadow had died and turned to large mud patches. Melanie's crosses throbbed in the dusk.

Drives to Dolores's house left me dripping in anxiety sweat be-cause none of my family had bands and weren't terribly concerned about getting them. It was like we were living in two different states. I felt they were deluding themselves. The panic tsunami was coming.

"No pasa nada," Dolores said, and laughed with Serena. "A nadie le importa dónde vivimos," she said.

After family dinner, I drove to my mamá's favorite tienditas, whose owners were on a first-name basis with her. There was no recognition of me, no sense of judgment that I didn't belong there like I would get from my sister, and no band scanners in the shops. Their absence relaxed me. It didn't last long.

One evening, a white bandless man yanked out his phone and

photographed the cash register station. Outside, he photographed the storefront and cars' license plates.

I spotted clusters of these cell-men walking the streets in zombie tandem twos or threes, notable for the fact they were white men walking in an area not known for walkers or white men. They disembarked from glistening black pickup trucks that sounded like asthmatic lions, roaming in prides up and down the avenue. Shop owners sometimes charged at them with broomsticks, garden hoses, or often their own cell phone cameras, tangoing in circles. Twice I had seen parking lot scuffles of men trying to throw punches with one hand and hold up their phone to record the encounter in the other. I used to think seeing white people meant gentrification, a sign the neighborhood was improving, becoming safer. I didn't know what this meant for my family's neighborhood, but I was sure it wasn't good.

I scoured the state's band website to see if new exemptions had been added to apply for one. Instead, the same disclaimer in bold red letters: "Eligibility subject to State, not Federal, approval." No parent with a US birth certificate equaled no band—no exceptions. I called a 1-800 number and after finger-punching through layers of protective automated menus, reached a live person, "Derek," who had a strong Indian accent.

"I'm sorry, ma'am," Derek said, emphasizing *ma'am*, "but you cannot get a band unless one of your parents has a US birth certificate. Are there any other questions I can help you with today?" It didn't occur to me to challenge this explanation, to pester and peel away, like a thumb scraping a paint chip, for a hidden loophole. I accepted this for an answer and hung up.

When this began, I was an American. Now I felt I was something else, someone ni de aquí ni de allá. I had been declared an uncitizen, forced to unlearn who I thought I was and what I could be.

At a press conference announcing ten million band activations, the state announced a bounty system that would allow anyone to claim a monetary award that led to the arrest and conviction of someone using a fraudulent band, or providing services to those using fraudulent bands. Those caught wearing fake bands could be tried and convicted, punishable with up to ten years in prison and a hundred thousand dollar fine.

That long ago snap reaction—*Good!*—was still inside me somewhere. But that wasn't what I thought.

A fake band. I'd never, ever do that.

Would I?

Thirteen

Dolores left a two-second message on my voicemail in which all she said was her own name. My mamá never left voicemails.

On the drive over, Mel told me about the band program being taught to her during class. "They're gonna have a big party when everyone in the class has one, because we're saving the environment."

"They said that?" I asked.

"Yes, and they asked us if our parents were wearing the bands, too, because if you aren't wearing one, you're not helping the planet." Mel hesitated, as if broaching a delicate matter. "Mom, why don't you have yours?"

"Mommy hates the planet right now," I said.

Inside, I dropped Mel on the couch next to Gonzalo, watching a soccer game.

"Hi, Abuelo," Melanie said.

"Where's Mamá?" I asked.

" 'Ta en el bedroom," Gonzalo said. It was unlike Dolores not to greet us when we arrived. The rare occasions she didn't were when she had massive back pain from her job. There were too many days when she had to work through her pain to count.

"Algo pasó con su chamba," he said.

"What do you mean, something happened with her job?" I asked. "Is she all right? Was she injured?"

"Pero, ta bien. Entra y habla con ella."

"Okay, I'll talk with her."

I set an open beer by Gonzalo's steady hand. Walking down the hallway, I heard Gonzalo ask about Mel's school day. I couldn't remember Gonzalo asking about my school days, but I was grateful he did it with his granddaughter.

Dolores's bedroom used to be off-limits. Once, I crept in when I was old enough to reach their dresser tops. Gonzalo had strong-smelling lotions, hair dyes, and a cologne that could have been called Pickled Bar Fire. My mamá had religious icons, a chipped wooden rosario, what I later realized were birth control pills, and a black-and-white photograph of an unsmiling Dolores with her own unsmiling mother (an abuela I never knew) in México, stand-ing by a bare, split thorn tree. I didn't linger, since their heavy, musty-smelling swap-meet comforter—a bear wrestling a nest of tri-headed snakes—gave me nightmares.

I knocked on my mamá's door, heard rustling inside. The blinds were drawn, with Dolores perched on the edge of her bed. She seemed to shrink in size as I approached. When had my mamá ever been this still, at rest, her body not at work?

"How did this comforter get uglier?" I asked. I sat next to Mamá, gripped the mattress for support.

"Después de treinta y siete años, creí que no tenía que worry más," Dolores said. "I thought, por fin, este es tu hogar también. Ahora, todos necesitamos a chafa piece of plastic para quedarnos aquí."

"Mamá, this is my home," I said. "It's our home."

"¿Neta?" she asked. "Yesterday, you being born here, enough. Today, they say a band, enough. ¿Y qué vamos a necesitar ma-ñana? Estas son las 'rules.' ¿Cómo se puede dar calabazas a las 'rules'?"

"Didn't you apply for citizenship?" I asked. I meant it as affir-mation that my mamá followed the rules and her application had been lost, misdirected, ignored. She heard it like a gut punch.

"Yes, I apply! How can I make this conversation believable to you?" she said, speaking fast. "Te enseñé las rules porque yo las obedezco. Hace años que vivo aquí. Tengo carro, tengo cantón, tengo familia, me comporto como gabacha. Pero todavía no es enough, y no soy, nunca podré ser como ellos. Who would believe?"

I didn't know what to say. I had a feeble explanation about how some rules mattered, while some didn't. Some clichés popped around, too: "good intentions," maybe, or "exceptions to the rule." Seeing my mamá this way, though, and applying my own intractable logic and sense of punitive outrage, I knew my feelings were irreconcilable. I had no birth parent, unlike Alex or Melanie, who was born here and, under these "What's old is new again" rules, me, and my mamá and father, weren't eligible for bands. A totem worth infinitely more than the plastic it took to make it. I heard my own words, spoken in a thousand debated conversations with my sister and other students during my college years, who were stunned at discovering "a Mexican like you." Not "pure enough" to be an ally, not pocha or successful enough to be a sellout, those simple, stupid words I had said echoing back in my face: *You have to go by the law.*

"¿Cómo puedo discutir esto con mi hija?" Dolores asked. "Es fácil decirle other things a una chava. 'Mija, eat your spinach.' 'Mija, finish your homework.' 'Mija, no te quedes embarazada, o duermas en el garage.' Soy un gallina por un chafa piece of plastic."

"Mamá, you can't think this way," I said. "People aren't acting, I don't know, clearly right now. They have a fever. We need to wait until it breaks."

Dolores grabbed my hand. "Hay un tramo desde el origen hasta el destino," she said. "Mi papá nunca se fue del cantón. But I did. I *left*. Y vine here, y me quedé here. Hace muchos años les bastaba con eso a los gabachos. Ahora, al menos para mí, eso ya no basta. ¿Por qué?"

Again, I didn't have an answer. I could imagine myself saying to Mel years from now what my mamá told me then: There's a moment when you go somewhere when you're more the place you are than where you were. Your grandmother's father never left home, but your grandmother Dolores did. She was young, hopeful, and ready to work and start a new family. She left, came here, and stayed here. For many years, and for many people, doing that was enough. Wouldn't Mel ask me one day: What did you do to help Abuela, Mamá? She would, because she is *my* daughter.

"Mamá, it's going to be all right," I said, uncertain.

"Ay, ¡no va! Tienes tanto miedo como yo."

"I'm not frightened," I lied.

"Tiemblas como un flan porque eres smart."

"Mamá, we can't hide in our houses. We have to work."

Dolores leaned her head against my shoulder. It felt warm and comforting, its weight a polished stone, and smelled of lilacs and soap. I needed a moment to weigh and accommodate my mamá's unexpected contact. Then Mamá cried, huffing in quiet sobs.

I had never seen my mamá cry. When I was a teenager, I worked desperately to make her cry over each imagined slight I felt I suffered. Why don't you cry over me, your own daughter? I shouted, while a quiet Serena watched from a corner, eating apple slices. Dolores said, *Llegará el momento en que tu hijo recuerde cada mal que me has hecho.* The memory made me wince with embarrassment.

Now Dolores said, "Mis jefes me despidieron. 'No band, no job.'"

"Mamá, that's illegal," I said. "We need a lawyer." I realized how ridiculous and out of touch this sounded the moment I said it.

My mother let out a dark laugh, and gave me a hard stare as if she wasn't certain I was her daughter at all. "Who do you pretend we are? With what money can we hire a lawyer? Cuando me dolía la espalda, I worked," she said. "Cuando me dolían las piernas, la cabeza, I worked. Todas las partes de mi cuerpo, las consumen, and I work. I keep working, for money, to pay the mortgage, to take care of us. Y ahora me dan calabazas. ¿Por qué? How will we live? What do I do?" Dolores wiped her eyes.

"They have to accommodate you," I said.

"¿Y por qué? A mis jefes no les gustan las palabras como 'accommodate,'" Dolores said.

I wasn't sure why I was certain. Things like this couldn't happen to us. Could they? Could they happen to *me*?

"I believe," I said, "they can't do this to you."

"¿Por qué no?" Dolores asked.

"Because you taught me," I said, exasperated, "that we always have to follow the rules!"

Dolores sighed, exhausted. "'Rules' son para nosotros. Nunca para ellos."

"Oh," I said, thinking. "What did papá say?"

"Ay, 'Don't worry, don't worry!' Está jubilado, y nunca sale de casa. Nothing matters a él," Dolores said. "Sí necesitara un band pa que le prepare la cena, ¡cambiaría de opinión imediatamente! ¿No necesitas un band para tu trabajo?"

Melanie shouted, "Goaaaaaaal!" from the living room. Gonzalo laughed, which made us laugh.

"They haven't asked yet," I lied, not wanting my mamá's worry to fuel my panic. "We'll see."

"Serena puede ayudarte," Dolores said. "Speak to her."

"Her help me?" I asked. "No, *I* help her. My sister doesn't— *won't*—help me. I can't even keep track of where she is. She treats your home like a hotel."

"Mula," Dolores said. "Ella me dijo que sabía cómo conseguir un fake band. She says she knows where to get bands that can pretend to be the real ones por los scanners."

A fake band. Within my grasp. The bedroom felt stifling. It was hard for me to breathe.

"Mamá," I said, "you could go to jail for a fake. Do you want a band that bad?"

"Estoy cansada de working," Dolores said. "Nunca acaba, el work. Siempre hay más to do, y menos fuerza y tiempo pa hacerlo. Nunca tiene fin. Pero hay que seguir. Sí no, ¿qué sentido tiene la vida? We work. Because *we must*."

I thought about this—*we must*—as we returned to the living

room. Melanie was silly wriggling on the couch next to Gonzalo, her band flashing light in time with her motion.

I was my mamá's child. I could help her. I *must*.

———————

I texted Serena about her potential band connection, when I heard the ash trees crackle in the morning's warm, dry "devil winds." They pushed flocks of wild parrots from tree to tree during my early-morning wall-measuring check. Every morning, the wall blotted out the morning sun. Missing it in my house made my joints ache. The entire home was cloaked in a funereal-black mugginess under the wall's shadow. The resultant chill had turned the floor tiles icy and congealed into an airless humidity that spread through the house. Overnight, my body was racked with waves of insomnia, migraines, stomach pain, and menstrual cramps. I felt like my body was being dissolved from the inside. Listening for the birds was the one joy in this house that made me feel human.

The birds swooped and dove in tornado funnels above my car while I drove Mel to school. I learned the story behind parrots roaming free when I first thought about moving to North Azulia, but had since forgotten it, inventing new narratives whenever Melanie asked why they were here. That day, I told Mel the last known band of pirates crashed a boat in the nearby aqueduct we drove over on the way to school, when it was a raging river, and set their stock of birds free.

"That makes sense," Melanie said. "Parrots are pirates' best friends."

There were plans to turn the area around the riverbed into a children's park and bike path, but lawsuits over a homeless en-campment kept that concept dormant. I'd signed an online peti-tion months ago, before I moved into the area, to create perimeters of chain-link fence meant to expel the fifty families living there. Instead, the encampment flourished, with dozens of tarps and a patchwork of multicolored tents, plywood structures, and hun-dreds of people dressed in heavy, accumulated layers of clothing regardless of the temperature. There was an incredible stench of ammonia and shit that forced me to keep the car windows up. Women tugged their children up onto the overpass and held up cardboard signs: WE ARE HUNGRY—PLEASE HELP.

"Mommy," Mel said, "did you read that?"

"Mommy's driving," I said.

"That woman said her family was hungry. Can we go there and feed them?"

"No, we can't."

"Why not?"

"Sometimes people are selfish," I said. "They don't save their money for food and use it for drugs, or alcohol. I have to focus on feeding us."

"We can't help anyone but ourselves?"

"I mean, no," I said, flustered. "It's good to help. But people have to want to be helped."

"She had a sign asking for help."

"Sure, right," I said. I found it hard to argue with Mel's direct kids' logic of absolute fairness this early in the morning on a single cup of weak coffee. "I mean, that can't be a nice place to live. That's no place for kids," I continued, surprised. "But they shouldn't be there."

"Where should they be, Mommy?" Melanie asked.

In the rearview, I saw Melanie's band jiggle and bounce around her wrist like a Hula-Hoop. Seeing the band gave me a pause in my thoughts, if not necessarily to reflect, but to form an impression of a changed mind.

"I don't know," I said. "Somewhere safe. Where their kids can go to school."

"Can they go to school with me?" Melanie asked.

"Sure, maybe," I said. "But they need a home. Somewhere safe."

"Can that be with us?" Mel asked.

"I don't think so," I said.

"And Daddy can't live with us, either?" she asked.

"No, honey," I said. "He can't."

"Oh," she said, "because he really wants to."

"When did he say that?" I asked.

"He let me stay up late, and we talked about how I was feeling and he asked if I missed him. I said I did, because I do, and he said not to worry, we would all be back together soon. Is that true?"

I parked at the school drop-off zone. "You and I are together right now," I said. "That's what I know."

Melanie unbuckled her own harness. "Make sure you tighten your band, it looks loose," I said.

"When are you getting your band?"

"Soon," I said. "When I have a free afternoon from work."

"I want ours to match," she said.

"Your dad already has one," I said.

"I know, but I want us to match. It only counts if we match, Mommy."

"We match, band or no band." I hugged Melanie. A car horn blared behind us.

"Okay, Mom, I gotta get the go!"

When I got to the office, a custodial crew was stopped at my office's security gate. Armed with a handheld scanning gun, our office guard, Eric, was squat-standing in front of four Hispanic women with buckets, tote bags of cleaning supplies, and a wet/dry vac. His band's light glowed from under his sleeve.

"No hay bandas," he said, pointing to his wrist, "no hay entrada." Talk radio had turned this phrase into a catchy viral song shared millions of times, teaching the Spanish translation of "no bands, no entry" to people who had up to this point no interest in learning any Spanish at all.

Walking into Karina's officle, I said, "You won't believe what that cabrón . . ."

Karina's shelves were bare. Her mortarboard was gone.

"Yes, Iris?" she asked. She wore a long-sleeve blouse, meaning I couldn't see her wrists. I hated myself for looking. "I'm working," she added, and tugged on her sleeves. Her attitude, and her things, were gone. She was trying to make herself invisible.

"Never mind," I said.

On my desk was a short memo from our company's property management corporation stating that, as a private business, it would soon require bands in addition to our company identification for building access. Any employees refusing to comply could be subject to termination.

The memo levitated on my desk throughout my workday, the words emitting their own frequency only I could hear, rising in pitch and intensity until I picked up Mel from after-care.

Driving home, while she sketched on butcher paper, I thought about how many secret back-door paths I could find into my office. I settled on crossing a dilapidated footbridge at the far end of the strip mall complex over a fetid artificial creek and duck pond, where I'd have to push through a heavy set of unlocked basement double back doors, then climb a series of fire exit staircases that echoed regardless of how softly you stepped. It would add about ten minutes to bypass a ten-second checkpoint.

Imagining this new journey kept me from seeing that something had changed outside my house.

The stone wall was gone.

In its place, twenty-foot-high copper slats, thin metal columns spaced about a foot and a half apart for a length of about one hundred feet. The bars glinted in the car's running headlights.

The bollards were bronzed with a smoggy copperish glaze, symmetrical in appearance from whichever angle I looked. I tried taking pictures of it with my phone. What came back were blurry white squares and error messages.

I touched its bars. A brittle, pewter grit coated my fingertips. On the slats themselves, finger-painted pink crosses, their color dripping down the metal.

"Who's doing this!" I shouted. "Who's doing this to me!"

I turned to Mel and said, "Go inside and pack a bag."

"Why?" she asked.

"Just do it, okay?"

I had seen enough horror movies to know when it was time to

leave—no, *run*—out of the house. I owned this property, but no mortgage payment or damage to my credit record or school district was worth this. We had stayed here long enough.

Above, the sound of wild parrots, their wings fluttering as they flew west, into the darkness.

Fourteen

I found a modest hotel in West Vecino that didn't rent to la gente de la calle where Mel and I could stay four, maybe five days before my monthly budget noticed. The carpets smelled like dog pee and cigarette smoke, but the tiny bar soaps were sealed in crinkly, unopened plastic wrap and the windows and front door locks weren't broken. Alex's house wasn't an option, and I didn't want to stay at Dolores's because what could I possibly tell my mamá that wouldn't make me sound insane? She was in grief from losing her job. *¿Asustada de una pared? ¿Crie a una mujer o a una miedosa?*

Mel liked that she had upgraded to a queen-size bed. She spread her maps across it and colored, uninterested in screen time. We shared greasy pizza and I let her stay up until ten p.m.

The next morning, I called the mortgage lender to tell them I was abandoning the house, but I kept getting cut off or circling through their endless not-helpful-at-all help menus. After dropping Mel off at school, I took a sick day, making appointments to see various apartments in the surrounding area. Nothing in North Azulia was available, so I took a second sick day. I drove around West Vecino and found a FOR RENT sign outside an ideal starter home with a tiny, open courtyard and a beautiful front lawn. It was a good hour from Mel's school, with no exterior walls or street-facing barriers anywhere. I called the number on the sign and agreed to bring a deposit check at six p.m.

I checked out of the motel and told Mel when I picked her up that we had a new place to live. "Does this mean I have to go to a new school?" she asked.

"Not for a while," I said. "We may just need to get up earlier in the mornings. But you'll love it."

I drove up to the new house on Challenger Lane.

There was a four-and-a-half-foot concrete wall out front. It was identical to the wall that first appeared outside my home months ago.

The wall hadn't been there this morning. It was there now.

The wall would follow me wherever I went.

It wasn't the house. It was *me*.

Leaving my house wouldn't solve the problem. It would just start things back from the beginning.

A wall would appear.

A wall would rise.

A wall would cast me in shadow.

I would lose what was left of my mind.

I had to go back to my home. *What else could I do?*

I leaned my head on the wall. It thrummed against my forehead, chattering my teeth. Melanie asked if she could play, so she slipped off her flip-flops and played on the perfect grassy lawn in her bare feet.

"Hurry up," Mel shouted, "I'm leaving! I'm leaving, leaving, leaving!"

Her band's light fluttered around her wrist like a Halloween glow bracelet, keeping her visible while she ran and jumped in the soon-to-be darkness.

I was desperate, with nowhere to go and no idea what to do next.

Hey, I texted Serena. *Mamá said to contact you.*

We drove back to the house around dark. I took the long way, hoping something would have changed when I got there. The slatted wall gleamed high in the air, catching the moonlight and trapping it on its bars. Why would it have changed? The wind blew through the bollards, making a shrieking, ancient whistle sound.

"The wall's singing!" Mel said. "Like a coyote! Owoooo!"

I waited until I'd put Mel to bed to check my work email. I knew my performance at work had slipped significantly in the past weeks. There—marked "Urgent!"—was an unopened email from several days ago.

Effective tomorrow, employees would be required to show bands to enter the office building. Anyone without a band would work remotely. A significant deduction would be made from our paycheck into a retainer fund until we received a band, whereby we would get our money back. Without a band in ten business days, I was subject to termination and forfeiting any monies from the retainer. I stared at that email and realized I had run out of options.

What can I do now? I screamed into a pillow to muffle the sound. I didn't want my daughter to hear me lose control.

A text from Serena roused me. She invited me to lunch tomorrow. For once, my younger sister had ideal timing.

After driving Mel to school the next morning, I took several wrong turns before I realized I had to drive back to the house to go to work. The wall was monstrous and blinding in the bright warm sunshine, like concentrated highway glare. Its bollards cast long slatted shadows across my house, keeping any direct sunlight from reaching me inside. The work-at-home morning quickly established a pettier workplace world whose computer interface amplified mundane tasks and problems. I winced at the ghostly metallic echoey pangs of a stuttering video conference. Dreaded the pleasant chime that preceded a manager's haggard face popping up like a boil on my screen, seething with resentment that I, for now, was being accommodated. I suspected a disciplinary file in my (or, optimistically, Irena's) name had been opened, my actions being documented, which would lead to my firing sooner than my ten-day extension period.

I met Serena at her go-to taqueria. There were metal security grates on the windows. The stand was located in a far corner of

West Vecino that bordered oil refineries and a truckers' gas station whose semitrailers kicked up swirls of gritty pinkish dust that sparkled like soap flakes.

I wiped down my side of an outdoor bench and table with some Kleenex from my purse. The sticky stains shredded the tissue. I wanted this to be a quick, formal conversation and thought of something neutral to open with.

"They're out of napkins," I said, and got a mouthful of disturbingly sweet pink grit on my tongue.

"Servilletas, por favor," Serena asked the girl through the black grate. "Here, princess, they have plenty."

"Is mamá trying to find another job?" I asked. "She doesn't have enough money to take care of three people." My sister being the third, of course.

"They've always saved money," Serena said. "Remember how they got us gifts when they were broke?"

"That was you," I said. "One Christmas in my stocking, I got coupons."

"You didn't! For what?"

"Milk, Froot Loops. Things I guess I liked."

"That had to be papá," Serena said. "He's cheap. That's why we came here for his birthday."

My sister told me this fantastic story she'd remembered all these years of how my father took us to watch fútbol at a pool hall we weren't supposed to be in because we were too young, then we came to this exact restaurant to eat. This is why this taqueria was her favorite, she said, because of all the memories the three of us shared here.

"I've never been to this place with papá," I said. "That was you."

"Was it?" Serena asked.

"We had different childhoods. I had rules," I said. "Then our parents got old and you got free rent."

"You're blaming me for when they had sex?" Serena asked.

Her blasé attitude infuriated me. "Mamá said you could help. Can you or not?"

"She's the one that got fired. Not you. No job means she'll have more time to babysit for you. Why do you care so much about mamá working all of a sudden?"

I was resolute about not revealing my insecurities to anyone, especially my sister. I tried not to connect the separation, the wall, losing Melanie at One-Shop, my own curbside detainment, the wall, the endless stares and questions about my identity, along with the accompanying questions I asked myself about who *I* am, the wall the wall the wall, while learning my ex-husband sneaked off to be a midnight bigot. Yet these events were a string of continuous waves that kept knocking me off balance, pushing me farther into the surf. How many more secrets could I carry until they were visible?

"Tell me how you can get the bands," I said.

"For mamá or you? Because mamá doesn't want one."

"How do you know?" I asked. "She just told me she had to work."

"She babysat some mocoso when we used to live at the old house. That guy cuts a huge discount for people he knows. But mamá found out how much they cost, even with the discount, and said no. 'No, no, muy caro, y no quiero meterme en un desmadre.'"

"So she hasn't changed her mind," I said.

"She's already going crazy sitting at home with Papá, but I can't force her. She thinks it's too expensive. But not you, I bet," Serena said. "No way you can keep your North Az job without a band. Not with that pendejo Eric, who thinks he's at La Línea. I know that fool's band's a fake. Nobody who listens to that much narco music has a parent that was born here."

"Don't you want a band?" I asked.

"Nobody in the shops on this side of town scans. My boss doesn't. The shop owners have to pay that cost themselves. Besides, I do my business every day without needing a band or a word of English. I'm not branding myself to make other people feel better about who I am. Okay, so maybe they'll come here eventually and when they do, I'll figure it out. Until then, fuck 'em."

"You can't live off of your part-time job in that house without mamá's income. And she doesn't have enough saved up to cover the mortgage," I said.

Serena stopped eating. "She told you that?"

"One month, tops. If she doesn't work," I said, "mamá and papá lose the house. You won't have any place to live."

"You just bought a house, so we could come live with you. I'm sure you'd let us do that, right?"

I thought about the wall and deflected. "You've had an open invite for months, but have never stopped by."

"I know you don't want us there," Serena said.

"Stop saying 'us,' " I said.

"So mamá and papá would be okay, but I could be out on the street?"

I watched trucks park, listened to their hydraulics exhale. "Tell me where the bands are, okay? Don't lord it over me. I'm trying to help. I could buy one for mamá without her knowing." *And one for me, too.*

Serena nodded. "There's a ninety-nine-cent store on East Gerkins," she said. Then she explained the process: the bands were sold in the back, by the bathrooms. Black-market bands popped up the day after the vote, but when los nacos saw how desperate people were to get them, the price skyrocketed. She didn't have an exact cost, but knew they were (a) super expensive and (b) my mamá's friend couldn't give me a discount.

"But I don't understand why you're trying to help mamá now," Serena said.

"What does that mean?"

"You and Alex voted for this shit, didn't you?"

It wasn't about me, I thought. *The bands were never supposed to be about me.*

Serena asked, "Can you at least explain your vote to yourself?"

When people spoke about "the vote" afterward, they did so with quote marks, a demarcation zone, extinction-level event the way grandparents said "Kennedy" or parents said "Nine-Eleven."

But the day didn't start out feeling that way. The morning I'd voted had felt insignificant. It was warm, sunny, and bright, like every day here. The path from my car to the voting booth inside the condominium complex's community room was about a thousand feet of bright, synthetic, insect-free grass, duck ponds and fountains, and faux cobblestone that felt springy but pleasing under my feet. I waited in line—the one person of color there—with güeros, who nodded at me and smiled. I didn't feel, as I often did, as if I was being evaluated.

When I cast my vote on the flimsy plastic touch screen, it was as easy as buying a diet soda at the movie theater, a brief moment of decision buoyed by the weight of my desire to be American, coupled with the moments I was denied my Americanness by voices that told me, *You'd belong here if you paled up* or *If only your accent lost a touch of that stretchy lilt.* Now here at last was a way that my identity and indeterminate brown complexion could be overlooked, and overcome, with a piece of bright plastic worn around my wrist. How simple, how perfectly American, and why wouldn't I want that, let alone *vote* for it? How democratic! I voted "YES," I want bands, I want this plastic signifier, I want to be proud of being an American, because I *believe*—I *am*—an American, and doesn't faith triumph in America, over love, understanding, and even peace?

I thought this, but couldn't explain it to Serena. This was the longest one-on-one conversation we'd had in a long time, but I didn't feel I could sustain the tennis match back-and-forth any longer. Arguing with my sister was like speaking to a faster, more opinionated, less informed version of me.

"I don't know how Alex voted," I said. "But I'm tired of having the same conversations over and over."

"Me too," Serena said. "That's family."

"I should get back to work."

"You can waste your money," Serena said, "or you can say, 'Fuck 'em,' too. Don't want to be trapped? Fuck the bands."

"Or maybe," I said, "things will change again. Maybe the bands will be recalled. Maybe they'll throw the vote out and things will go back to the way they were. Maybe they'll change their minds."

"This is your last chance," Serena said.

"What will it take?" I asked. "What could change their minds?"

Serena said, "Waking up us."

Fifteen

I withdrew five hundred dollars from my bank's ATM for several consecutive days. The machines, unlike the human tellers inside, allowed a customer to opt out of using a band for withdrawals via an extremely inconvenient and time-consuming captcha process. Taking out the entirety of Melanie's emergency savings funds (which I *would* pay back) didn't make me broke, but my dwindled account balance could now see broke-ness around the corner.

I was detained three additional times for not wearing a band: once, walking away from the ATM by a too-friendly bike patrol downtown; then in a supermarket parking lot when I made a night trip for Pepto Bismol and had to explain my bouncy jig as a "crabby stomach"; and, last, a terse encounter outside a tiendita.

"Don't come around here if you don't have to," an officer said. "People don't like being confused."

My first detainment felt like a significant event, but then I got the hang of it. Each subsequent one felt somewhat anticlimactic, seemed to rankle me a little bit less than the one prior, to the point I expected detainment whenever I saw a police officer and began involuntarily rolling up my sleeves (I still wore them in public, though they didn't help) and gestured my arm up in the air from twenty feet away, like a referee that had witnessed a foul. It wasn't harassment if I wasn't following the rules. This was simply the cost of not having a band.

It took four days of ATM withdrawals to collect what I thought would be enough money to buy Mamá's and my bands. The Dollar

Central store was at the tail end of a gentrifying downtown street that stopped at the fancy pasteles-slash-record store, cut off by East Gerkins, where a string of tienditas with tinted windows and dusty awnings sold knockoff Adidas and Nike gear. It was one of five vintage storefronts that wasn't destroyed in an earthquake years ago. Dolores used to bring me here for school supplies when it was a national five-and-dime chain. Then, it was a special occasion store for me. I would race to aisle five and stock up on plastic binders, multicolored folders, and "college-ruled paper, mamá, because I'm going to college!" There was a soda fountain, an ice cream machine, and a lunch counter with stools I sat on and spun, my swinging feet close to but never touching the floor.

One day, the lunch counter, the stools, and the ice cream and soda machines were gone, the five-and-dime's signage was removed, its sun-bleached letters left behind in a faint outline on the roof awning, and Dollar Central took its place. The linoleum floor puckered until it bled an unsavory sludge of greasy residual cleaning fluids, and the store smelled like a vinegar that went bad. I cried when Dolores dragged me by the wrist into the store and pouted when she bought my sixth-grade clothes there, too.

"I hate this place!" I screamed. "Everyone here is on welfare!"

That familiar stench hit me about ten steps from the front door, the acrid exterior eye-watering tang of a building drenched in urine, surrounded by an atoll of garbage mounds.

There were more white people inside the store than I remembered. Many of them had tattoos, and two were working as cashiers, each checking out long lines of customers, their shoulders slumped, fists gripped around taut purse straps, baseball caps slung off in frustration. Merchandise scanners panged a slow-drip beep, but there were—*impossible!*—no band scanners installed. Kids screamed and melted down, something I would normally attribute to distracted parents on their cell phones, but the cashiers were moving slow enough that their lack of motion looked like a special effect.

All I need is a band, I thought, *and I'll never have to come in here again.*

A grid of anemic overhead lights somehow dimmed the store. Freezers contained rows of single-tray meals with the same brands and color schemes I remembered from my elementary school friends' fridges, easy-to-make food for kids left home alone. The horrible linoleum was gone, peeled away to the gray concrete floor underneath. In a designated kids' section were neat stacks of children's shirts and jeans on clean metal shelves. I pretended not to skim for potential outfits and bargains. Delicate kids' shirts had iron-on decals of whales and dolphins. *Actually, that would be cute for Mel.*

It took two circuits before I saw, next to the fifty-cents-or-less markdown aisles, a doorway to a corridor blocked off by a stack of cardboard boxes. A prieto without a band slid the boxes over, passed through, then slid them back in place. In the corridor were three doors, two of which were restroom doors covered with zigzagging red and blue tape. The third door had a cardboard sign: ANILLOS.

Was I breaking the law, walking through this door?

It was a large windowless room that contained the store from my memory. The linoleum was scuffed with tar marks and in a corner were dirt rings where the lunch counter stools used to be. Water stains spider-webbed across chipped ceiling tiles, then down onto fake wood paneling. There was an overwhelming stench of citrus room freshener. My nostalgia hadn't softened my impression of this place. I longed for nothing that used to be here and wanted to run straight out of this room and back into what my life had been. Except that life wouldn't be out there without a band.

Cardboard boxes overflowing with bands in plastic baggies were stacked in a far corner. Next to them was a scanning machine with its insides exposed. A man dangled a band with tweezers over the machine until it beeped, then dropped it in a plastic bag. Someone's number was called. A hunched ruco snapped a band around a young boy's wrist, then walked him hand in hand out of the room. An armed security guard stood in the corner, scrolling on his phone. Things appeared organized and efficient.

"Hola, hello," a woman holding a hand screen said. "Are you buying or selling?"

"Buying," I said. "I have some questions about how they work."

"Sure," she said. "Grab a band from that box in the corner, then wait for us to call your number. Shouldn't be long."

"Any band?" I asked.

"Yeah, just grab one. You can't do anything with it anyway until we turn 'em on."

I fingered the band in its pouch like a contraceptive, then stuffed it in my purse, as if it was worth anything inactivated. I unfolded a chair from a neat pile and set it near an empty corner. I enjoyed waiting, and was better equipped to wait than anyone I knew. It had never been an annoyance for me. Waiting forestalled inevitable confrontations.

I wanted to text Serena a last-minute question—*This seems sketchy*—but didn't want my sister to call me a rule-following coward. I knew I was tougher than she gave me credit for. I fingered my envelope of cash to remind myself it was there, and where I was, in the back room of a dollar store, waiting to purchase black-market identification. It seemed inconceivable a short time ago that I would be here, in a position where I felt I had no alternative but to break the law. Or, as I saw it, bend a new law just a bit. I reminded myself that, though I would directly benefit when I got my band, I was doing this for my mamá, and for Mel. It *had* to be for Mel.

Part of me toyed with mentioning this purchase, this whole back-room operation, to Alex, to see if he would at last break his cover and acknowledge what he was doing with his early mornings. What would outrage him more: An illicit band ring in his former in-laws' neighborhood, or his ex-wife getting a black-market band of her own? Perhaps that would be the catalyst for him to stop telling Mel we were reconciling. I could be objective and acknowledge that Alex's nocturnal activities were part of the reason I was here. He was, in fact, succeeding at something he believed in. It hurt, but I was less outraged by his promoting hatred—and it must be *promoting* rather than *believing*—than the fact he did it in secret.

My God, I thought, *how sick is that? Why was I still making excuses for him?*

There was no feeling of desperation or rock-bottom-ness here. Instead, things felt procedural, like waiting at the DMV I wondered, *Are they here for the same reason I am?* I had trouble stereotyping who they were outside this room—their reasons for getting the bands—a skill I once valued to keep me safe, but that had evaporated. I thought I would be in the company of TV-style drug dealers in wifebeaters wearing sagging pants and flip-flops. But these people were adults in business slacks and designer sweats. Children absorbed in their phones. Every skin color was represented here. How many of them were like me, walking around in fear for days, weeks, sleepless, uncertain, paranoid? What was their breaking point? What gave them away to others? Their arched, thick eyebrows? The wideness of their eyes or noses? Did they stand out next to their Anglo husbands and wives, some of whom were here, holding their partners' hands? I knew the stakes to get a band even if my sister didn't. My sense of reality was the biggest thing I could lose. What else was left but my own dignity?

A young man my skin color named Jim called my number and sat me at his desk. A plastic screen was tethered to his waist. He was dressed in a collared, untucked blue denim shirt with tan slacks. Jim could have been selling me a cell phone.

"¿Qué necesita, señora?" *What to be offended by first—him thinking I only spoke Spanish or that I was an abuela?*

"I'm not that old," I said. "I speak English."

"Great, me too. What do you want today?" His fingers performed a rhythmic tapping on his screen that didn't break stride.

"I need a band," I blurted out. I felt an overwhelming sense of relief, saying it aloud where I wouldn't be judged. "I didn't think it would be this easy."

"We go where the people are," Jim said.

"I used to shop here as a kid," I said, my nostalgia now loosening me up. I was doing something illicit, a shade dangerous. How easily I could talk with criminals! Serena thought *I* was the uptight one?

"Isn't that something," Jim said, his fingers never breaking stride. "This location's the only one that's a literal back room. I was telling a colleague the other day, 'Why don't I go to our location out by the beach and you come to West V and work in a back room?' A space with some windows would be nice."

"You'd be worried about somebody seeing, I suppose."

"That's giving people a lot of credit."

He punched more buttons on his screen. "We're almost done," he said. The experience, no matter how I tried to inflate it, was banal, akin to when I bought an extension on my service contract for my phone.

"So these bands really work?" I asked.

"Nobody would be here if they didn't," Jim said. "Which kind do you want?"

"I thought there was only one."

"There is through the state," he said, and punched more buttons on his screen, "but here you can get a blank slate with the utility company, the cops, wherever you need a reset."

"I guess a fresh start would be nice if you're in trouble," I said, attempting my best version of back-room small talk.

"Wipes are overrated. People have lost their minds," he said. "But 'never waste a good crisis.'"

"I don't have problems with anybody," I said.

"That's fine. You change your mind, those upgraded bands are worth the extra five thousand."

Five thousand? I held in my breath.

Jim stopped typing, and sensed my body stiffen. "It's ten thousand for the basic band, another five for an alternate ID. You can shop around, but we're on the low end."

"Yes, I knew that," I said, uncomfortable with demonstrating ignorance even in a black-market storeroom. I was several thousand dollars short. Briefly, I entertained taking a massive cash advance against my credit card limit, but I still wouldn't have enough. Was I getting ripped off? How could I "shop around" for a black-market item?

Hearing the band's cost shifted something inside me. I couldn't afford one for Dolores, let alone for both of us. No wonder my mamá couldn't rationalize the cost, regardless of whatever discount she could get. Ten thousand dollars for, what, exactly? A disposable piece of plastic that might not work or could be obsolete in a month or two?

"I understand," I said. "Thanks for your time."

The relief of not having to spend a large amount of money to make an illegal purchase was overwhelmed by not seeing what the next step on my path was. Walking out, I had no backup plan, and that terrified me. I wondered if Mel realized how valuable the band she twirled everyday around her wrist was. How had she not lost it?

Then I remembered the band in my purse. I was about to turn around and return it, when I weighed its lightness in my hands. If only I could activate this band somehow. Or trade it with someone with a working band.

What if I traded this band with Mel's?

It was a horrible, unacceptable thought. I spun my mind for a loophole. I thought of those safety videos on planes where, in an emergency, you're instructed to put on your oxygen mask before helping others. I'd watched those videos while nervously gripping my armrests and said, "I'd never put my mask on first before Mel. I don't care what the videos say." Alex replied, "How can you help Melanie if you're passed out?"

How can I help? I thought.

I held up a kids' shirt with appliqué stars and a poorly sewn-on baby elephant. The same two cashiers scanned items for the same two lines of customers.

"I can't wait," I said.

Sixteen

When I picked Melanie up from school, she unzipped her bag. "I did this for you."

On a handmade card, Melanie had drawn a big planet Earth decorated with pine trees that reached the sky and, around its equator, a large gold band, capped with a bow.

"You drew this by yourself?"

"We took, um, suggestions," Mel said. "Principal Jessica said we should put a band around the Earth."

"It's very nice," I said.

"Yes, I think so, too," Mel said. "Mommy, do you still hate the planet?" She waved her hands around on her screen, the band on her wrist like a glowing dot that bounced over the words from children's sing-alongs. The glow was distracting, a weight I could feel from the rearview mirror.

"Not today," I said.

"So you're getting a band, too?" Melanie asked.

The un-activated band was in my pocket. There was no need for a complicated heist. I ran through various scenarios: asking for it at the park before Mel went on the swings or running through the water fountains, or insisting I hold on to it while she played in the sandbox, then a furtive glance at Mel while I switched her band with mine. Or a swap after Mel went to sleep would do it, then a shocked discovery in the morning that Mel's band had stopped working. I could pass with Mel's lighted band for a few days and, while they canceled and reset Mel's old band, maybe I could find a cheaper fake band elsewhere. It wasn't a permanent solution, but could buy me some time. That's what I needed now—just a little more time to figure out a new life.

Of course, if I asked Melanie for her band, she would give it to me, though not until finishing an epic-length question and answer session. *But what kind of mother did I think I was?* There was no way to view my actions in any way other than black or white, right or wrong. I wanted to feel as little duplicity as possible, but I didn't want to lose my job and my ability to support my family. I wanted release from the pressure of being observed, scrutinized, and surveilled. I did not want to run back to Alex. I wanted to feel like a whole person again, a whole mother to Melanie. These were the reasons I told myself I was doing this.

"Soon, I promise," I said, voice cracking. I ran every rationalization for borrowing—no, *stealing*—my daughter's identity. They pinged back hollow, coarse, self-serving.

We arrived home. Melanie collected her butcher paper maps and ran inside, completely unfazed by the blinding sun's reflection off the wall. I sat in the car, the wall's steel bars casting shadows on my face. I felt disgusting and sleazy, and slammed my fists against the steering wheel.

In the rearview, I saw glimmers of sunlight amid the undulating leaves of a tree. A calm came over me. *You're doing this for Mel.*

When she was asleep, I unplugged Mel's band from its charging station, then connected my dummy, un-activated band to the power cord on her nightstand. I wondered if it would beep, blink a hostile flashing red sequence, or do something to betray its status. Instead, it lit up a sickly gray that ran in a circle, as if searching for a connection.

I clasped Melanie's band around my wrist. It seemed to contract, as if tightening on its own, then I found the adjustable band loop and loosened it a notch. The band glowed gold. My relief was an immense rush of anxiety-dissolving endorphins, and my body shivered in a long exhalation.

I waved the band left to right in the bay window's reflection, watching it trail light through the dark, in the shadow of the wall. It looked like another arm was outside, its luminescent glow mimicking my movements and reflecting off the wall's shiny bollards.

I stopped waving my arm. The reflection took a second or two longer to stop its movements. My sense of touch and balance left me, and I leaned on the cool kitchen counter for support.

I couldn't see the band reflected in the window anymore. It was gone.

A sunrise drip fleshed out the shapes in my bedroom. The band charged on my nightstand, its circle of light continuously swirling in a ring while I stroked its plastic rim. I couldn't get back to sleep. Too much of a giddy "first day of school" feeling, but more comforting, familiar. I could keep my job. I could get my old life back.

I was headed into a new and unfamiliar situation—back to the way things were before. Before the bands. Before the election. This time, I could learn to live my life better. I could read Mel a book one grade above her level each night, build a kite with her and fly it on an endless beach, download an app to teach her chess, and have her explain what was on her dozens of butcher paper maps that I hadn't bothered to look at until now.

I would change all of this. Once the bands were gone, I would salvage the hours I thought gone.

Through the bay window, the wall hadn't changed, but I could see more of the morning peeking over its top and through its slats. There was a confidence surging inside me, the way you feel when a song from your youth catches you by surprise in a grocery store or a commercial. If I blinked, I could imagine the wall gone, my view restored, my life back to normal.

I clasped Melanie's band around my wrist. It pulsed an amber-ish gold. My beautiful new day was here. Again.

"Mommy, you got it!" Melanie said, running down the hall. "Thank you!"

"Why are you thanking me?" I asked, hugging her. "Come on, you're running late."

"Mommy, mine's not gold anymore, see?" I checked Mel's wrist, and felt the crevice in Melanie's skin where the band left an indentation and a tan line. "It's blank. It's not any color," she said.

I was careful about what to say. I didn't want to trick Melanie into thinking she broke it, but didn't want a long interrogative back-and-forth, either.

"Honey, have they scanned your band at school?"

"No, but Principal Jessica says—"

"Mommy can talk to Principal Jessica, okay? If there's a problem, they can call me and I'll handle it for you."

"We're a team!" Mel said. I winced when she said this.

"Okay, let's get the go," I said.

I thought I would be nervous, disoriented, about slipping back into my routine after working from home. Instead, I was overwhelmed with a flurry of nostalgic senses and sights that felt comforting. I strode past Eric, making sure my band was at his eye level, then flung open his push-button barrier without waiting for him to clear me through. It was empowering, until I heard the loud clang and echo of the emergency back-door staircase I used to sneak up and I had to double-check that the band was functional.

Karina's things weren't in her officle. Nobody had seen her that day or could remember the last time they had. She probably was moved to another section, or had she been assigned to work-at-home status, too? Searching for her I became aware that unlike other similar bands I wore that tracked my sleep or physical movement, I was always conscious and aware that Mel's band was squatting on my wrist. Its trivial weight never disappeared.

Alex called me before noon. It was unexpected to hear from him while I was at work. When I started this job, he used to drop off veggie sandwiches for me at lunchtime with a note asking for a date after work. Back then, I couldn't wait to feel nostalgic about my husband. That was a long time ago.

Now I panicked, thinking Mel had already been found out.

They couldn't scan her band at school and contacted Alex first because *of course they would.*

"My parents are going out for drinks tonight," he said. "I know it's last minute, but Gonzalo said they could watch Mel. That is, if you'd like to come."

"You're asking me out," I said, a statement. I hadn't confronted him since I saw him hobbling from house to house in the dark, making his bigoted Easter Bunny rounds. I couldn't erase that image of him, so pathetic, so lost, from my head.

"My dad suggested this new wine bar in North Azulia," he said. "I told him I'd check with you." The thought of drinking with these three was nauseating, but I wanted to keep things civil between us.

"Okay, I'll be there," I said.

"Really?" he asked. "They're doing some special promotion tonight. Show the band, get half off your first drink."

"That's fine," I said. "My band's activated. Turns out the website was wrong about what you needed to get it turned on."

"What did you need to do?"

"Does it matter?" I asked.

"No, I was just wondering what we missed. Maybe we can get dinner with my parents after."

"Are you fine spending this much time with your father?" I asked.

"It's better. I have to put more effort into, I don't know, listening. I'm trying."

"That would be good for you," I said. "And Melanie, too."

"I'm still his son," he said. "You can't change family, right?"

"Serena says the same thing. Actually, I think she said you can't change who's your family. But you can change what you tell them about yourself and who you really are. Do you think that's right?"

What was right was Alex simply telling me who he really was. To explain why he was driving around at night planting hate messages and why he had drifted out so far from me and his child. I didn't want to reveal that I had to spy on him to learn this whole other side of him that I never knew existed after so many years of marriage. When had that chasm opened up? I wanted my ex-husband to reveal this hidden side of himself to me properly. I would reward him with kindness and compassion if he told me the truth.

Alex said, "I'll let you get back to things."

I hung up.

After work, I waved to Eric with a healthy "See you tomorrow!" and pushed his security arm so hard it misaligned from its swing hinge. I called Dolores en route to the wine bar and asked for Mel.

"How was school today?" I asked.

"Boring," Melanie said. "We had to make more Earth cards."

"Did anything else happen?" I asked. "Anyone ask about your band?"

"Yeah, they checked it."

"Who did?"

"It couldn't scan," Mel said. "They asked me a couple questions and after a while they stopped."

What questions had they asked her? It didn't matter what Mel's answers were because the more information she gave me, the more anxious I would grow. I tried to ignore the expanding brick in my throat and forced myself to breathe.

I said, "If it's broken, I'll fix it, okay? That's what mommies do. Mommy will be very happy to see you when she gets home."

"Good. I like happy Mommy. I gotta get the go," Melanie said.

The wine bar was a midway point on a manufactured "Italian" citywalk promenade whose cobblestone pavers were, per a factoid sign, made from a high-grade recycled composite plastic that absorbed footfalls. I loved wine bars because I appreciated their officious camaraderie. They were my secret getaway spots in the last year of my marriage. Dolores watched Mel for me, and I would sit with a glass of Barolo, read a book for an hour, and *simply be left the fuck alone*.

I wanted a muscle-relaxing, memory-evaporating buzz tonight. I didn't want any awkwardness with Alex's parents, wasn't eager to take the bait in any of their attempts to engage me in current events, or what was happening in my life. I imagined I was a better kind of person now after everything that had happened to me in the past months, a stronger mother who would speak up when someone said or did something wrong.

Then I remembered I had my daughter's stolen band around my wrist, felt it seize and tighten.

Inside the wine bar was a long zinc counter, velvet stools, Fellini movie posters, and tiny porcelain dual chamber bowls for olives and olive pits. Alex and his parents waved me over, their wrists bandless. Kevin, who had three empty wineglasses in front of him, hugged me. His gentle physical contact stunned me. I asked the bartender for a glass of their driest white. He leaned behind the counter for a band-scanning gun. I arched my wrist for him to reach my band.

"Hey, no," Kevin said. "She's way over twenty-one. She's with us."

The bartender apologized to Kevin. There was no menu signage about specials for band wearers, but I didn't ask Alex, who appeared relaxed and tried to rub my shoulders until I grabbed his hands and set them on the bar. I didn't feel as if an interrogation was imminent from Alex's parents, other customers, the bartender, or anyone, really. I felt I was, at last, a part of the crowd. I was back to being a blend-in person, a stock photo inside an unsold picture frame. It was perfect. I almost felt a part of Alex's family, an invitation I now didn't need to fear would be revoked because their acceptance wasn't important to me anymore. The band had made my invisibility possible again.

We adjourned to a four-top table next to a large window. The conversation was lively, spirited, akin to a major celebration, as if I had finished a marathon and they were reveling in my exhaustion.

"We're happy you two worked everything out," Kevin said.

Alex's head was buried in his phone and he either didn't hear his father or ignored him. *So that's what this was about.*

Alex couldn't see how badly I wanted to annihilate him, but before I could conjure an excuse to leave—or flag a waitress for a bottle to go—an African American man in a heavy down jacket and soccer shin pads shuffled up to our window on the street outside. The man shouted and pointed at our table, tapping the glass with his fingers. Kevin made eye contact.

"You're encouraging him," Cynthia said to Kevin.

Kevin stared back with a pained earnestness that communicated fear. His face flushed and his hands trembled, as if he would be ripped through the glass if he turned away. When the man stumbled off, Kevin coughed out a fake desperate laugh. "My taxes at work," he said.

We curdled into an awkward, tense silence, broken by each of us round-robin checking, then pocketing, our phones. Alex texted me, *I can explain.*

I excused myself to the bathroom, undid the band, and set it on the wet sink to wash my hands, then strapped it back on.

The gold light flickered, then died. I had set the band in a large puddle of water I didn't see.

I tapped the band with my fingers, shaking it like a stopped watch. I held my breath, trying to maintain a steely resolve, imagining myself a heroine from a slasher movie, the last survivor trying to stay calm while she's unable to start the getaway car with the oh-my-God-it's-flooded engine.

"Come on," I said, tapping the band. "You're fine. Don't be stupid. This is real. Please."

The band smoldered out a meek amber ring of light. A faint pulse. Then, life.

———

I left Alex at the wine bar. Walked out of the bathroom, past him and his parents staring at me with bemused expressions, down the soundless fake cobblestone street, unconcerned if Alex was chasing after me (he wasn't) and straight to pick up Mel. I was so angry with Alex that seeing the wall creep into view didn't faze me. I was relieved I wouldn't have to think about Alex again. Any lingering feelings I had for him were extinguished.

The next evening, Alex was standing by my car after work, holding Mel's hand. He was becoming the worst ex-husband, there when I least needed him.

"Daddy got me from school!" she said. "He met all my teachers."

Incredible—still a better divorced father than a day-to-day one.

"Mel, wait for me in Mommy's car, okay?" I said. When she was inside, I said, "Alex, it's not your day. And I don't want to see you unless it's your day."

Alex looked me over and smiled. "I'm proud of you," he said.

The bastard was *smiling* at me. It was the first time I had seen him genuinely happy in who knows how long, as if he were a teacher who taught me a lesson that had only now dawned on me. If my complete and utter detachment from him was what it took for him to at last find his happiness, I wish it hadn't required sacrificing so much of myself. I shivered and wondered who this stranger standing here was and how much was actually left of me.

"Where did you get your band?" he asked. "I know the rules. There's no loophole. If there were, I'd have found it for you. Did Serena hook you up?"

"Why, so you can turn me in to your midnight neighborhood weenie watch buddies?"

Alex nodded, or shook his head no. I couldn't tell which. "I'd have gotten you one where I got mine."

"What the hell does that mean?" I asked.

"I want to ask you something," he said. "But not here."

"I have nothing to say to you," I said. "Mel and I are going home."

"It won't take long," Alex said. "Follow me in the car. You'll like this place. Hear me out, then you and Mel can go. Okay?"

I sighed and got in my car. We drove in tandem to a gardening shop in North Azulia that I had never seen despite it being no more than a ten-minute drive from my house. Birdbaths and rock water fountains funneled into a tributary that ran into shallow wishing ponds. Lemon and fig trees shed and flickered sunlight off their leaves in the breeze. Stone obelisks, chrome pinwheels, and decorative glass orbs were set next to stone and small metal benches to sit on, like what you'd see at a child's grave.

Alex and I walked across a footbridge. I let Mel run up ahead on a gravel path. "Mel misses home," Alex said. "She misses us."

"I don't miss you," I said, and meant it. "What are we doing here?"

"Kevin came here illegally. My mom, too. All our bands are fake." I understood this information should land as a massive betrayal, a "gotcha" moment. Now it felt like a puny afterthought.

"That means nothing to me," I said. "They're your parents, not mine. Mine were honest about who they were and they're in real trouble. I'm sorry, but I really don't care about who your parents are or what happens to them. I'm sure you all have top-of-the-line fake bands, so everything will work out."

"I want it to work out for us, too," Alex said. "We love our daughter. It's the right thing for her. Neither of us want to raise Mel as a child of divorce."

"I can't be the wife you need," I said. "And you're not the husband I want. We'd need so much marriage counseling, separate therapists. And I can't be with someone who terrorizes people under cover of darkness like a coward."

"Say the word," Alex said. "If you two come back, everything stops and we work on our marriage together."

"I don't believe you," I said. "You're too far gone."

Alex said, "We're the best version of parents Mel needs when we're together. Mel needs us together. You don't want Mel to grow up like me. Come back."

I wanted to say, *Fuck you.* I watched Mel play in a peaceful oasis.

What I said was "Let me think about it." *What the hell was wrong with me?*

Alex hugged me, then kissed Mel goodbye and left.

A strong gust ran through the wind chimes. Sunlight cast shadows on one of the stone benches, and in a flicker, Brenda was there, watching me.

"Look at you now! Fun!" she said.

The pinwheels rustled and shook. Brenda was gone. I looked
again and saw Mel running to me.

"Mommy," Mel said. "Can we go home now?"

"Sure," I said.

"I mean, our real home?"

"We'll see," I said.

I thought about Alex's offer on the drive back. Because that's
what it felt like: a proposition, not a declaration of undying love.
Despite the gulf between us, I knew we still ordered and framed
our worlds the same way, by pairing lessons and logic with punitiveness and punishment. It was what we both felt a child needed
to become a healthy, independent adult. It was what I had always
felt was best for Mel, because it was the way Dolores had raised
me and I thought I had turned out well. But I sure didn't feel like
a resilient mother now, and was less certain at this moment if this
was who I still wanted to be. Everything felt clearer, but also more
confusing.

Mel was asleep when we drove up to our house.

The wall was gone.

I stared, incredulous, then called Alex.

"Okay," I whispered. "Let's give this a try."

Seventeen

That night at sunset, I felt around where the wall had once stood, my arms out in front of me as if I were searching for a light switch. Tamped the dirt down where it had grown, my bare toes digging into the grass that died in its shadow and the soil that had seemingly swallowed it up. I inspected every inch of the property, including the berm of dirt that had outraged my neighbors and hadn't been moved. I walked on the pathway that the wall had intersected— back, forth, back, forth—and half expected at any moment to run headlong into an invisible barrier that would smack me on my ass. I kept seeing a black impression, a blinding negative, where the wall once was but was not any longer.

Mel said, "It's not gone. It's hiding."

The wall *had* gone. Where?

I stared from my bay window late into the night, as if waiting for a delinquent teen who'd stayed out past curfew. It didn't come back.

The next morning, I knew right when I woke up it hadn't returned. The house was drowned in sunshine and an incredible warmth. I needed socks to walk across the baking floors.

I sat in the kitchen, staring out my glorious picture window at a beautiful, gleaming white sunrise, its sinewy light and heat flooding the house, waiting until Mel got up.

"Come here," I said, and pointed. "Mira. It's still gone."

"Does this mean we're going home?" she asked.

"Maybe," I said. "But first, school."

I tried not to feel as if I was surrendering one dream to sleep-walk through another. I was doing this for Mel.

I arrived at work still shrugging off a dream. There was a note attached to my computer terminal. I was being reassigned to another office, K-17, and would need to work late. I texted Alex to pick up Melanie after school. He said, "As you wish." I had *just* forgotten his dumb pop culture references.

I never memorized my location by number, and it took several circuits of the "bullpen" before discovering K-17 was, in fact, Karina's space. It was stripped bare except for Karina's mortarboard, which I found behind a cardboard box filled with power strips and extension cords. Its hand-decorated sequins that spelled out the words *Orgulloso nopal en la frente* flaked off and fell on the floor when I touched them.

I asked several coworkers in close proximity where Karina was. *Do you mean Irena? She was fired. About time, too.*

I've never met anyone by that name.

Sorry, I thought you were Karina.

I was, of course, not Karina. I had plopped Karina's mortarboard like a paperweight on my new desk, and stared at it while I waited for my computer to update. *Orgulloso nopal en la frente.* Cactus on the forehead, or as Serena translated it: someone who looks so Mexican they have a damn cactus growing on her forehead. But it's also someone who hates herself and her race so much she wants to assimilate into nothingness.

Someone like you, Inés, I heard a voice say. But whose voice? Serena's? Brenda's? My own?

I rubbed Mel's plastic band around my wrist so intensely my fingertips smelled vaguely of fish oil. I would give this band back in a heartbeat if things could just go back to the way they were. Before the bands. Before the wall. Before I fell out of love with Alex. That's all I wanted. I didn't believe in the power of prayer, but as I sat there listening to my computer's fans whir through various cycles of grinding noise, I asked, *Please, let me go back home.*

At 5:01 p.m., employees left their workstations in a rash of snapped power switches and incensed sighing. I could see the building exhale its workers into a gauzy, objects-are-farther-away-than-they-appear dusk. Their backs were humped over, their shoulders hunched, their hands a tremble from carpal tunnel, symptoms present in my own body, too.

I held Karina's mortarboard, then slid it into a desk drawer. *I know who I am.* My band's face clinked my desk.

My phone vibrated walking to my car. Several times in succession, a packet of texts and messages delivered at once. Before I could check them, I picked up Alex's call.

"I need you to come home right now, please," he said, his voice a sprained-toe panic.

"Which home?" I asked. "What happened?"

"Mel's been detained."

I remember thinking, before his explanation faded into a buzzing hum, how odd that he used the word "please." It was polite, deferential, as if Alex had a gentle surprise waiting for me. That was the last thing I registered before I felt myself empty out, as if my soul broke free and exited my body, whose physical shell retained the muscle memory to drive back to my home. The one I had made with Mel. The one tether to reality I had was the plastic band, which I tapped on the steering wheel, its gold "on" light a steady beam as a bauxite dusk faded.

When I turned onto the street, my house was behind a sixty-foot-high bollard wall.

Its rusty poles vibrated a hideous nails-on-chalkboard screech when the wind hit them right. As I walked aside the wall, I could see the motion of bodies moving, falling, and running. Body parts, severed limbs, screaming faces were flash-baked into its scaly metal surface, captured in midair, reaching up, reaching *out*. Scattered atop the wall, colored glass shards and a tinsel of galvanized double barbed wire. At the base, monolithic black flagstone slabs.

I slid my hands up the gritty slats and, arms raised above my head, touched the cool metal bollards. I slapped one hand against them, then slammed the other, harder. Shards of broken glass rolled off the top of the wall and shattered by my feet. My hands found a cacophonous rhythm, slapping the wall until my hands bled.

I screamed as the blood trickled down the rusty slats and sprayed the ground in dewy flecks.

Palm trees bristled moonlight off their waxy leaves. I saw the flutter of blinds and curtains from my distant neighbors' windows and knew I was being observed with varying degrees of curiosity and fear.

Something brushed my feet. Leaving bloody handprints on the wall, I picked up Mel's Tigger and Snoopy chanclas. I could smell my daughter on them.

I tried turning the porch light on, leaving a blood smear on the switch. No power. No water, either. All the utilities were shut off.

Alex had forwarded the voicemail Principal Jessica had left on his phone. I listened to her in the darkness reciting the details of Mel's detainment with feigned concern. Alex was ten minutes late picking Melanie up from after-care, where, somehow, she was able to wander away and was picked up by a police cruiser. The police officer scanned her band, which came back dead. Instead of returning her to school, she was taken to the police station where, upon a second scanning, the inoperative band read as fraudulent hardware. Melanie was then remanded over to a separate holding facility for a violation of illicitly using state services. The school couldn't offer any additional information as to Melanie's whereabouts, but Alex would be contacted by the state authorities within seventy-two hours with further information.

"Unfortunately, you weren't at the designated pickup point at the appointed time, and your daughter didn't have a function-ing band," Principal Jessica told Alex. "I'm afraid our responsibility ends here."

When I finished the message, I slid Mel's stuffed toy and chan-clas across my dining room table, a smear of blood and skin ribbons behind them. Granules of wall rust peppered my blood trail and made a prickly sound as it crinkled across the table.

I was only a few minutes late, he texted. *I swear. Been trying the app for hours, but it's down.*

"Even when you need to apologize," I said to no one, "you can't say the words."

Listen, he texted. My cell phone glowed with his stream of excuses. I flipped the screen over, casting the house in darkness, and gave myself one hour to cry.

I cried for an hour. Then I started dialing.

Eighteen

My 911 call was no more than a minute or two.

"My nine-year-old daughter is missing," I said to the operator. "I need your help."

"Okay, let me collect some information and we'll send someone over," a voice said.

I relayed the information from Principal Jessica's voicemail in a clear, straightforward way, as if accounting for a missing delivery at work. *Be clear, be unemotional,* I thought, *and you will get help faster. Follow the rules.*

"I'm sorry, ma'am," the voice said, "but this number is for emergencies only. If your child has been detained for a nonfunctioning band, you need to contact that specific police station during business hours for more information."

"I don't know what station has her," I said, hearing my own urgency rise. Could this voice hear it, too? "I don't have a station, or a name, or anything. I need the police to help me find where the police took my daughter. She's a nine-year-old child."

"A detainment isn't an emergency," the voice said. "I'm sorry that I can't help you." I was disconnected.

I sat at the kitchen table, the wall slicing moonlight into my house, and using a spare external battery I kept charged for emergencies, compiled a potential list of police stations. Alex sulk-texted me until one a.m., when he realized I wouldn't reply. While I researched, on the border of passing out from exhaustion, I slapped myself awake and told myself, again and again: *This is your fault.*

I tried keeping my drowsiness in a corner, but the crash, when it came, would be spectacular.

After an hour or two of sleep, I got up at six a.m. and left messages at fourteen different police stations. Then I called Principal Jessica's office in ten-minute blocks until she picked up at a quarter to nine. Jessica recited the information from her voicemail with identical wording and a vaguely concerned inflection.

"Jessica," I said. "What's your last name?"

"I'm sorry?"

"You're an adult, right? And we're not friends. Tell me what your last name is."

If he were here, Alex would be waving his hands in a broad "Don't do this!" gesture, mouthing, "Stop!"

"Iris, I think you have more important things to focus on right now."

"You're not going to help me find my child, and since you'll never see Melanie at your school again, I want you to tell me what your last name is."

"Hart."

"I have never met a Latina named Jessica Hart before," I said.

"My maiden name is Guerrero," she said, "Mrs. *Prince.*"

"It's Soto," I said. "*Ms. Soto.*" It felt weird, but right, to say my name. "Thank you for losing my child, Ms. Hart," I said, and hung up.

In the cold, slatted darkness of my house, I changed into an outfit that would be taken seriously at a police station. Conservative long-sleeve blouse, checkered slacks, black flats, discreet earrings, no makeup.

A morning text from Alex said, *I could finally log in to the app. It said Mel is at your home. That means she was returned safe, or you swapped your band for hers. I am her father and want to know. Which is it?*

I waited for inspiration to supply me with a devastating comeback. Several moments passed. Instead, there was the silence of our house without my child in it, an absence of Melanie's morning squeals of delight at being awake; her happy dance, a variation of the Snoopy dance that Alex taught her, when I prepared her lunch box; her whining when I couldn't find her favorite sock and shoe combination. The silence was more than a weight. It was a vacuum that extracted the oxygen I breathed. I did not have the air to stay in that house.

I called in sick to work on voicemail in a dispassionate, disaffected tone. Then I texted Alex: *Don't judge me.*

I heard the children singing in classrooms. These happy voices and perky handclaps kindled in me an incandescent furiousness and shame. I stalked the blossom-lined paths of Leland Elementary's campus for a lead on Melanie's whereabouts. I imagined how difficult and fruitless this search could be.

It took five minutes to find a lead. An upbeat playground monitor wearing a shaggy cardigan heard from security that Melanie had been "picked up." I expected a pantomime of downcast eyes and limp, mumbled apologies describing how my nine-year-old child was put into a police car instead of being held on school property until Alex arrived. I wanted shame. But the information was volunteered almost gregariously, as if I had asked for directions to the spa at a resort.

"The station on Baxter is where I'm guessing they took her," the aide said, jangling a large key ring. "The band should make her easy to find. Did you download the app?"

I stroked my wrist, felt Melanie's band scratch the tip of my radius bone. I was aware of both its lightness, how it slid down in a permanent gesture of escape over my hand and fingers, and the moist contact its sharp, untrimmed band edges made chafing my skin. Its weight was a delicate force—a mosquito's pulse—that led my body, pulled me, arm-first, into my car, then, after a blinding, sun-soaked drive, up the steps of Baxter Station, located at the end of an industrial parkway clotted with tractor trailers. The police station—square, white, no windows—could pass for any of the businesses in this corporate park alley. Its purpose was given away by the flagpole out front, with its accompanying police and American flags creaking in a dry breeze, set at half-staff. I couldn't remember when I'd last seen a fully raised American flag.

I sat in a soundproof glassed-in waiting area. Trucks drifted by like old clipper ships on a special day at a marina. I sweated on a long uncomfortable plastic composite bench and desperately wanted to lie down for a few moments. Just a few moments to compose myself. That's all I needed. The bench had metal seat dividers that kept anyone from lying down. These outdoor benches were everywhere in North Azulia. Whenever I spotted one, I shoulder-tapped Melanie as if I'd spotted a rare animal that would gambol away if she didn't look quick.

See those benches, I'd say, *they keep us safe. Bad men can't sleep on them.*

Having stayed up through the night, I flinched at my memory, dodging it like one of a flurry of insistent fireflies as my sleep-deprived thoughts stumbled on and recounted moments where I fell so easily into a binary of "good" and "bad" people with Melanie. I'd had a screaming match with Serena when I heard her tell Melanie never to go in a car with a policeman because they could take her away, forever.

"Run away," Serena said. "Obedece a Mommy, a Daddy, el maestro, but never, *ever*, a la policía."

"Stop telling her lies!" I'd scream. "You're going to get her killed!"

I know Mel happily went into that police car. I shifted on the hard bench, over and over again, and wondered where my daughter was.

Hours passed until a police officer walked into the waiting area and extended his hand. Officer Gordillo was a model of courtesy as he led me to a cool, air-conditioned, windowless room lined with community history books and black-and-white photographs of firemen and policemen picnics. I was grateful for the change in temperature.

Gordillo's boilerplate assurances were reasonable, conscientious, and despite my own momentous sense of panic and concern, a temporary calm rolled in, washing over the places inside me that were angry, muting my instinct to press with outraged questions. It was a one-sided monologue that could have occurred on the phone with me pressing *1* each time for more options only to be cycled through to an automated response.

"I'm sorry, but your daughter isn't here," Gordillo said. "You will receive information as soon as she has been officially processed."

"I'm sorry, I can't tell you where she is," Gordillo said, "because I don't have that information. I can assure you she is safe and being cared for."

"I'm sorry, I can't do anything else for you," Gordillo said, "but I will be happy to take down your and your husband's information."

How easily the apologies dropped from his mouth. He produced a tinier-than-expected notebook from a chest pocket.

"Is there anything else that you think I need to know?" Gordillo asked.

I could see the wall outside my house. Its image produced an actual sound in my head, a high-pitched, ear-ringing howl.

I shook my head no.

"We appreciate you stopping by, Iris," Officer Gordillo said. He had a strong, close-of-conversation handshake and a warm smile. "It's what any good parent would do." I thought I would shout and scream at him to help me find Mel, but how could I argue with disinterested courtesy? Over the past few months I had encountered no one but friendly strangers who breezily chaperoned me from one atrocious consequence to the next.

Driving home, I realized Officer Gordillo took my contact information and trailed off into a murmur, not promising to follow up if he found anything. I rotated the experience around in my head and was left with an empty void, as if I had traded something valuable I fleetingly had for nothing.

With the power out and Melanie gone, the house was a museum to grief. Here was the space, by the pantry, where Melanie pleaded for cookies. Near the microwave was where Mel air-guitared waiting for her food to finish when she thought I couldn't see. The

living room couch was where I tickled her hard enough that she
gasped for breath.

I lay in Mel's tiny bed, curled up with her Tigger, now stained
with my blood. From somewhere outside the house, I heard an
abrasive talk radio program whose volume rose the more I zeroed
in on the voice, which relished its own angry rapture. I heard the
word "band" repeated, the *buh* sound in "band" a relentless percus-
sive punch in the air, *buh buh buh.*

I lost count of how many *buhs* it took before I screamed, "¡Vete!"
I fell asleep.

It was past midnight when I awoke. My thoughts were wiped, a
hangover blank, as if I had to relearn who I was, and that Mel was
indeed gone. A large moon reflected light off the wall's bollards,
slapping shadows of its bars throughout the house.

Not a sound to be heard. Nothing of any worth was here. My
home was empty.

So this is what it means to feel safe.

Nineteen

On a high shelf, behind a garbage bag of Melanie's old stuffed animals, was a musty-smelling weekend bag. It was an anniversary gift that was packed once for a weekend trip we didn't take because Alex had an unexpected work commitment. Using my cell phone light and almost dead external battery, I was packed in fifteen minutes.

The porch light was on outside Dolores's house. She sat at a high-top table near the kitchen, watching Gonzalo, who was watching a soccer match on the couch. Dolores saw me carrying a travel bag and nodded. I kissed her on the cheek, nodded at my father, then went into the spare bedroom. I felt the shy, self-conscious, insecure parts of being sixteen years old again, as if I were dressing for a big Saturday night party and didn't want Dolores to measure my skirt.

While I unpacked, I overheard Dolores and Gonzalo's conversation. Gonzalo asked Dolores if I was okay, and she said, "Ta bien." I appreciated the easy rapport my parents had indulging a lie about their child. I didn't have the energy to explain I didn't know where my own daughter was, and had no one to turn to, as I was disgusted with Alex. I feared Dolores's anger, when I told her, would be overwhelming. Much like I did in high school when facing an unpleasant situation, I skipped dinner and went to sleep early.

The rattle started down the hall, a marimba-style knocking on the house's security window bars, then a jangle of pellets rolling inside a large tin bucket. I was in a liminal space between sleep and waking.

Brenda was in the doorway. She didn't materialize. There was no fading into being seen. It happened the way infatuation or terror arrives. One moment, nothing, the next, she was there, present, unavoidable.

"Vete," Brenda said.

I couldn't rationalize speaking to her. I closed my eyes, screamed into a pillow, pinched myself until my thighs hurt.

"Are you done?" Brenda asked. She had covered her ears. Her voice was a warble. "Vete."

"I have nothing," I said. "That's why I'm here con mis papás."

"Ve a casa," Brenda said. "Why do you keep looking for the dead around you? If you want her back, ve a casa."

"¿A dónde, Brenda? ¿A dónde quieres que vaya?" I asked.

"Al lugar where she can come out and play," she said.

"B, lo siento mucho. ¿Por qué te fuiste?"

"Porque somos americanos, ¿verdad? We're *Amur-i-cans*, remember? Fun!"

The sun slid through the bedroom window's bars, casting my shadow on the wall as if my body was a sundial needle. I remembered it was called a gnomon, a word I learned when I dropped Melanie off for her first day of kindergarten.

Welcome gnomons in training, Mel's teacher had said.

I don't want to be a gnome, Mel said.

Okay, I said, *you can be the sun. Let me see you smile.*

Brenda smiled. Disappeared.

I was in bare feet and oversize pajamas, standing by my closed bedroom door. I smelled a grease slick of dinner from the kitchen. *How long had I been out? Did I miss the entire day?*

I was holding my phone. There were a seething flood of unanswered bold type subject line work emails in my inbox. I hadn't called in sick, had no idea how much trouble I was in, if I had been suspended, or fired.

Then Alex sent a text. *I know where Mel is.*

Embedded with his text was a link containing Melanie's holding facility's address and a six-second video clip of her "detainment." Her hands were locked behind her back with a doll-size plastic zip tie. A police officer hauled Melanie into the back seat of his cruiser like a sack of laundry.

"Are you taking me home?" Melanie asked, delighted. The video ended.

It was surreal to hear Melanie's voice after two days of her being gone, like a scream had followed me home from a scary movie and waited until I was at my most relaxed to thunder out of the walls.

I replayed the video in a loop. There was my daughter, trapped on a screen. Hearing the joy in my daughter's voice—*Police officers are your friends*, I'd told her over and over—produced a monstrous wave of motion sickness and loss.

This was how total powerlessness felt, an inconsolable loss that took an actual bodily form. My grief, fueled by imagining the scene of my daughter's arrest—the immense relief she must have felt when she saw the approaching police car, waving it down and proudly reporting her name, address, and her parents' names to the officer, just like I had told her to, surrendering herself without fear or hesitation into the arms of the man who then picked her up like my baby was a stray dog—became a living thing, a weighted shadow suffocating and smothering me with so many catastrophic possibilities. When did she know she wasn't being taken home? How unrecognizable was the drive to the detention center? Did she panic? Had she cried? Was she hungry? Confused? Scared?

Would I see my daughter again?

Packing a bag for Mel, I told Alex, then realized I didn't want him to come to my parents'. *Meet me at my house. We're getting her tonight. Bring a flashlight.*

I reached for the band and felt it strangling my wrist.

At the kitchen table, Serena shoveled food with one hand and talked to Dolores with her mouth full.

"Mamá, I'm going out," I said. "I'll need your help later with Mel."

"We're not tu niñera," Serena said, and scrolled her phone with a spastic thumb movement with her free hand.

I grabbed Serena's phone and slammed it into the kitchen sink. Gonzalo started out of his plush television-watching chair. Dolores bent her head down, as if in prayer, anticipating a fight.

"What the fuck is wrong with you, pendeja!" Serena screamed.

"Mamá, ¿la oyes?" Serena pleaded. "This is what I'm talking about!"

"¡Haz lo que dice tal cual! ¡Basta, ya!" Dolores said.

"Melanie's desaparecida," I said.

"¿Qué? ¿Desde cuándo?" Dolores asked.

"A few days," I said.

"¿Días?" Dolores said.

Gonzalo turned off his television. "¿Qué pasó?" he asked.

I fingered my band, its golden ring of light hovering around my wrist.

"I did this," I said. "I swapped bands with Mel to keep my job."

I heard my family gasp in fury at me, then embarrassment for me.

"I made a horrible mistake," I said, "but I know where she is. I need all of your help now. Please."

Dolores said, "You cannot think about yourself right now. Get her, then come home. Pero no vuelvas sin ella. Ahora vete, egoísta."

"Mamá, wait," Serena said. "Iris was scared."

"¡Fuera de aquí!" Dolores screamed.

It was just after sunset, but the streetlights hadn't turned on. There was a dry, shrill ringing in my ears while I drove through a darkened North Azulia. American flags listed in a whispered breeze. So many houses here with white picket fences. Too short to obstruct a view, but tall enough to frame how much of the property was yours. They were like the frame around the picture of your house. How perfect they seemed.

That was all I had wanted when I bought a house. A simple white picket fence.

I hated every fucking fence I saw.

At my house, thick layers of rust flakes from the enormous metal poles snowed on my windshield like ashes from an explosion in the sky. When I thrummed the poles with my fingers, they panged like the sound you hear when the ocean has rushed back from shore.

Standing underneath the wall, I could see it curve as it stretched into the night sky, leering at an angle that made me feel it could collapse in a wave of bronze and blue-pink metal. Lining the wall's base were black and red spray-painted crosses, forming a barbed-wire pattern.

I emptied my overnight bag to pack things Melanie might need. In went her blanket, her pillow, her night-light, and several changes of clothes and chones. I added some of her favorite treats and gummy snacks, along with carrot sticks, ranch dipping sauce, several water bottles, her favorite Velcro-fastened sneakers and, on top, her Tigger and chanclas. They would be the first things she'd see when I knelt by her, opened the bag, and whispered to her, *I'm sorry. Mija, I am so, so, sorry.*

I was ready, I lied to myself.

I called Alex, but got his voicemail message. I redialed on a loop, but hearing his voice for the tenth time convinced me that I didn't need him with me. I *wanted* him to come. I wanted Melanie to see both of us there waiting for her, and to embrace her so tight we'd dissolve the past two days off of her. Then I could look at Alex and confirm what I already knew. I didn't need to be married to Alex, or married at all, anymore, but I couldn't reach this conclusion unless he accompanied me.

Alex texted, *Will get there as soon as I can.*

I can't wait any more, I wrote back. No reply. So I waited anyway, staring at the shadows cast through the wall and watching how they moved throughout my house.

It was dark when I heard Alex's car brake in the driveway. I caught a shadow of him, floating across the lawn as he stared up, up, up, agape at the wall.

"My God," he said. "When did this happen?"

"It's always been there."

"Impossible," he said. "I would have seen it."

"I'm just telling you my truth," I said.

Alex shivered as he came inside and set a bag of take-out food on the kitchen table.

"You stopped for burgers before coming over?"

"I was starving," he said. "But I won't eat if you don't want me to."

"I'm turning myself in," I said. "I'm going to tell them what I did and see if I can exchange myself for Melanie. El toma y daca. I want you to come with me. When I'm arrested, you can take Melanie home."

Alex sat down on the couch and sighed.

"I can't go with you," he said.

I sat next to my ex-husband in the dark.

"We have to bring our daughter home. We have to do this together. Do you understand that you don't have a choice?"

Alex fiddled with his band. "It wasn't supposed to be this way," he said.

"I won't turn you in," I said. "If that's what you're worried about. I don't care that you or your parents got fake bands."

"You're too damn judgmental!" Alex shouted, taking me by surprise. "The only thing that reaches my dad now is politics. This shit is personal to him. He was caught three times crossing the border. Said coyotes raped a cousin of his. After that, he said he was going to become an American or die trying."

"Then por qué chingados does he think the way he does?" I asked.

Alex was incredulous, almost laughing. "Why do you?" He paused, then said, "I don't know how much of his stories are true. But a son has no choice but to believe his father and take care of him. I thought if I went to one of his political meetings and kept an eye on him, I could make sure he didn't get too deep into things. I had some beers with his friends at a pool party."

"You got recruited with chelas at a chingada pool party?" I asked.

"They were family guys. Like me. Nobody was shouting, like people do online, nobody was blaming anyone. They seemed rational, logical. It was about keeping our neighborhood safe. That's always been so important to you. Hasn't it?"

"You're right," I said. It was what I had thought and believed for too many years. I was nauseous, ashamed.

"One of the guys asked me to do a recon," Alex said, "because they had success in Kevin's neighborhood. He seemed normal. Who turns down a nice, normal guy?"

"Sure," I said. "But we both know better now, don't we?" I said, and patted Alex's hand.

He winced. "We were just gonna take pictures. Someone looked sketchy, we'd see if they had a band. Take a picture, nothing else. My dad saw how involved I was getting. We were talking more, fighting less. Then one night his friend Ron saw someone we thought was trying to break into a car. The guy didn't have a band, so Ron said, 'What are you doing here?' Then Ron pushed him. The guy tried to run. I think I tripped him, but I swear I didn't mean to. Ron threw his head against a curb. He was loving it, so he didn't stop. That wasn't me, okay? I didn't believe people when they said, 'It happened so fast.' But they're right. I lost myself for that half minute of time. I didn't try to stop him, but I didn't know where I was, either."

I was speechless. None of the words I knew in English or Spanish carried the requisite heft I wanted them to.

"Are you sorry?" I finally asked.

"Of course," Alex said. "Because none of this is hurting the people that were supposed to be hurt."

I said, "Gonzalo would be so embarrassed of you."

"I don't know what that's supposed to mean. He's not my father or anything."

"Right. Because if he were, he'd say he had no son."

Alex nodded, and fidgeted with his hands.

I grabbed my car keys and Melanie's bag. "I hate you right now. You couldn't begin to understand how deep my hate runs for you. But I need you by my side. Come with me and get our daughter. Please."

Alex stared at me with a naive, childlike fear. "I can't get arrested. I'll lose my job and my parents won't understand. They're not like your parents."

I fingered Mel's glowing band around my wrist. The plastic made my body feel both tiny and immense.

"My dad says if we wait a week they'll release her to the closest emergency contact," Alex said. "It probably isn't even that bad for her down there!"

I had the words for this moment now.

"I was afraid for myself, not my child," I said, "and I did something a mother's never supposed to do." I thought there would be an enormous cathartic release at this admission. Instead, shame, but no release. "Voy a encontrar a mi hija and I will try and make it right."

He said, "What do you want me to do?"

"Didn't you hear me? I said, 'my daughter.' I can't decide for you anymore," I said, shocked at this realization. "Go do what you want. You don't have to be a father anymore."

"Mel needs us together!" Alex shouted. "Will you please listen to me?"

I swung open the front door. "Don't run into the wall when you leave. I'm glad you can see it now."

Twenty

The drive to the holding facility was illuminated by a glowing mist of amber sodium light, fizzing up and over the night horizon like aged fireworks, and the faint glow of my cell phone's GPS directions. The location used to be a One-Shop Mega Center. The building's signage was stripped, but its old lettering was visible. My headlights caught swirling coiled rivers of concertina barbed wire flowing amid steel pickets attached to chain-link fences that lined the store's miles-long parking lot.

There was a steady parade of drab school buses with blacked-out windows unloading people. Up one ramp marched adults shackled together at their ankles, and up the other, a chain of shuffling children tied together with plastic zip ties, dragging their juguetes, blankets, and backpacks. Above were blinding floodlights. Armed security guards paced the perimeter in poisoned ant circles.

I parked the car, stabbed my knees into jagged pebbles on the ground, and threw up. I knew, in a feeling akin to a stroke, how limited my own imagination had been in understanding all of this. I wasn't ready to see what was inside.

The entrance was One-Shop's former outdoor-gardening section. Next to it was a storage area where chain-link-fence pens contained pallets of thin Mylar "blankets." Arranged in long, orderly rows were glass-door coolers stuffed with hundreds upon hundreds of nonmatching children's sneakers with torn soles and chanclas, disintegrating chamarras and blue jeans, tiny pocket Bibles, toothbrushes with travel-size toothpastes and mouthwash bottles, filthy mottled cobijas with Disney characters on them (there were many, many cobijas de Elsa), leather wallets, piles of wrapped chocolate candy bars and tuna fish cans, cheap burner cell phones, plush peluches and teddy bears, and braided serpientes of multicolored rosary beads piled hundreds of feet across. These were the possessions of people who had traveled many, many miles, and ones, like Melanie, who hadn't prepared to travel anywhere.

I was funneled into a maze of temporary corridors, twelve-feet-high contiguous white-canvas barriers. I didn't have permission to witness who was detained here. On the floor, every six feet, were red tape arrows directing whoever was on this path to stay on it.

There was an endless, cry-wail echo, a torrent of agonized shouting and exhaling, floating above me, up in the cavernous roof, the sound falling down on me like icicles. A steady trash compactor rhythm of metal on metal, endless clang and clash hydraulics, doors being opened, then slammed shut.

While I walked I saw these things scattered on the floor like bread crumbs:

Foil-sealed cups of tuna salad with vegetables.

I am remembering Mel in my arms that first day home from the hospital. Her skin smells of papaya and buttery snow.

A cache of drained, knife-punctured botellas de agua, swaddled in torn pink Disney toallas de playa.

I am bouncing a six-month-old Mel on my knees, swaddled in an oversize leopard print coat on the first cool day of fall because Dolores said, "Every girl deserves a leopard print coat."

Stacks of folded bootleg polo shirts.

Mel is guiding a colored piece of glass in her hands, watching the light it refracts onto the wall as it floats around the room like a butterfly.

Piles of torn Bibles, Nuevo Testamento, held together with neon-green cording.

Mel is running on the beach, away from me, headed for the water.

At the final corridor was a child's stuffed toy, un gato negro with a concha coin purse in its patas. I had a coin purse like this. I don't remember where it went, but I held it in a picture, the one picture from my youth that survives in my memory. I was in one of my two church outfits. Dolores told me to "smile, damn it, smile," so I stuck my index fingers into either side of my mouth and hooked my lips into a smile.

In the photo, Brenda was by my side.

An echoing chorus of children crying. Sobbing. Screaming. Or was it laughter? I couldn't tell the difference between pleasure and agony. *Why couldn't I?* On the ground, I stepped on and crunched into pieces an ivory coxcomb with the letter *M* etched on it.

Around a corner was a desolate "Control Dispatch" area, where human sounds were masked by an air-conditioned chirr. An officer with a name tag, GARZA, drank from a miniature cardboard cup as she tapped at screens behind a broad reception desk. Painted above her was a mural of a beautiful green valley that said CASA MADRE in letters several feet above the land. Between the words "Casa" and "Madre" was a quote: "Sometimes losing a battle you find a new way to win the war."

There was a television, playing a home renovation show that I once was addicted to, and a single door with a thick glass cutout. Behind it, an endless white corridor with track lights.

The waiting area was a sealed container. I realized this was the space in the old One-Shop where I'd taken Melanie to see the massive Christmas displays. Melanie would sing "Frosty the Snowman" to each snowman she saw.

Officer Garza slid her cup aside, leaving a coffee residue trail on the counter. "Step forward, ma'am," she said.

"Where is everybody?" I asked.

"Visitation hours are closed. Come back at eight a.m. tomorrow. Or are you notifying? About someone we need to pick up, or someone selling or dispensing fraudulent state equipment?"

"My daughter is here. I want to take her home."

"We don't release people at this facility. Anyone arrested has seventy-two hours to obtain legal representation followed by arranging a time and date to set up a state hearing. All releases are handled at that time."

"No, my girl can't stay here," I said. "She's in the wrong place. She's a child."

"We're equipped for both adults and juveniles at this facility."

"She doesn't belong here," I said. "I got a link to a video of her arrest, but she was wrongly detained. She has a legal band," I said, hesitating. I could stop here and not say anything else. Garza stared at me, curious or sleepy.

Then I said, "I don't qualify for one. But my daughter does. I took hers."

"You took your daughter's band?" Garza asked.

"Right," I said. "I want to trade myself for my daughter."

Garza laughed. "Trade? We don't 'trade' for people, but if you want to voluntarily answer a few questions, I can get your information."

"Okay," I said. "As long as you let my daughter go."

I unlatched the band and rubbed my wrist, self-conscious and, suddenly, cold. I placed the band on the counter with gentle, bomb-handling hands. Garza dragged the band on the desk through a puddle of coffee.

"Be careful," I said.

"Don't worry about these," Garza said. "Wait here a moment."

Garza spoke into an intercom, her voice garbled into a robot-like gibberish. A series of hydraulic locks in the door behind her opened.

"Would you follow me?" she asked.

I followed her down a bright hallway with many doors. Garza stopped at one, which opened without a key, and I was led into a drowsy rectangular room with four chairs and a coffee maker. Garza motioned for me to take a seat in the corner, then sat next to me, blocking my exit.

"I'm sure you've been through a lot, so I won't keep you here all night," Garza said. She set a scanning plate and Melanie's band on the table in front of me.

"When can I see my daughter?" I asked.

"I need to get your details first," Garza said. "One thing at a time."

"She's only nine," I said.

"Oh, she's a *big* girl, then," Garza said. "Look, we don't torture people. I'm sure you raised your daughter to take care of herself."

I thought I had. I didn't know anymore.

I was flooded with an irrational sense of relief and gratitude as I gulped down three cups of bad coffee. I rattled off my vital information and a glib summary of how I took Mel's band. Garza asked me to repeat the story, over and over, to see if I changed or added anything in its retellings. I don't know how much time passed. Ten minutes? Two or three hours?

Finally, Garza ran Melanie's band over the scanning plate, but couldn't get it to produce the satisfying ping. I wondered whether sliding it through coffee damaged it.

"This band doesn't read, but I inputted what you told me into the system," Garza said. She twirled the band around her fingers like a tiny lasso.

"Is it broken?" I asked.

"These things have a high failure rate," she said. "But wearing it is what counts, right?" Garza flipped open a large recycling bin and sling-shotted the band into it.

"When can I take my daughter home?"

"That decision isn't up to me," Garza said.

"I broke the law," I said. "My daughter didn't do anything. There's no reason for her to be here. Let her go and take me instead."

"Do you think we're doing hostage exchanges here?" Garza said, and laughed. "I can't authorize your daughter's release because you decided to follow the law when it was convenient for you."

"You said you needed my information," I said. "I gave that to you. I've told you everything I know."

"I don't believe that's true," Garza said. "And this is hard to say because you seem like a good person. You told me when you came in that your daughter had a 'legal' band."

"I said that?" I asked. "I don't remember."

"You did," Garza said. "Did you at one point acquire or wear an 'illegal' band?"

"I don't understand what you're asking me," I said. I was right on the line between consciousness and a blissful never-ending sleep. "Please let my daughter go home."

"You're what we call a 'P-minus.' Parental defection," Garza said. "It's been happening all the time since this system went into effect. Nobody blames you, all right? But there's a lot of bad people out there taking advantage of the system. You're a good person, right? You believe people should follow the rules here, don't you?"

"I do," I said. After all that had happened, I still believed this.

"You're really no different than me," Garza said. "I mean, c'mon, *hermana*." She grasped me on the shoulder. A shiver tore through my body. "If you give me some information about what you know about illegal bands, I can help your daughter go home. Don't you want to get her home right now? I don't know any mother who wouldn't do everything they could to take their child home."

I thought about Serena, and the operation behind the dollar store. *Would Serena forgive me? Would mi mamá?*

"When I hear a name," Garza said, "your daughter can go home. I promise."

I squeezed my eyes shut, took several deep inhales, whispered, *I'm sorry.*

"Alex Prince," I said.

"And who is he to you?"

"My ex-husband," I said. "I told him if he helped me get a band, I would agree to reconcile."

"And do you know who was helping him get bands?"

"His parents," I said. "Kevin and Cynthia Prince. I have their contact info, addresses, everything."

Garza clasped my forearm. "Is there anyone else we need to speak to? Because obviously we'll need to speak to Alex, Kevin, and Cynthia to corroborate what you told us. For their safety."

"Nobody else," I said.

"You did the right thing," she said. "I'm proud of you. Let me get all this info in the system and I'll see where your daughter is."

She left the room. For how long, I don't know. She returned

with barbecue potato chip breath and a stack of smelly carbon papers.

"Sign in the indicated places," Garza said, then detached a small coupon. "Top half of that says you have signed out your daughter, bottom half is to get her a replacement band. The P-minus—sorry, the 'Parental Defection' statement—says that your child has legitimate state citizenship, but that you do not and will need to self-report to any of the facilities listed on there for processing."

"Self-report?" I asked.

"We're attaching a tracking device on your ankle," Garza said. "Again, we don't normally handle releases or arrests here, but we're handling this differently because of the information you volunteered tonight. You have twenty-four hours to make arrangements with your job, make sure someone's looking after your daughter. If you don't turn yourself in, or if the device fails or is tampered with, an immediate warrant will be issued for your arrest. Sign again here to confirm you understand what I've said."

I didn't understand at all, but I signed a greasy screen with my fingertip. It took several tries before the screen read my touch. The gesture, and the coffee, made me feel light-headed, an unreal person.

I was escorted back into the waiting area. "We'll call you when we've located her," Garza said.

"You don't know where my daughter is?" I asked.

"She's here," Garza said. "There's not a lock on any of their doors, though. Any child can leave their assigned area at any time. But they don't. You know why? Because they're well taken care of."

I zoned out to the sound of Garza's endless keystrokes. I stared up into the fluorescent lighting, trying to deaden whatever senses remained active. I poured more coffee—cool, acrid—and drank gratefully. I had imagined myself as the kind of mother who would shout, scream, pound a desk, leap over a counter and grab someone keeping me from Melanie until a crew of unseen security personnel emerged and dragged me away, kicking, fighting. Then I was overwhelmed by how futile any such gesture would be, and by how pointless counting time was while I waited. My daughter could come out in three minutes or fifteen hours. Nothing was under my control and it never had been.

Garza left, replaced by another officer. My sleeplessness mugged my conscious thoughts. I lost track of the hours, or how long I was nodding in and out of consciousness. My location within the One-Shop meant that, like a casino, it was impossible to confirm the time. The television's monotonous spiels were broken by unexpected, staggering notes of metal grind outside the waiting area, and a colony of marching whispers. Objects of massive girth and bulk were moved and dropped on concrete floors. The air-conditioned buzz faded, and I could hear the faint echoes of children wailing in breathless, endless waves.

Was that Mel I overheard crying?

A shuffling and pacing of foot soles slapping the floor. Loud alarms blared, rang, pierced the eardrums, then shut off in a fixed loop at what could have been hourly or minute intervals. Echoed shouts of "Sit down! Shien-te-say, uh-or-ah!" Faint murmured laughter. Then, drifting over me like a passing storm, an incredible odor of unwashed bodies and fetid perspiration. An eye-watering ammonia vapor masking the tang of shit. Acrid piss and rotting meat and fresh paint.

You would think it would be a relief that all I could see was a blank wall in front of me. It wasn't. Imagine the worst stench you have ever inhaled. Sounds that would pulverize your eardrums into deafness. Put them together into a horrific assault of pain, misery, and degradation.

Now picture all of this happening to your child. Then accept that they are happening to your child because of a decision you made. It was *your* fault.

This was my fault.

My body chose to cower at the scary part of the movie, waiting for some kind of comforting sign that it was safe to uncover my eyes, that the worst was over. That comfort never came.

A fleeting image, no more than a moment, broke through to

me: Melanie sitting in the corner of a chain-link cell. She wasn't tethered to a pole or scoured with bruises, but she had a blank, emotionless face. She had no idea who I was.

I heard Brenda whisper, *Go home now.*

I felt a rough male's hands fumbling around my ankle, and someone attached a lump-sided box with a blinking red light. Then a loud *clang.*

"Who's there?" I shouted myself awake.

"Your daughter is here, ma'am," a new officer said. A small group of people in the waiting room were sitting on the surrounding benches. When had they come in? "Once we scan a new band for her, she can go."

From my uncomfortable bench seat, I saw a scrawny child in a pale, unfamiliar, long-sleeve cardigan. I ran, fell to my knees, and grabbed a stiff, unresponsive Melanie, smelling smoke in her once black hair that was silver in this light.

I hugged her, whispering, "Are you okay, Mel? Oh God, I'm sorry, I'm so sorry."

Melanie stared at me and didn't reply. The sound of a false-band-scan chime—three computer burps—repeated while I was on my knees.

"Mel, are you okay? Talk to me. Please."

Melanie stared back at me. The scan screen emitted the same broken sound. *Burp. Burp. Burp.*

Then, a pleasant microwave oven three-chime *beep.*

"We're good," the officer said and attached the band to Melanie's wrist like a collar. "I'm using the last hole on the bracket so it won't slide off. Don't forget your P-minus forms. I put them in a sealed envelope so you won't lose them."

Instinctively, I wanted to say, *Thank you.* Instead, I held Melanie's hand, cold and limp in mine, and walked us through a separate passageway of chain-link fences and stocked coolers of footwear, clothing, and blankets. The yelling intensified while we walked. Melanie said nothing, her band chafing my wrist.

"Mel, honey," I said. "Are you okay?"

Melanie didn't flinch or motion to cover her face. Her hair looked shock white in the sun.

"Let's go home," I said. I had said this phrase a thousand times without thinking, but the word "home" suddenly had no meaning.

It was a fading day outside. The tracking device felt scratchy and awkward on my ankle. While I was driving, I shielded my eyes. In that temporary blindness, I had another idea, a new picture of what "home" was, but had trouble articulating it. It wasn't a house, that was certain. The carefully curated experience I thought my house was—the hardwood floors, upgraded appliances, the cutesy motivational sayings scattered throughout the bedrooms, and that damned bay window view, blocked by and in the shadow of the wall—felt worthless. That wasn't my or my daughter's home.

I texted Serena. *I have Mel. We all have to leave right now.*

Why? Serena asked.

I gave up Alex and his parents for selling fake bands.

You really did that? Serena replied. Then: *!!!*

To buy time, I texted. *I'm sure they'll give up my name, your name, and our parents, too. We need to leave. Right now.*

Did you tell Alex I told you about where to get fake bands?

No, I said. *You're my sister. But he figured it out. Do you believe me?*

A long pause. *Yes.*

We all need to leave here tonight, I wrote. *I want you, Mamá, and Papá to come with me for a few days until everything dies down.*

You serious? Where?

I wrote, *No idea.*

Why are you doing this? Serena asked.

You coming or not?

Serena texted, *You're crazy.*

Then, a moment later: *Let me think about it.*

On the drive to Dolores's house I avoided asking Melanie about her detention. I asked if she wanted to stop for pistachio ice cream, her favorite. She stared out her window, not speaking, her gaze inscrutable.

"We're going to Abuela's, okay?"

Inside, Dolores and Serena hug-rushed Mel. Gonzalo stooped over, brushed her head, and asked, "¿Quién le tintó el pelo?"

"I don't think it's dye," I said.

"What did they do to you in there?" Serena asked, crying. "Puedes decirme." Melanie stared at us and didn't speak.

"¿Por qué no dice nada?" Dolores asked.

"She hasn't spoken since I got her," I said. "But it's okay. She'll speak when she's ready. How about you all? Are you ready?"

"¿Listo pa qué?" Gonzalo asked.

"Did you tell them everything?" I asked Serena.

"They didn't believe me," Serena said. "They think you're loca. I think you're being loca, too."

"¿Qué pasa con su padre?" Gonzalo asked.

"Tiene a fake band, también. His parents aren't citizens," I said.

"¡No mames!" Dolores said. "¡Sus padres eran mojados!"

"I told you!" Serena said. "So you're not getting back together with Alex because his folks weren't born here? Damn, that's cold, blanquita."

"He wouldn't come to get Melanie," I said. "He thought if he went, he'd get caught. He didn't want to take the risk."

"¿Te dejó que le recobraras a su hija *by yourself?*" Dolores shouted. "¡Que no se le ocura pisar el suelo de mi casa!"

"No, it's okay," I said. "I understand." And I did. "But we all need to leave. Now. I have a little savings. It won't last long. But you have to trust me. You understand?"

"Sí, entiendo," Dolores said. "Voy contigo."

"You will?" Serena and I asked.

"Claro," Dolores said. "I will come with you."

"Me too," Serena said. "Fuck it."

"Ay, ¡cuida tu lenguaje!" Dolores said. "Y no vengas si vas a discutir con tu hermana todos los días."

"Look," Serena said, "we're okay right now. And I should go because papá ain't coming."

"¿Papá?" I asked. "¿Vendrás conmigo? ¿Con nosotras?"

"Eh," Gonzalo said. "A mi me cuesta salir, you know? My sight, my body. Todo débil."

"¿Vas a abandoner a tu hija, a tu nieta, porque no quieres salir del sofá?" Dolores shouted. "¡Apaga la chingada televisión and acompaña a tu familia!"

"Papá, mamá won't be here to take care of you," Serena said. "None of us will."

"Claro, tienes razón," Gonzalo said. "Pero tal vez es hora de volver a casa. Mi única casa es México. Con el padrino. Es como si nunca lo hubiera dejado. I want to go home. To México."

"Ay, ¡él está hablando con un muerto!" Dolores said.

Before, I would have been hurt, stunned, to hear my father say his only home was México. What was our family? Where was our home, then? Now I understood.

"Papá should go where he wants," I said. "But, familia, come with me."

Dolores quickly filled a couple garbage bags with her and Serena's clothes.

"Nunca he ido a ninguna parte," Dolores said. "¿Por qué tendría un suitcase?"

"I have luggage at my house," I said. "We can pack there. Let me finish with Papá, okay?"

While Dolores and Serena sorted their clothes, I grabbed Gonzalo a beer. "Papá, I'll get the remote control for you," I said.

"No quiero ver la TV," he said, and asked me to guide him into the master bedroom. He sat on the edge of his bed, afraid to mess the taut and still hideously ugly bedspread.

"You're always taking care of yourself," he said. "That's why I say nothing. Only speak when you do something bad. But you never did! Even when you were little, you were not scared of anything. First time we took you to kindergarten, you thought you were going to live at the school and cried. Dolores said, no, you come home to us each day. Then you said, 'I can do this, Mommy,' and ran inside. I had to chase you with your bag."

"You were there my first day of school?" I asked.

"Claro," he said.

"¿Por qué no te recuerdo? Puedo recordar a mamá si I think about it, pero no a ti."

"No lo sé, but I was there!" Gonzalo said, and laughed.

My father wasn't bitter or angry about being absent from my memories. How humble he was in accepting his forgottenness. Would I be that accepting if Melanie couldn't remember the extravagant and carefully organized birthday parties I arranged, the cornucopia of Christmas gifts, the mountains of packages that seemed to expand each year? All those important events crucial to Melanie having the perfect childhood felt worthless, trampled by me and Alex separating, the wall, the bands, and the unseen and unknown moments of my daughter's detention, planting a trauma deep inside her that could blossom into pain and terror for months and years ahead. Could Melanie forget those experiences the same way I had forgotten my father from my important moments? I would wipe myself from all of her memories if it could help Mel forget the past three days. Or was there an opportunity, if I found a new home—the right home—for Mel to heal?

"Papá, you rest, okay?" I said. "Mamá will return soon, in a few days."

"Quiero acompañarlas," Gonzalo said. He leaned back on the bed. "Soft!" he said. "¿Podrías apagar la luz, por favor? It's too bright."

I saw my father's chest struggle in the darkness, slowing until he was asleep. I kept the door open a crack, to let the hallway light in, the way Dolores had left my own bedroom door open when I was young. I closed my eyes, and either imagined, or remembered, my papá standing behind my mamá at my childhood doorway, watching over me together.

Twenty-One

Driving the familiar route from Dolores's house with a clunky plastic weight on my ankle, and a knowledge this could be the last time I traveled these streets, I thought I would be flooded with a sentimentality that privileged the basic things I took for granted. There, the corner gas station, no longer part of my routine. That corner where I turned to Melanie's school. I searched for any semblance of emotion or connection. What kicked back was resentment, an impatient loathing at how small and insignificant this clean, tidy, oh-so-perfect neighborhood and these streets seemed. Coveted luxury cars appeared cheap, like flimsy toys made of tin. The houses on the roads to my cul-de-sac looked dreary, emaciated, haunted. I remembered how I marked off the final turns to my house as a sign of safety and security. Two more turns until the American flag mailbox on the corner, one more turn until I could exhale and become myself, until the wall changed that and took those feelings away. I clicked off the turns with a breathless anxiety. I wasn't coming home. I was leaving a house I despised.

The wall, as if it sensed my disgust, had grown to monstrous proportions. I couldn't see where it ended. Its gleaming copper slats throbbed under my headlights. A sharp, ear-ringing howl vibrated the air as a fierce wind sliced through them.

"¿Cómo ha pasado esto? ¿Nadie vio nada?" Dolores asked, touching the bollards.

"I don't know," I said. "I guess they couldn't see it."

"Why didn't you tell us?" Serena asked, stunned. "Is this why you've been such a bitch?"

"It didn't start out this way," I said.

I got their trash bags out of the car. Around the wall were fresh makeshift trenches with water, creating shallow moats. Saguaro cacti climbed out underneath the wall, their arms bent over in a death crawl, their cores split into a rancid pulp. Dead plants festered and rotted throughout. Lining the pathway up to the house were curlicues of barbed wire.

Dolores stared up at the wall's peak. "No puedo ver dónde acaba," she said.

I clutched a silent Melanie by my side.

Serena activated her phone light to guide our walk. She cast our family's shadows on the slats and the ground behind them. Our silhouettes ran along the wall, from left to right, then back again.

Inside the darkened house, I rummaged bags out of the closet for Dolores and Serena. "The utilities were cut off," I said. "Serena, keep your light on."

In Mel's bedroom, I set out a duffel bag. "Mel, pack five of everything. Calcetines, chones, T-shirts. Voy a ayudarle al abuela, okay?" She sat on her bed and stared out her window at the wall.

I helped Serena and Dolores pack. Then I knocked on Mel's doorframe twice fast. Melanie was sitting in the same spot, staring at the blinds covering her window. On the bed, atop her duffel, was a sheet of paper with two colored-in hands and a colored pencil.

"Mel, I thought I told you to pack," I said. I unzipped her bag and found neatly packed clothes, in lots of five.

"I'm sorry," I said. "Of course you packed."

"¡Mija!" Dolores shouted from down the hall. "¡No podemos salir!"

I grabbed Melanie's bag. "We're coming!" I said, and led Melanie out of her room.

Outside, tall metal bollards sprouted like fresh saplings in the pathway out of the house. We breathed heavy in the darkness. Dolores and Serena held their bags, uncertain.

"When did this happen?" I asked.

"I didn't hear anything," Serena said. "There's barbed wire everywhere, too. No way to go around. Maybe Mel could squeeze through."

"Where's she going to go?" I asked. "To our neighbors? They won't help."

"Are we trapped here?" Serena asked.

"Podríamos esperar hasta mañana," Dolores said. "¿Quizás desaparezca?"

Melanie held my hand and said, "We can go."

"Mel, we can't fit," Serena said. "Estamos atrapadas."

"Mamá," Melanie said, "hold my hand."

I said, "Vengan acá and do this with me."

Dolores, Serena, and I created a hand chain. We lined up behind Melanie, like a string of children crossing a street. Melanie guided us through a tight barbed-wire corridor that lined my house's front door path right up to the wall's metal slats.

"Leave the bags," Melanie said. Dolores shook Serena's suitcase out of her hand and it landed with a thump on a loose stone.

"Vamos a casa, Mamá," Melanie said.

Then I watched Melanie walk through the wall.

Her band caught on one of its slats and fell to the ground, its light dead.

I followed, but I tripped to my knees and sank into a sludge emanating from the ground. My forehead pressed against the wall, which thrummed and vibrated.

Visible through the slats was a jagged, wind-slapped desert. A maze of walls sprouted from the land, hundreds, thousands of feet high, aflame and glistening like burning coals, blockading the just and the unjust. I had an unslakable thirst and couldn't blink my eyes. In this almost dead moment, I had an instantaneous recall of my life choices, the innumerable wasted moments where I "kept score." I tried speaking, but my mouth was dry, my body feverish, aging, decrepit. I felt I was being absorbed into the wall itself, as if it would bury me whole.

I let Mel's hand go.

"Ayúdala," I said, gasping for air. "Help my daughter."

Melanie grabbed my hand. She tugged harder, and I felt my wrist lodge between two bars. They chafed me like old vellum.

A soupy rumble and pucker shuddered the wall. Its bars creaked and moaned with a chorus of crackling metal fatigue, like power lines humming before they pop in a storm. Metal shards fell off the wall's uppermost heights, cutting wind as they screamed down to the ground, shattering amid the wall's slatted bollards in loud exploding puffs.

Another tug from my daughter, and the resistance on either side gave way.

I walked through the wall. Then I pulled Dolores and Serena through the wall with me.

Across the cul-de-sac, porch lights turned on. Front windows illuminated in urgent succession. I grabbed a jagged hand-size shard of wall, sliced off my ankle bracelet, felt the cut against my skin, and smashed it against the bars.

"Mamá," Melanie said, "we can go."

"Everyone in the car!" I said. "Mel, get up front!"

I revved the SUV in reverse, its headlights capturing the wall shimmying in a breathtaking multicolored shock-wave pucker, undulating up through the air, popping the glass fragments at its top. A rainstorm of glass shards pelted the car. I sped out of the cul-de-sac, seeing in my rearview mirror the wall disintegrating, like sand dissolving into a black ocean. There was a strange absence of sound, and an aluminum-scored horizon line snapped in a mushroom-shaped ring of light.

How stunning the wall was in its nonexistence. It took me a moment to accept that it was gone. *What could grow in that ground—that dry, dusty earth—now? One that had been shrouded in cold, dark shadows for so long? Was any life possible?*

I saw Serena in the rearview mirror trying to film behind me. She told us, matter-of-fact, there was someone standing underneath the wall. "Una chavita," she said.

I flinched, saw Melanie sitting by my side. I knew I hadn't left her behind, but in that instant, I had to be sure.

"Brenda," I said.

Melanie said nothing, cradling her Tigger. Her Snoopy chanclas dangled off her feet. When had she found them?

Speeding onto a freeway, I saw glittering rows of brake lights, scattering ahead in clusters until they thinned out and our car seemed to take flight. Up ahead, spray-painted in large, gaudy letters on a peeling billboard: ISN'T THIS THE GOLDEN STATE?

I stared at my mamá and sister in the rearview mirror. *This is what it took to be a family together.*

Oh.

Okay.

Twenty-Two

Dawn rose, a headache of awareness, over undulating waves of orange and purple poppies on ascending and descending hillsides.

I had been driving for hours, my mamá and Serena asleep. My teeth chattered as I drove. How long had I been awake? My road numbness made me think the poppies had an unhealthy pallor, or were an illusion, until I saw pockets of stopped cars, commuters on their way to work, waving their camera phones aloft in back-and-forth motions, as if they were sanctifying the ground they were recording.

"It's pretty," Melanie whispered.

"What'd you say, honey?" I asked.

She's speaking. We're okay. At last, we're safe.

The poppies faded into crisp dry fields with billboards advertising corn, wheat, and soybean farms. Signs announcing towns with dry, direct names, anchored by derelict gas stations, abandoned churches, and skeletons of barns. A red billboard with white lettering said: BAND TOGETHER! A golden ring linked both words.

Our fuel gauge flashed red. "We're filling up. Pee and get food if you want."

"Where are we?" Serena asked. "Parece un ghost town."

Melanie said, "We're going the right way."

After gassing up, I parked in front of a busy complex with six mini hybrid fast-food restaurant combinations and a gift shop that had, inside a large bucket, Confederate flags a thousand miles from a former Confederate state. The flags had large white words on them: HERITAGE NOT HATE. We were the only brown people here.

"Mel, quédate cerca, okay?" I said.

Back from the bathroom, Serena photographed the Confederate flags, then called our mamá over. "¡Cuando las banderas necesitan un subtítulo, es obvio por qué you lost!" Serena's laugh was an explosive boom in the market. Several white people did a double take.

"Hurry up," I said.

Standing by my driver's-side door was a middle-aged white woman in a stretched-out T-shirt, flip-flops, white socks, and orange sweatpants.

"You were speaking Spanish to that little white girl," the woman said, pointing at Melanie. "Are you her mother?"

"Please move away from our car," I said.

The woman stared at my bare wrists. "This little girl doesn't belong to you," she said.

"*I am her mamá,*" I said, trying to holster the gun barrel in my voice. Our family got inside the car. The woman stood behind it, held up her phone, as if the gesture was a threat—*I'm going to tell!*—and filmed us. She shouted to a clerk in the store, made a "Call someone!" gesture.

I started the car, furious, exhausted, and concerned. The woman held up her free hand to signal "Stop."

"She won't get out of the way," Serena said. "We're boxed in."

"¿Qué quiere esa loca?" Dolores asked.

"She's mad," I said. "Stay buckled up."

A police car with its flashers on stopped and a brown-skinned officer approached. I waved him over. He ignored me and spoke to the woman behind our car. I watched them talk in the rearview. The officer approached as I opened the driver's-side window and turned off the ignition. The woman held her phone up like a shield and continued to record.

"¿Cómo está, señora?" Officer Ortega said.

"Did he call you señora?" Serena asked. "You're an old woman now!"

"I speak English," I said.

"Okay, ¿habla inglés?"

"I just said I speak English," I said. I tried, hard, to strip my voice of anger, fear, and adrenaline. What was left, and did it sound real?

"Ma'am, this lady reported that inside the store you were speaking Spanish. So which is it that you speak, English or Spanish?"

"I'm bilingual," I said, "as apparently you are."

"By necessity," Ortega said, "which is none of your concern. This lady heard you speaking Spanish, which is very unusual around here, and asked the staff to make a phone call because she believes you're not the child's mother. You have identification on you?"

"Identification that my child is mine?" I asked.

"Ma'am, I'm trying to help you all out, okay?" Ortega said. "If you help me out, I can help you out and you can be on your way."

"I'm recording all of this," Serena said.

"I don't have a band, but I have a physical driver's license," I said. "You can speak to my daughter, too. I don't know what else I can do."

Ortega noted my wrists and handled my license. Then he peered inside the car. He wasn't rude, but he wasn't listening to me, either. I realized, in the two or three seconds he evaluated my license, that he could send us on our way, or this could spiral into a longer, more complicated situation. I kept my frustration from scrambling atop my insincere politeness by biting down hard on my inside cheeks.

"Where are you headed today?" he asked.

"We're driving," I said.

"Anywhere in particular?"

"We're passing through."

"But you don't know where to."

"I don't need a destination to drive," I said.

"Do any of your other passengers have bands?"

I acknowledged we didn't.

"Okay, I need everyone to step out of the car, please."

We got out. Ortega asked for Serena's phone.

"I have a right to record this," she said.

"Not while you're being detained," Ortega said. He confiscated

Serena's phone and shut it off. The woman recording put her phone down, but continued to watch us. "I need each of you to turn around and get on your knees," he said, etching a line by his car with the toe of his shoe. "Then put your hands behind your backs. This is for your safety and mine."

"This is illegal," I said. "What you're doing is against the law."

"Why don't you let me worry about what's illegal," Ortega said. "Now, do you want to tell me where you're from?"

I said, "Ni de aquí ni de allá."

Dolores said to me, "¿Cuándo te convertiste en tu hermana? No hagas olas. Escúchalo."

"Ma'am, you need to stop speaking Spanish in my presence right now," Ortega said, "or I'm placing all of you under arrest."

"I'm sorry, Officer," Dolores said.

"So, you speak English fine, too," Ortega said.

Ortega allowed Serena and me to help Dolores kneel. Then he zip-tied our arms behind our backs. The tie chafed the spot where my band used to be. Melanie's zip tie slipped off her hands. Ortega fished out a handful of small rubber bands from his glove box and stretched them around Mel's wrists.

The woman who initiated the call held her camera up, as if to start recording again. She then snapped several pictures of our family on our knees. "All right, keeping us safe!" she said, and gave Ortega, typing on his keyboard, a thumbs-up. He didn't break typing stride and thumbs-upped back.

We were on our knees for minutes. Customers entered and left the mini-mart, sometimes pausing to gawk, then walking around us. In my restraint, and my inability to help Mel, my body went numb. Then my feelings, thoughts, and emotions followed—all dead, like a power outage.

Dolores bent her head over, spent from kneeling on the hard asphalt. A couple of tears plopped on the ground.

"Mamá, ta bien, ta bien," Serena said.

Seeing my mamá cry, I whispered, "Basta. Nunca llores delante de un gabacho. Okay? Basta."

Dolores sniffed, nodded. "Tienes razón, mija," she said.

"The adults are now in the system," Ortega said in a bored, procedural voice. "Each of you now has a summons to appear before a court here in town. If you fail to show up, the state will issue warrants for your arrest."

He undid each of our zip ties, unrolled Melanie's bands, then gave each of us a carbon paper slip. Rubbing her bruised hands, Melanie said, "Thank you."

"No le des las gracias," I said. "No nos ayudó."

"That's a really bad attitude," Officer Ortega said, starting his car. "You're not teaching her right." He drove off, down a vacated Main Street overgrown with weeds and plywood, out-of-business corner stores, a boarded-up post office, and a three-story clock tower in a square with vacant storefronts. The second-tallest building had a limestone faceplate that said it was once a paper mill, instead of the Penny Saver Goodwill store inside it now. This land appeared cancerous, skeletal.

They will chase us away to keep things this way.

"You speak louder in Spanish," Serena said.

"Oh," I said. "Really?"

"I like it, hermana," Serena said.

Dolores leaned against our SUV. "Mamá, ¿qué pasó?" I asked.

"Nada, solo es que necesito ponerme derecha un poco," Dolores said.

"You're not standing, you're leaning," I said.

"Maybe we could get a couple motel rooms somewhere," Serena said. "Since we don't know where we're going?"

"We're almost there," Melanie said.

"You know?" Serena asked.

"It's not me," Melanie said.

"Where are we going?" Serena asked. "Everywhere is gonna be like here."

"I trust my daughter," I said.

We drove back onto the freeway.

Twenty-Three

Some hours later, Serena said, "None of us knows where we are, Mel. You think you could give your mommy a hint?"

Mel looked hopefully at me.

"I'll drive until you tell me to stop," I said. "I believe you."

Mel picked up a sheet of thick butcher paper by her feet. It was a crude but incredibly detailed map—trees, roads—drawn in her hand, that corresponded with the land we were driving.

"When you see her," Melanie said, tracing a finger on the paper, "pull over."

"Who, honey?" I asked. "Who am I looking for?"

"Her feet won't be touching the ground," Melanie said. "That was the game you played with her. Whenever her mommy drove you to a place, you both lifted your feet off the floor of the car. The last one who dropped her feet won. You always won because she'd put her feet down first."

"Mel, no mientas, okay?" Serena said. "Mommy necesita saber a dónde vamos. We've been driving a long time."

"Mel's right," I said. "Brenda did that."

We drove into midday on four lanes, then into an early dusk on two.

I saw a road sign for a national forest. Up ahead was an unoccupied booth with its toll arm raised. I drove on, past a thick herd of parked motorcycles and a flagpole that creaked the American flag at half-staff, listless in a small breeze.

I turned on the headlights. The road rose in elevation and the car strained. The mountains and yucca trees inched closer to the road, so much more vigorous and thriving and *alive* than the painted nature facades of North Vecino. Up around the curve was a tiny inlet. There, I saw a girl in a bright, flowing sunflower dress whose body was aglow in the waxing moonlight.

"Mamá, you see her?" Mel asked. "Mira!"

"We're here," I said.

"Where?" Serena asked. "Are you making this up?"

We got out of the car, bristling with the biting wind and a sudden drop in temperature.

"I see a path," I said.

Dolores said, "No sé por dónde ir."

"Are there rattlesnakes out here?" Serena asked.

I spotted her, sprinting up a craggy rock face.

"¡Vengan!" I shouted. "Yo sé el camino."

I held Melanie's hand as the four of us climbed a harsh, steep mountainside. Rocks twisted and cracked our ankles. Up over the last jagged crest was an unbound desert valley below that spread out as far as we could see, infinite and endless.

"¿La ven ustedes?" I asked.

Together, we saw a girl running amid white flowers exploding in the darkness.

"¿Qué son?" Serena asked.

"Flores Reina de la noche," I said. "Florecen una vez por año."

"¿Y ese momento es ahora?" Dolores asked.

I said, "Florecen pa Brenda."

Icy desert winds whipped around our bodies. Stars flooded the night.

"Voy a trazar el cielo, Mommy," Melanie said.

"Empieza por allá," I said. "Veo Orión. La Estrella del Perro. Y Gemini, los gemelos."

"Ay, it's getting cold, mija," Dolores said.

"What do we do now?" Serena asked.

I said, "Déjenme abrazarlas. Por favor." Long afraid of touch, I huddled my family into a taut circle, clinging onto my mamá, my sister, and my daughter. I shivered as I felt our bodies become weightless, as if each of us was holding the others up.

I said, Las quiero a todas.

I love you all.

I said, Ya no tengo miedo.

I'm not afraid anymore.

¿Puedes oírme, mamá?

Can you hear me, mamá?

Soy yo, mamá.

It's me, mamá.

Me llamo Inés.

Thank You/Gracias

Jofie Ferrari-Adler, Carolyn Kelly, Lauren Wein, Jonathan Karp,
and everyone at Avid Reader/Simon & Schuster

Susan Golomb

Lisa Page and the Jenny McKean Moore Writer-in-Washington
Professorship at George Washington University

Art Omi, NY, Spring 2019: DW Gibson, Carol Frederick,
Chef Rita, Hanan Elstein, and Haro Kraak

Wilton Barnhardt and The Barnhardt Center, Raleigh, NC

Dani Shapiro, Arlo Haskell, Meg Cabot, and the Key West
Literary Seminar Residency

The City of Key West, Florida

The Rockefeller Foundation Bellagio Center, Bellagio, Italy,
with special acknowledgment to Pilar Palacia, Alice Luperto,
Bethany Martin-Breen, and Sarah Geisenheimer

The English & Creative Writing Department at Indiana University,
Bloomington, with special thanks to Samrat Upadhyay,
Bob Bledsoe, Doug Case, Patty Ingham, Michael Adams,
Vivian Halloran, Jonathan Elmer, and Ed Dallis-Comentale

Morgenstern's Books, Bloomington, Indiana—
the value of an excellent independent bookstore
to a community cannot be overstated.

Michael Dumanis

Marina Antić

Stephanie Li

Sam Chirtel

Helena Viramontes

Lan Samantha Chang

Viet Nguyen

Kiese Laymon

Brian Leung

Dan Barden

Jaime Paglia

Hernan Diaz

Hercilia Mendizabal Frers

Daniel Maurer, Christopher Maurer, Maria Estrella Iglesias,
and Lucia Ezeta Lopez

Mi familia: Adriana, Kereny, Natalie, Aurora, Candido,
Dillan, Marco, Itzel, and John

Dr. Adrian Armel and Katie Armel

With love, awe, and gratitude to Erin

My Name Is Iris

BRANDO SKYHORSE

Introduction

My *Name is Iris* is a dystopian novel set in a near-future America where second-generation, Mexican-American Iris Prince is working hard to provide for her daughter and achieve the life she's always dreamed of. As the plot unfolds, she finds herself facing two obstacles: a mysterious wall that has appeared in her front yard and her lack of a mandatory identification wristband available only to those who can prove parental citizenship. As the nation further divides itself into those who have bands and those who don't, discrimination and hate quickly evolve into violence, and Iris finds herself making difficult decisions and taking risks to protect her daughter and herself.

Topics & Questions
for Discussion

1. In chapter one, Iris Prince immediately lets us know she was born in the United States and she's the daughter of Mexican immigrants. Why do you think the author made Iris a second-generation immigrant rather than a first-generation immigrant? How does it make the elements of the plot more frightening?

2. While describing her new neighborhood in chapter two, Iris says, "I wanted to live where the land had no memory. I had earned the right to forget who I was, too." What kind of life is Iris building for herself before the wall appears in her yard? How does her new neighborhood compare to the neighborhood her parents live in?

3. In chapter three, the wall appears in Iris's yard overnight. Discuss the way Iris's understanding of the wall evolves from a physical object to a loaded concept.

4. Discuss Brenda's role in the novel. How does her death influence the way Iris moves through the world? What is unique about the moments when Brenda's ghost appears to Iris?

5. Initially, the wristbands are presented as a useful piece of technology meant to track local utilities and replace driver's licenses. However, they quickly become something much darker.

Do you see the wristbands as an evolution of our current technology?

6. In chapter ten, Iris, Dolores, and Serena go out for dinner and are denied service because they do not have bands. Why was this scene so painful? How did each of the women deal with the situation?

7. In chapter twelve, a national frenzy erupts after the incident at the One-Shop. Discuss the ways in which extreme supporters of the band use it as a rallying point. Can you find similarities in any historic or current events?

8. Iris and Serena were not only raised very differently but also have disparate outlooks on life. Compare and contrast the two sisters. Are you different from your siblings?

9. In chapter sixteen we learn Alex is using a counterfeit band. Were you surprised by this revelation considering his involvement in extremist groups? How does it influence your perception of his character?

10. When Melanie is detained by the police, Iris must reckon with the decisions she's made and the lessons she's taught her daughter. How does this moment change her? Have there been any moments in your life that drastically altered the way you view the world?

11. In chapter one, Iris says, "I don't live for my daughter. I live to never let her doubt for a moment that she is loved and she can be fearless." How does this statement influence Iris's actions throughout the novel? By the end of the book, do you think Iris kept her promise?

12. What is the role of hope in a dystopian novel like *My Name Is Iris*?

Enhance Your Book Club

1. In chapter eight, Iris contemplates Esteban's *Star Wars* anecdote and wonders about the "people over the years that have disappointed and denied him his own reality because he was the wrong kind of misfit, the wrong kind of outsider or, perhaps, as a darker-skinned Mexican, the wrong kind of person of color." Each of the Mexican American characters grapples with their *latinidad*; compare and contrast each individual's search for identity.

2. Share other dystopian fiction novels you've read and discuss the essential elements of the genre.

3. Spanish language is a big part of the novel. Not only are slang words used in Iris's first-person narration but entire conversations are held in Spanish. Make a list of the words you looked up and share them with the group!

A Conversation with Brando Skyhorse

The events that transpire in the novel feel all-too-possible. What was your inspiration when you first sat down to write *My Name Is Iris*?

In summer 2016 I was struck how, at that time in America, the word "wall" had ceased to be a noun and had become part of an advertising slogan, an irresistible chant that was selling not just an idea of security, but a particular idea of fairness. To be more secure, "we" will construct a wall, but this security that "we" seek will be paid for by another country—a "them."

I was struck by how seductive this image was—a wall that will somehow solve not some, but all of our problems!—and how this object was a thing that literally divides two sides into a "we" that was right, and a "them" that was wrong. It's not a leap to see how this idea helped our country harden into and accept the fierce binary of social networks we have today.

The more I thought about that word, "wall," the more I wondered what would happen if someone who believed they were an essential part of our "we" learned (to borrow from Hemingway "gradually, then suddenly") they were part of the "they" instead? This book is about one woman's journey from "we" to "they."

While you've written fiction before, the dystopian elements of the novel are a departure from your previous work. Were there any

dystopian books that informed your writing process? Did you do any research for the book?

Exit West by Mohsin Hamid was an excellent influence in learning how to layer fantastical elements atop realistic situations. I was also drawn to what it would be like to live in the shadow of a wall that grew out of the ground, so in December 2016 I visited Belfast, Northern Ireland, and toured the Peace Wall that divides Protestant and Catholic sections of the city. I also researched the history behind Oxford's Cutteslowe Walls, built in England in 1934 to divide two housing estates of different classes. I focused my reading not just on walls but on the aftermath of walls—what potentially remains in areas where demarcation and dehumanization are seen as essential to a community's survival.

There is such a rich cast of characters throughout the story—many of them women. Which character was the easiest to embody? Which the most difficult?

Much of my fiction finds its voice through women characters. I was raised by my mother and grandmother, so I gravitate to rendering day-to-day life through a woman's eyes. I knew early on that my protagonist was Iris, and I also knew she would be both the easiest and most challenging character to write. "Easy" in that many of Iris's thoughts, feelings, and emotions are sentiments I heard expressed by my own family growing up. "Hard" in that much of what Iris expresses is not what I think or feel, and I knew that her bluntness could make some readers uncomfortable. I'm writing about uncomfortable topics and ideas so it felt disingenuous to create a main character you would want to be friends with. What I wanted to do instead was create a character who was doing her best to survive in a fictional system and society that rewards fear and punitiveness. Would any of us fare any better?

What is at the core of Iris's thoughts and feelings is a fervent belief in an identity that is based on what she is *not*, instead of what she is. It's an identity based on fear and not hope. My place as Iris's narrator is not to judge her but put her in situations where she learns the steep cost fear extracts and see if she can find a way out from fear to learn who she really is.

How did you balance the themes of fear and hope in the novel?
Each of us are guided, I think, by our relationships to these two essential feelings of fear and hope, which define our brief existence on this planet. Fear dictates to you a never-ending stream of facile solutions to complicated human problems. What Iris learns in this novel is that while fear is easy, it comes with an enormous cost. Iris believes fear made her "success" as an American possible when in reality, Iris's status was as secure only as far as those around her were willing to view her as part of their "we." Once the band system was introduced, the fear around Iris's life became streamlined, manageable, easy. Fear never really solves complicated problems—it only shifts the burden of those problems around.

Hope is inspiring to us because it is so much harder to do. Hope requires hard conversations, painful self-reflection, and a constant nurturing. It's hard work not to demonize others and to empathize with their pain and struggles. There really is no "we" and "they"—there's just "us," but as a species, humans succumb to fear much more easily—and much more quickly—than they embrace hope.

Iris's journey is one from fear to hope. She must lose everything in order to understand what hope is and how transformative it can be. I don't know what happens to her after this novel ends, but I know she has the courage to lead herself and her family with hope, and not fear.

Spanish is an important part of the novel. How is it key to understanding Iris and her family?
I spent a lot of time constructing Spanish-language scenes throughout the book so that someone who doesn't know Spanish can understand what is being communicated. It was also important, though, to render these conversations between these three generations of women in as honest a way as possible.

Iris feels that in order to be successful—to realize the full potential of being "American"—she must deemphasize her relationship to her language, to the point where she is cautious of when she speaks it and to whom. For her, speaking it in the wrong place, at the wrong time, to the wrong person, could lead to a series of judgments or assumptions, something that would be anathema to Iris, who simply wants to blend in. Much of this belief came from her mother, Dolores, who wanted Iris to put her head down, behave, and follow the "rules" she believed her daughter needed to succeed in America. Iris's younger sister, Serena, has a different relationship with Spanish. To her, it's an integral part of her identity, something that Iris feels will inhibit Serena's ability to achieve success. Between them is Dolores, who is also English fluent but is uncomfortable using it because she assumes (wrongly) she is not "good" at speaking English and doesn't want to run the risk of daily embarrassment. So while Dolores has been able to construct a daily life where she does not need to speak English, she also understands this decision has limited her life options in a way that her daughters' lives are not.

While each character in Iris's family is fluent in English, each of them has a different relationship with Spanish, and I wanted this to be another way for a reader to understand who these characters are and their place in this world.

Throughout the novel, we are introduced to many different Latinx characters with different political and social ideologies. Why was it important to represent this?
It's crucial that representing marginalized communities means rejecting any monolithic depictions of identity. Each character in this novel, depending on their age and gender, has not only a different relationship to America and American-ness but to their own specific identity. This has been my experience in real life, and I wanted my fiction to represent this complicated reality, too.

Is there one idea or concept in the novel that you'd like readers to consider more deeply?

I teach fiction every year to amazing undergraduates and graduate students at Indiana University Bloomington, and the cornerstone of that teaching is to imbue their creative thinking with empathy. That is, by learning as much as you can about who your characters are, what they want, and where they're from, you can better depict where they want to go on the page.

I want every reader of this book to reconsider any group they may have branded a "they" and to weigh this question: what would I do if, tomorrow morning, I became a "they"? We are experiencing as a society a global deterioration in empathetic thinking, which I attribute to social media misinformation. Online, we are rewarded for prioritizing our ability to *fear* one another over our ability to *learn* more from—and about—each other.

Social media is the greatest fear-and-misinformation system ever created in human history—but it doesn't have to be. Can we learn a way to prioritize empathy over fear? I don't know if social media is ready to create new ways for us to do this, but reading fiction is the best way I know to cultivate empathy. This is why I read, write, and publish books.